C000007301

JULIE DUNDON *and* BARABBAS

Terrific yarn
& a great laugh

JULIE DUNDON and BARABBAS

The Beginning

JD LYNN

Copyright © 2015 by JD Lynn.

Library of Congress Control Number:		2015909627
ISBN:	Hardcover	978-1-5144-6104-4
	Softcover	978-1-5144-6103-7
	eBook	978-1-5144-6102-0

All rights reserved. No part of this book may be reproduced or transmitted in any form or by any means, electronic or mechanical, including photocopying, recording, or by any information storage and retrieval system, without permission in writing from the copyright owner.

This is a work of fiction. Names, characters, places and incidents either are the product of the author's imagination or are used fictitiously, and any resemblance to any actual persons, living or dead, events, or locales is entirely coincidental.

Any people depicted in stock imagery provided by Thinkstock are models, and such images are being used for illustrative purposes only.
Certain stock imagery © Thinkstock.

Print information available on the last page.

Rev. date: 06/26/2015

To order additional copies of this book, contact:
Xlibris
800-056-3182
www.Xlibrispublishing.co.uk
Orders@Xlibrispublishing.co.uk
713305

Chapter 1

Holy Thursday 2009, Dublin, Ireland

In the late afternoon, a shaft of sunlight moved across a filthy floor. Overweight, balding, and terrified, Laurence Power, handcuffed to an iron bed, prayed its march would stop.

But time, his time was slipping away. At least they'd told him why he was here—money, of course, their money. He'd tried to explain that in recent years, banks didn't just 'mind' people's money any more. No, not nowadays, not with deregulated capital zipping worldwide at the touch of a button and with derivatives and leveraging and contracts for difference (CFDs) and credit default swaps (CDSs) and other exotic financial instruments.

And hadn't they heard of Lehman Brothers's collapse last year and the global financial tsunami? And worst of all, Ireland's panicked government guaranteed everything with money they didn't have. Madness everywhere—never enough sleep and endless meetings with jittery clients, government departments, and the slavering media.

No, it was all an act; it just seemed they were solvent. He was chairman, and he should know. A whole floor in the Financial Services Centre meant nothing and was worth nothing today. They'd asked about the villas, the private jets, the parties, the yachts, the helicopters, the chauffeured limousines, the trophy wives, and the private schools.

Then they tortured him methodically until they were satisfied, satisfied he had nothing left to give, but not about their loss. Their simple logic was that the money couldn't just disappear. If his bank lost it, then somebody else had it, and however it was done, they had to have it back.

They showed him daily newspapers. He was headline news: 'Leading banker kidnapped—ransom will not be paid according to sources at the bank and the Garda'.

But it was, but not enough—two million instead of ten. They were disappointed—not because it was theirs personally, but because it belonged to their movement. They explained this calmly as he lay in his soiled underwear, and then the quiet one shot him through the left eye.

Good Friday 2009, Dublin, Ireland

'Oh my god!'

The heavy oak door slammed shut. Heads turn to see a bewildered young woman. The air full of the cloying smell of incense, candles, and packed humanity.

Voices shouting,

'Crucify Him. Crucify Him. Release unto us Barabbas!'

That name of all names burst a dam of pent-up emotions. Blinded by the sudden rush of tears, she reached out for support.

Then the gravelly smoker's voice from a large middle-aged woman, 'Move in here, love. Jahney, you look like you've seen a ghost.'

Julia Dundon had pushed through the nearest doorway to escape a sudden downpour and found herself in the middle of the Good Friday ceremonies in Clarendon Street Church.

Julie squeezed in and, after a moment, started to follow the ceremonies in the leaflet she found in front of her. She closed her eyes and remembered the words her mother taught her as the priest moved from one station of the cross to the next.

'We adore Thee, O Christ, and bless Thee because by Thy holy cross, Thou hast redeemed the world.'

Like Alice stepping through the looking glass, Julie saw herself sixteen years before as a little girl in the small town of Katoomba in the Blue Mountains of New South Wales.

Her parents operated a fruit farm along with some sheep, cattle, and horses. It was the horses above everything else she remembered most, and how they came to influence her later life.

Her earliest memories were of her father as he came in from the fields, lifting her and placing her astride his horse's neck just in front of the saddle. She would have been three or four at the time and needed only to close her eyes to have those memories pouring back—her father's male scent of sweat and tobacco, the sound and smell of horse and leather and hooves striking sparks from the flinty path that led to the yard.

Then pony shows and gymkhanas, rosettes and cups, and endless sunny days before it got too hot to breathe in the upside-down weather world of south east Australia.

The local school and the boarding school of the Franciscan nuns in nearby Sydney were all influences on the girl she was and the young woman she had just become. Being an only child, she was adored by her parents but somehow avoided the worst extremes of puberty by loving them unconditionally.

All this was shattered like a storyline in a cheap novel when Julie was summoned to the mother superior's study. There she found Sister Carmel biting her lips, tears running down her cheeks.

'What's wrong, Reverend Mother? Why are you crying? Oh my god! Don't say it. Please don't say it.'

'My child, my child . . . God, give us strength on this dreadful day. It's your parents. I'm afraid they both perished in a brush fire that's been burning for the past week. It's the same every year. The wind shifts, and in a moment, those who were safe are suddenly at risk. Pray with me for their souls and that God may reveal His intentions to us in our hour of need.'

Julie ran screaming from the study and had not set foot inside a church until this very day in Clarendon Street, Dublin, Ireland. Her own tears ran down her face as she contemplated what she had come to Ireland to do. Her little friend Sarah was always reminding her that revenge was a dish better eaten cold. She would be patient until she could kill the man who had destroyed her and everything she held dear. Her heart and soul ached from the betrayal and all because from the beginning, his only real interest was to get control of possibly the greatest racehorse of modern times.

Chapter 2

Julie's mother, Molly, had a brother living in Western Australia by the name of Jimmy 'the Nag' Monahan, a tall, bony, bald man with a prominent Adam's apple. Jimmy lived with Susie, a short woman of immense energy and bosom, with frizzy once-blond hair. He only ever called her Wench, but she insisted they were married. They were the oddest, most unconventional couple in a continent full of oddballs.

With the funeral and legalities finalized, Jimmy brought Julie to live with them in the quaint townland of Balingup, Bridgetown, Western Australia, about three hours south of Perth. Bit by bit, her shattered little world was mended by the love of these two crazies and a new kid goat called Michaul.

Their rambling old house of pine slabs and its thatched and galvanized roofs looked like a drawing from a nursery rhyme. Giant fig trees with bursting purple fruit provided a wonderful canopy of shade. Creepers of rose, ivy, and honeysuckle covered everything. Susie christened it Bramble Cottage, which summed it up perfectly. The birdsong from these home acres carried on from dawn till dusk as each species contributed their share of noise. The Nag had a wonderful way with nature. His horticultural tunnels, where he grew exotic blooms for far-flung markets, were a marvel of engineering. They called their enterprise Midship Industries as a salute to Jimmy's past. He organized the work in such a way that he could spend the most of his time doing what he loved most.

Working with horses was Jimmy's all-consuming passion, and his tough and tender old heart swelled with joy as he watched his little niece share his love of these magnificent animals. Jimmy and Susie were childless—or unblessed, as they said—and so poured a reservoir of love on their very own little orphan.

Jimmy had served his national service in the Royal Australian Navy and loved to use as much sailor talk as Susie would tolerate. When calling the first shift of mostly migrant itinerant workers, their waking ears would first hear a bellow of 'Hands off cocks, put on socks!'

And so began another magical day in the kingdom of the Nag and the Wench.

Jimmy had a separate out farm of about a hundred acres. Here he indulged his gift and talent for breaking and schooling every variety of horse in the book. And that was a very big book indeed when you consider that every strain of horse had to be imported from the first mount of the first governor of the first colony at Botany Bay. Few of the original purebred sires and mares survived the long and arduous journey from England to the new territories. The original gap was filled by importing stock from South Africa, India, and other more-settled parts of the British Empire.

As wars and outposts proliferated, so too did the demand for workhorses and remounts. Farmers and stockmen on the new continent took to this task with a will and soon had a reputation for producing hardy, versatile animals immune from fevers from every form of stinging, biting, and sucking insect in their own country and across the vast empire on which the sun never set.

The cobblestone yard surrounded by loose boxes; the smell of oats, straw, and dung; and the living sounds of living horses in all their moods were intoxicating to the lovely eighteen-soon-to-be-nineteen miss. Her aunt and uncle watched and wondered how she would turn out, but so far so good. She was a late developer—all elbows and knees, huge brown eyes, and a sallow complexion that had avoided the worst excesses of the dreaded spots and pimples that ravaged young girls the world over. She was tall for her age, and her dark-brown hair in a ponytail completed the picture of a healthy, attractive young woman in the first bloom of her beauty.

Jimmy and Susie enrolled her in the local secondary school where she had just completed her second-level examinations. There she met Sarah Bright, who would be her friend, enemy, friend again, and soul mate to the bitter end. They planned she would stay with them for a further two years before setting out for university.

All that was in the future, and nobody could have suspected the train of events that began the day Davey Beckett drove into the yard, towing his battered old horsebox.

Chapter 3

'Nag, take a look at this fucker before he ends up in a can of dog food.'

'Why, certainly, Sir David. Allow me to be of service to the bollix who still owes me 500 dollars ten months later.'

'Struth, Nag, but you are one cranky old shitehawk. Look, I hadn't the guts to pass you by. There's something about this fucker, something worthwhile, but he's got me beat. You take a looksee. Maybe we should snip him. Be a shame though. Here, take a gander at his papers. They're fair decent for such a wild bastard.'

'Black Knight out of Salome—well, shiver me timbers, young Davey lad. I must say I do admire your cheek. Now get the fuck—sorry, Julie, sorry, Wench—outta my yard before I really do get cross!'

'Fair dinkum, Nag! I knew you'd blow a fuse over these scrips. Funny thing is, though the paper appears dodgy, the dirty deed was done, and the bloods confirmed by the Racing Board. Here's the printout signed by the chief pox bottle Harry Richards hisself.'

'So you slipped Salome under the wire and got her covered by Black Knight? Will you go shite, Davey, and stop annoying me? As if anyone could slip one past that Fort Knox over at Ballymore Stud.'

''Twas'nt that hard, Nag. My nephew, little Dickey Beckett—y'know, Tom's youngest—well, he was supposed to get the apprentice jockey's job, and guess what? He gets gazumped by some prick pal of the gaffer, and when he complained, he got a whip in the face from old Bill Burroughs hisself. He was itching for a shot at those bastards. Only thing is, he blabbed to Burroughs daughter Miriam after a row they had while he was shagging her. Don't ask, Nag, don't ask. Someday he'll dig his grave with his own prick. He legged it when she ran to her da, crying and whingeing. We had the mare. She had the foal. We tried everything 'cos we knew he was the business. We just couldn't manage him. Only thing is, we might have ruined him. You're the last chance saloon, Nag. It's either that or the knacker's yard.'

The Nag stared long and hard at D. Beckett, Esq. He knew Beckett was a waster and a chancer, but he also knew him to be an excellent judge of horseflesh. 'Before I take a look, Davey, I'll give you one chance and one chance only to tell me the truth. Now, for the first, last, and only time, what's his problem?'

'We couldn't break him, Nag—pure and simple. And he's got the killer eyes of a fucking shark. Lemme back him out, and I'll show you.'

The Nag gave the nod and watched as Davey unloaded a black-coated colt into a small saddling corral just off the yard. Holding the horse tight and short on the bridle, he waited as the Nag started his long and careful appraisal.

Good definition; nicely formed; 15 hands, would definitely grow out to 16 plus; good, strong tendons; dancers' dainty feet; the chest a bit broad for the narrow back; a fine, noble head with deep black eyes that never strayed. The Nag, without a word, climbed the rail and sat on the top alongside Julie and Susie.

Davey slipped off the halter and waited in the centre of the ring. There was total silence for a short moment as man and horse eyed each other. The colt then wheeled away and started in a blur of movements to drive Davey relentlessly towards the rail. No kicking or rearing or dramatics, just the single-minded pursuit of the hapless man in his sights. Davey was eventually cornered, and the horse slowly started to lean in, transferring his weight bit by bit.

'For fuck's sake, do something, Nag. He's trying to fucking kill me.'

The Nag, with a noose at the ready, had walked the top rail and, in one fluid instant, secured the colt's head. With the help of his brawny foreman, who was watching and enjoying the show, they dragged the horse from the unfortunate Davey, who sat in the dust, wheezing and clutching his chest.

'I was right, you useless piece of shit. You've ruined a gift horse. Now we'll never bloody know.'

They turned as one to see a large red-faced man incongruously dressed in tweeds and wearing a cream panama hat.

'Why, shiver me timbers, if it ain't Mr William Burroughs, master of Ballymore. With a little notice, I'd have piped you aboard myself. What can I do for a fellow shipmate?'

'Nag, would you fuck off with that *Navy Lark* shite? I've been tracking Beckett and the colt for a while now, and I intend to get what's due to me. Plus the wife's on the warpath. Seems Beckett's nephew's put our Miriam up the duff. Non-stop snivelling and slamming doors—no peace, Nag, no peace whatsoever in a man's home.'

With all the makings of a Mexican stand-off staring them in the face, Susie, the voice of reason, invited them all to the house for a cool glass away from the searing sun.

After many hours of raised voices, the clinking sound of raised glasses was heard as a satisfactory compromise was reached.

1. Burroughs would copper-fasten the papers and make sure the colt was properly registered.
2. At Nag's insistence, Julie would be the registered owner.
3. Beckett would ensure his nephew Dickey stood by Miriam Burroughs and clear off when told, which would be about a month after the birth.
4. The Nag would run the syndicate, which gave him half of the share; Burroughs, three-eighths; and Beckett, one-eighth.
5. The Nag would meet all expenses, provided that;
6. The colt could be broken and be fit to begin training.
7. The name they chose was to be on the first random page of the Monahan family Bible.
8. That name was Barabbas.

After the deal was struck, Burroughs took the Nag aside.

'We can trace Black Knight's bloodline back to Rockingham, who you know arrived in NSW from the old country in 1799, but get this, Nag. We can also trace Salome back to Diamond Jim Campbell in 1908. That bastard was the greatest cross-breeder ever. He took the Cape horse, Basuto pony, Java pony, Arabian, and barb, threw in the Norfolk Roadster, and gave us the Waler—probably the toughest, gutsiest breed of all time. Now if that clown Beckett hasn't royally fucked up, we could have something here, Nag.'

The Nag did break the colt but wasn't entirely sure his homicidal nature was cured as well. However, he did discover that the colt was an entirely different animal when Julie's kid goat was about.

Chapter 4

And so the heat of the Australian summer waned. Christmas, with its fraudulent cheer, came and went, and everything in Julie's world seemed unending and timeless. Time crept slowly in fortunate people's lives, and from this well of certainty, memories are drawn that never fade.

The new year began as a seamless continuation of the old, hot, very hot, and humid. However, there was an imperceptible hum of gathering energy in their little world in south-west Australia.

The principal reason was that the colt Barabbas was now almost two, broken, trained, and blowing their brains with the speed of his early-morning trials on the 3-mile gallops. Little Dickey Bennett, protected by the Nag from the influence of his uncle Davey and Burroughs's boot from his arse, was in seventh heaven. Barabbas tolerated him on his back at all times, and when the Nag shouted 'Go!' in the early-morning mist, the two melded as one in a blur of utter perfection.

After yet another record run, the Nag turned his face to the rising dawn and was heard to say, 'Thank you, God, for letting me live to see this day.'

The only spoiling note was that Barabbas wouldn't tolerate being patted or petted after such a performance and only wanted to be with, as the Nag said, 'that fucking goat'.

Back in the yard, Julie was the only person he would come to when called and take an apple or carrot from her hand. Julie had stroked and talked to hundreds of different horses in her young life. She had a natural affinity with them, but the fixed, cold look in Barabbas's eyes made her shiver. She was the only one who could feed him by hand, yet she always felt he was barely restraining himself from biting a piece of her arm.

She often wondered what Davey Beckett had done to this magnificent animal to make him so unapproachable. However, the Nag's theory was that there was such a thing as bad blood, and it came out every so often in humans as well as in horses.

Chapter 5

The Bridgetown spring show was a phenomenon. Calling it the spring show in March in Australia was part of its crazy magic, and over the years, it took on a life of its own. And now the Bridgetown spring show was to south-west Australia what the World Cup and Formula One was to Victoria and neighbouring New South Wales.

A sleepy rural parish would be transformed annually for one week only into an internationally acclaimed venue for commerce, gambling, and horse racing. A select committee would be in continuous session, fine-tuning everything until the giant marquees start to arrive in the last two weeks of February. International event organizers vie with each other to be chosen to organize for any one of the most-recognized brands in the world. All the international banks, breweries, jewellers, fashion houses, and turf accountants are represented. Most of them hated being there, buried in the countryside far from the sleazy glamour of their regular bright lights. On their coattails came the flotsam and jetsam of so-called society. The very air was changed with this annual invasion, changed from tranquillity to desperation.

Sixty-five years ago, this juggernaut came into being because Bill Burroughs's father was in the right place at the right time. He was at that time heavily involved in import and export in Fremantle Harbour. One bright morning, he saw some horses being offloaded from a P&O steamer and looking very much the worse for wear. He made enquiries and learned that two out of forty thoroughbred horses had perished due to atrocious weather on a voyage that left Cape Town bound for Melbourne.

These were top-class animals from all over Europe intended for the Melbourne Racing Festival. Indeed three of them were entered in the Melbourne Cup itself. Wealthy European owners and trainers were sick, sore, and tired of the boasting braggarts and their fucking Melbourne

Cup. Now here they were in Fremantle, 3,000 miles from their destination, with their animals in a sorry state.

Jonathan Burroughs saw an opportunity. He called a meeting of the owners and principals. He hired a luxury coach and brought them to the family's stud farm and vineyards in Balingup. The place was in pristine condition as he proudly showed them around his many fine facilities. Over a lavish dinner washed down with the best from the family cellars, Jonathan made the pitch of his life.

He proposed the horses in Fremantle be brought to his stables, fed, nursed, and exercised back to fitness. As there was no hope of making Melbourne in the time remaining, they would have their own festival of racing right there in Bridgetown. A challenge would be issued and a vast publicity campaign would be started to entice Australian racehorse owners (of which there were many) to compete against the cream of European thoroughbred racehorses. With his audience gobsmacked, Jonathan, as if inspired or possessed, got their written agreement to his proposal.

The rest, as they say, was history. The venture was a stupendous success and became the essential first port of call for foreign horses to rest up, get acclimatized, and take on the best of the local talent before moving on to Melbourne. Such was the success of the Bridgetown venture that even the advent of air transport did not deter owners and breeders from flying into Perth to earn their Australian spurs before the ultimate Australian test of breeding and stamina at Melbourne.

The Melbourne racing people were quick to see and seize the Bridgetown opportunity. They began sending promising horses themselves, and soon friendships and business deals were made. The area around Bridgetown was ideal for breeding, and soon prominent owners, including the Arab sheiks, set up outposts of their vast stud enterprises.

Things hummed along nicely even with an odd interruption like the Second World War. There was the occasional tragic suicide of some poor soul losing everything in the myriad gambling opportunities that roared day and night. Old Burroughs was so well connected that he got annually renewable state and federal licenses for drinking and gambling for twenty-four hours for the first week in March.

Sometimes the odd murder happened, but not very often. Nearly always, a girl or a married woman would be involved, which showed that the lesson of Eden was still to be grasped by *Homo sapiens*.

Chapter 6

Julie would be nineteen in the first week of March, and like any healthy young woman, she had a natural interest in the opposite sex. One night and not meaning to, she overheard the Nag and Susie discussing what they should do to inform her and protect her from sexual harm.

'Struth, Susie, our Julie is filling out.'

'What can you possibly mean, Nag?'

'Don't torment me now, woman—you know, like things, women things, boys, men, and their bits and pieces. My nerves are stretched, worrying about her. What if she turned out like Burroughs's daughter all due to ignorance? It's down to us, Wench, to make sure she's well tutored about all that sort of thing.'

'Rest easy, Nag. I've been guiding her since she had her first period. She's young and healthy and surrounded by nature. She's been watching mares being covered and stallions being teased since she was a young girl. Plus, she came to me the time she caught some of the young grooms wanking themselves looking at horny magazines. It's all part of life, Nag. It's called growing up. We can't keep her in a cage. It wouldn't be right.'

'Too right you are, lass. She's a free spirit, just the way her mam and dad would have wanted.'

Julie's birthday on 2 March fell this year on the first Tuesday of the month, a day after the opening of the Bridgetown spring show. The show always started on the first Monday in March, with a truly gargantuan parade. The major horse-breeding countries funded by their governments participated with floats and fireworks to the delight of thousands of locals and millions of viewers on satellite TV.

Julie had finished a disappointing second in a gymkhana event and was coming to terms with the universal truth. She had been outclassed by an older, semi-pro, and better-prepared competitor. The Nag and Susie were biting their lips to hold back their disappointment. Luckily, she had pre-qualified for her most important event, the WA cross-country junior trial scheduled for later in the week.

But for now, racegoers of every stripe were anticipating a vastly more important event not only locally but also nationally, as word had seeped out of an exceptional two-year-old about to take on the best of the old and new world in the Bridgetown Derby. Even the name suggested something dark and dangerous. All were intrigued by the rumours and eager for a first glimpse of Barabbas.

Julie, having changed to an elegant, cool, slightly flared summer dress, was making her way with best friend, Sarah, to join the Nag and the Wench in William Burroughs's private box at the famous Balingup Racecourse. At the entrance to the grandstand, Julie was giddy with excitement.

'Sarah, I'm hopping on one leg. Got to pee. See you upstairs.'

With that, she charged into the ladies' room, grateful that for once the usual queue was absent. In a trice, job done—hands washed and skipping out the door.

Somebody touched her shoulder from behind. 'Don't turn round. Don't move. Your dress is sorta caught up.'

Julie stopped, didn't turn, slipped her hand behind, and found that her dress had caught in the waistband of her panties. Adjustment made, she turned and felt a million-candlepower shock from the vision before her. The bright sun betrayed no flaw in the male perfection grinning at her. She experienced the full Mills and Boon effect of dry mouth, stab to the lower stomach, and shaky legs.

She did a mock curtsy. 'Why, thank you, kind sir, for sparing my blushes. Now, if you'll excuse me, my family are waiting for me to join them for the next race.'

'Indeed, my lady. Well, until your gorgeous blushes have abated, allow me to introduce myself.'

She could not refuse the outstretched hand or the pools of laughing blue eyes. Fifty thousand volts shot up both their arms.

'Stephen Doyle, late of Bridgetown in the County Wexford.'

'Julie Dundon, currently of Bridgetown, Western Australia. Where in the UK would I find Wexford?'

'Ah, Miss Dundon, not in England, but in God's own green acres in the south east of Ireland.'

'Forgive my ignorance, Mr Doyle. The Irish people I've met around the stables speak with a very different accent sometimes difficult to understand.'

'There's a reason for that, Miss Dundon, which I would love to explain if we could meet up later—maybe after the big race?'

Just then the Nag charged up.

'Got to weigh anchor now, love. We're needed in the parade ring.'

'Goodbye, Mr Doyle, nice to meet you. And thanks again.'

Something clicked. Stephen shook out the creased race card folded at the Bridgetown Derby. There, wearing No. 2, was Barabbas, ridden by R. Bennett, trained by J. Monahan, and owned by Ms J. Dundon. He rushed and pushed his way through an enormous mob to get to the parade ring.

A hush was what he first heard. Nobody called for it, but it arrived as suddenly as the gap between a flash of lightning and the crash of thunder on a sultry afternoon. He stood up from his battering-ram crouch as he reached the rails. Eight purebred racehorses were being paraded by male and female grooms, coats and tackle all gleaming to perfection. Jockeys in colourful silks talking to owners and trainers in the centre, all shaded by drooping eucalyptus. Brilliant darts of colour as parakeets and other exotic birds flitted between the trees. The style and glamour and hats of wives and girlfriends a technicolour feast for the eyes.

Then from the arch and into the hush came a magnificent black-coated animal, all 16 hands on dancing feet and barely held by a red-faced Nag Monahan. They did one full circle until the colt stopped and refused to move. Only then did Stephen notice the young woman step forward. The horse nuzzled her shoulder as she talked softly and stroked his muzzle. The horse had not been agitated before and was not agitated now. Stephen could only describe it as self-contained calm.

The young woman looked up, her broad-brimmed hat falling back on her shoulders. The sun picked golden glints from her dark-brown hair. Stephen suddenly had the strangest feeling that somehow in the future, their lives would be inextricably bound together.

'And they're off!'

Three words intoned on racecourses the world over as man and horse compete with every sinew. At full stretch of 18 feet, a velocity of 53 feet per second, and each weighing approximately ¾ ton, the nine runners and riders thundered past the stand on the first circuit of the 2-mile track. The ground shuddered as they turned right up a long sloping climb to the top of the course. The course commentator was intoning the names, pedigree, and progress of the tightly bunched pack. The Bridgetown Derby was one of the signature events for two-year-old novices and carried the third richest purse in the entire country. The winner would be guaranteed a starting place in all upcoming group 1 events and, if successful, a place in the classics.

With a mile to go, the blistering pace had taken its toll, and four horses fell back, then another and another. Half a mile to go, and the crowds were screaming and shrieking and urging their fancy of the final three. Suddenly, a black shadow detached from the bunch and effortlessly pulled away yard by yard, clods of flying turf streaming in his wake. Barabbas had arrived, smashing all previous records, already a legend in track and field by the manner of his victory. He would never again be given odds to merely win; such was the esteem of the Australian bookmaking brigade, whose hard hearts just know when something special had come into their lives.

Stephen Doyle slowly tore up his betting slips as he contemplated his folly. Everything on the nose of Viviscal, the well-fancied but beaten favourite. An avid gambler, he had studied the form and travelled especially to Bridgetown to get the best price from the on-course bookies at the track. Looking again at the race card in his shaking hand, he couldn't believe the signs he had missed.

Most punters are superstitious in one way or another, but Barabbas; Bridgetown, for God's sake; and the colours purple and gold . . . Was it a late entry? No. No baby excuses. Calm, calm, please be calm, as he fought to suppress the uncontrollable murderous rage coursing through his veins.

All his life, he had struggled for control. He dreaded the onset of Mr Hyde whenever that dreadful demon ruled. A troubled past had his character in perpetual conflict with itself. In a daze, he found himself at the rails of the winner's enclosure. How did he get through the mob of overexcited well-wishers, ambulance chasers, and stage door johnnies? He was not to know that somewhere in most people's subconscious, a primitive fear would turn them away from the dark force radiating from such a rage.

White as a sheet, he slumped down in a dead faint.

'Make way. Make way. Give the guy some air. Call the medics.'

'Get him in here—yeah, inside the ring. The medics outside will never get through that mob.'

Stephen was passed over the rail and carried to a shaded area by strong and willing hands. In spite of his protests, he was ordered by the on-site doctor to stay put, drink fluids, stay out of the sun, and take it easy. Propped against a jacaranda, he would now have a grandstand view of the presentation ceremony.

'Struth, Wench, this is gonna be the hardest part. How're we gonna get that black bastard calm enough? He's never had to walk through a wall of noise like this. Any other horse in this fucking—sorry, lass—world would be ridden to the winners enclosure by his fucking, fucking—sorry, lass, sorry—jockey.'

'For the love of God, man, would you ever calm down? We've gone over this time and again. Julie and the goat will be just fine.'

And so it appeared; the riderless Barabbas was led through the throng of euphoric race goers, cameras flashing like millions of disco lights. What a sight; as the deep-dark colt was led by the bridle on one side by a striking young woman and on the other by the burly red-faced Bill Burroughs wearing his trademark cream panama, and out in front, high-stepping in style was Michaul the goat, led by a grinning Davey Beckett. Davey—washed, shaved, and sober—had, like the prodigal, returned from the brink to claim his little place in the sun.

Just then, Davey, waving to well-wishers, let the lead slip through his fingers. The goat was off in a flash, and the effect on the horse was instantaneous. Barabbas surged forward, dragging Julie and Burroughs in his wake.

Stephen Doyle, in one fluid motion, gathered the fleeing goat as it ran past. Carrying the rank-smelling, struggling animal, Stephen walked back towards the excited crowd trying to calm the agitated horse. As he walked, Stephen talked and crooned to the goat until it was no longer struggling in his arms. Stephen then presented the goat to the horse. The two animals touched noses as the tension dissolved.

The Nag, Julie, and the Wench tried to mouth the word *don't* as Stephen reached out to stroke the horse. Amazingly, nothing happened, just a man stroking, talking, and blowing into a horse's nostrils. The Nag slapped Stephen's shoulder as he led Barabbas out a side gate and back to the stables with the goat's lead firmly tethered to his arm. All the others crowded around Stephen, offering every form of relieved congratulations. The incongruous thought of the hero cowboy rescuing the damsel from a runaway buckboard somehow crossed his mind.

'Come with me, young man. You're joining us in my box after the prize-giving.'

Stephen, his survival antenna quivering, was dwarfed by the man mountain that was William Burroughs, who led him towards the presentation area with a meaty arm draped across his shoulders.

Chapter 7

Later in the owners' box, champagne from Burroughs's estate flowed like proverbial water. Although pressed and pressed, Stephen, a nearly teetotal, accepted only a token flute of the bubbly brew. He didn't want or need alcohol; what he did want and desperately need was money. As the drink-fuelled excitement grew, Stephen's looks, bearing, and affable manner marked him out as a bloke, a mate, a topman in a man's world. In response to Stephen's innocent questions regarding the form for the remaining races, a veritable mountain of tips and inside information were immediately forthcoming.

Living on his wits as he did, Stephen was an expert at reading character traits. Poker men called them 'tells'. Wealth was wealth—OK in the abstract—but to certain people, cash was king. Some wealthy people never seemed to have or need cash and were always borrowing from others. But Bill Burroughs had the need. He had the need of the feel of a wad of cash in his pocket. He liked to peel notes from a huge wedge for doormen, waiters, and flunkeys. The wad was in his left front trouser pocket tailored deep and wide in a flattering cut.

Stephen waited and watched and followed Burroughs every time he went to the gents. This was a situation where lady luck either smiled or frowned. The first two visits were stand-up jobs. On the third visit, Burroughs entered a cubicle. And as Burroughs locked the door, the door to the right opened.

The departing client had hardly set foot outside when Stephen hustled him with a 'Sorry, mate, bloody emergency.'

Burroughs dropped his trousers and, with a sigh, commenced his business. Stephen lay down on his back next door and gently eased his hand under the partition. *First time lucky,* he thought as he felt the gaping opening of the trouser pocket. *Don't think, just do. Slowly insert two fingers, then four. Out comes the wedge neat as a nut. Stand up, dust down, flush, and out, cool as a breeze.*

Stephen Doyle was back in business. He slipped into the service area of a catering tent and quickly skimmed the roll.

Five grand Australian, give or take. Out to the betting ring armed with the best of information. Shit or bust. Three races to go. All or nothing. What to do? Three separate bets or a roller coaster three-win treble?

He was definite in his own mind about Freebooter and Redman and Magnier, ridden by R. Beckett (Barabbas's jockey) and, joy of joys, owned by W. Burroughs. Deep in thought, he literally bumped into Dickey Beckett as the latter made his way to the jockeys' preparation area. Not yet dressed in racing silks, the lad looked half his age; he smiled in recognition.

'Fair play, mate. You saved mor'n one slice of bacon today. Uncle Davey is rat-arsed in the beer tent an' keepin' his head outta sight.'

'Not to worry, mate. Glad to help. What's the spoof on Magnier? Any point havin' a major punt?'

Dickey leaned close. 'Bet the farm. This is the Gaffer's tickle. Barabbas was different, short to average odds. This one was backed at 20's. You can still get him at 10's.'

'Fair fucks, Dickey. Do the business, and there'll be an extra slice for yourself.'

'Don't shake hands, mate, just in case. See you after the race.'

Stephen, back in Burroughs's box, was giving off vibes of positive energy, everything enhanced, magnified, and alive. Every female in sight was drawn to him. It was as old as time itself. He had risked everything—the rewards unknown, the price of failure unthinkable. He exuded male scent and power, both caught by female receptors honed since time began.

'You missed the commotion, young Doyle. Burroughs had the police around, claiming he'd been robbed. Gone off to look at mugshots or some such carry-on.'

This was from the Nag, who was by now in high good form, relaxed for once at the word that Barabbas had settled back in his old box.

The following two hours were greater than any imaginable narcotic to Stephen with the tension and the reckless feeling of a high-wire act without a net, all the while being conscious of the presence and scrutiny of Julie, her uncle, and especially, her formidable aunt.

Freebooter duly obliged in tremendous form, leaving Stephen
tingling with anticipation. Redman was a different matter. He was clearly
the superior horse, but the jockey managed, or mismanaged, his ride and
struggled for the line with barely a neck to spare.

Stephen's contradictory nature was such that by the time the next
race was called, his persona had completely altered. Now he had retreated
Zen-like into himself. Sounds came as if from a muffled distance. His
heartbeat slowed, and his blood seemed like ice in his veins. On a
different level, he knew that the rest of his life depended on the outcome
of the next race.

All he heard through the noise of the throng was "winner all right-
Magnier by two lengths".

Like the sun suddenly appearing after days of gloom, Stephen Doyle
was transformed. He had been irresistibly charming to his host, the
Monahans, and especially Julie, but he very shrewdly decided not to press
his luck. He realized they had a lot to plan and discuss concerning the
future racing career of Barabbas.

Remembering an advice from a teacher long ago ('Don't dither,
Doyle'), he approached Julie, her aunt, and her uncle.

'Thanks for a lovely day and for looking after me. I'm staying at the
Coachman's for a few days. Would you please join me for dinner any day
before Saturday? It would give me so much pleasure if you could manage
it.'

Taken aback and noticing Julie blushing furiously, the Nag and Susie
exchanged looks.

'If we can, we will. We're straight kinda folks, Doyle—no bullshit on
our menu. Got a lot on, not least Julie in the cross country on Friday.
Better still, you call out to the farm. Everybody hereabouts knows where
we are. See ya, mate.'

Chapter 8

The Barabbas syndicate gathered that same evening for dinner at Bill Burroughs's family estate. Opulence, taste, and luxury—though not easy to balance—were all in evidence. Burroughs had fully blown his temper but had recovered good humour after the pickpocket affair.

'Cops said I was honoured. Only the fuckin' prince of thieves' hisself could've dipped me. Now to business. Do we stick to our 2-mile plan or try for the Golden Slipper at 1,200 metres? Big risk, folks. We always figured him for a 2-mile stayer, maybe three tops. We don't want to ruin a shot at the Melbourne. What do ya think, Nag?'

'Julie, the Wench, and myself talked this out with young Dickey before we came over, Bill. We're all pretty much agreed that you only get the proper spoof on any horse when he's under the hammer, and we saw what Barabbas was capable of today. The way we see it, if he fails at Sydney, we and everybody with half a brain will see he's for the longer distance. No harm done. But if he clicks, Bill, if he clicks, the sky's the limit. Dickey says he could barely hold him. We have just enough time to get him ready for Easter.'

With all agreed, the master of Ballymore closed the meeting, instructed his butler to decant the Ballymore Estate's reserve, and joined his other guests for pre-dinner drinks. The celebration of Barabbas's first success was a typically long and loud Australian affair.

Chapter 9

The following morning set in motion unimaginable events. The Nag inadvertently drove over Michaul the goat.

Nursing a mammoth hangover, he reversed his VW pickup over the animal that was, but shouldn't have been loose in the stable yard. Unfortunately, although fatal, the collision did not immediately kill the unfortunate goat. Instead, he bleated in agony until Susie, seeing the dire necessity, rushed out with a kitchen knife and cut the animal's throat. The reaction from Barabbas's stall was immediate and terrible. Great chunks of oak were being kicked out of the rails and door in his box.

'Everybody, quick, for fuck's sake, before he kills or injures himself.'

People streamed from every quarter, and eventually, the maddened horse was subdued. Experienced hands applied ropes and halters. The padded horizontal rails installed for this purpose were closed in and secured. The Nag had borrowed this method from observing the steers and broncos being prepared for entry to the rodeo ring in the USA. The vet was on hand to administer a sedative. The Nag dithered, totally opposed unless all else failed.

Julie, frantic with worry, tried everything she ever knew to soothe the manic animal. Eventually, the Nag dragged her away.

'Give over, darlin'. He'd kill you in a sec if he could. Hop into that pickup and drive like the bats to the Coachman's and get that Doyle back here. I saw what I saw yesterday, and I think he's got the gift.'

The journey was a blur. Julie braked to a halt outside the hotel. Leaving the engine running and the door swinging open, she ran across the lobby to the reception. Before she could open her mouth, she spied Stephen emerging from the lounge. He was talking and seemed to be walking away from three oriental gentlemen. One of them grabbed him by the sleeve of his linen jacket, and all three surrounded him. Lots of finger-pointing and up-close intimidating gestures—all were noted in one glance by Julie as she hurried over.

'Excuse me, gentlemen. I need an urgent word with Mr Doyle. Please excuse us.'

With eye contact broken, the palpable air of tension dissolved.

'Mr Doyle, my uncle asked me to fetch you without delay. Barabbas's goat has died accidentally, and the colt has gone berserk. He seems to think you may be able to help.'

Stephen drank her in—eyes flashing, cheeks flushed, hair gone wild, chin up. Perfection.

'I'll do whatever I can, Miss Dundon, and glad to. C'mon, let's go. As my old granny would say, "In the name of God, His holy mother, St Anthony, and all the saints".'

With hearts singing on a shared adventure, they agreed as they drove to suspend the *Miss Dundon* and *Mr Doyle* formalities. Julie explained the situation up to leaving the yard. Deep in thought, Stephen barely noticed the almost-suicidal driving of Julie as she tried to both keep her eyes on the road and on the gorgeous hunk beside her.

Arriving at the yard, Stephen huddled with the Nag. He praised the trainer for resisting the temptation to inject the horse with a sedative.

'I'd only ever consider it myself for something fatal, Mr Monahan— and then only before I had to use the humane killer.'

'We're agreed then, Doyle. See what you need. He's well and truly secure. Don't think he broke nuthin', but you'll see.'

Stephen and the Nag inspected the colt. While indeed secure, the animal had eyes rolling, sweat pouring, and mouth frothing and was straining against the restraints. Stephen then walked to the top of the yard to a five-bar gate leading to the gallops. Another gate opposite the track led to a large oval area completely enclosed by the gallops. He opened both gates. The sun now high in the heavens was beating down, throwing everything in sharp relief. Taking off his jacket, he proceeded to roll up his sleeves.

'Mr Monahan, I agree the situation is dire. The animal could do terrible damage—ligaments, breaks, pneumonia, all manner of things and some that may not show up for a long time yet. I'll gladly have a go. I've a good idea what needs to be done, but I'll need your cooperation and a free hand. No time for bullshit now or prima donnas either.'

The two men sized each other up as men have done for centuries. The Nag, with forty years' experience, knew in his gut that this situation was possibly beyond him and with a lot, maybe everything, in the balance. A minute passed.

The Nag stuck out his hand. 'You're on, Doyle. Do what's needed. Tell me what you want me to do.'

A flurry of activity followed. Everybody was cleared away, including the horses in the other loose boxes. The dead goat was already gone, the blood hosed away. Stephen asked for the goat's blanket, said he would be as long as it takes, and headed back into the stalls.

An anxious Bill Burroughs had arrived with Davey and Dickey Beckett and Miriam with babe in arms. They all congregated in the vast old kitchen in the house at the lower end of the yard. Susie pressed all manner of refreshments on them as they settled down for the long wait. An hour passed, then another, and just before the third, Stephen emerged from the shade of the stables, leading Barabbas on a short rein. The colt walked quietly, coat gleaming, ears pricked, and head bobbing behind the tall young man striding confidently across the lower yard.

The kitchen emptied en masse, the inhabitants barely daring to breathe as they virtually tiptoed to the upper yard. Man and horse crossed the gallops, and the man closed the gates behind them. The small crowd climbed the steps to an observation stand used for time trials on the gallops. They watched as the man stroked, talked, and breathed the breath of the young colt. Five minutes passed and then ten. The watchers, not a word passing between them, looked on, enthralled at the sight of a maestro at work. They knew they were witness to something special, often spoken of but seldom seen. Watching closely, the Nag anticipated the defining moment before the others.

'Go on. Go on, you fucking beauty.'

As if released by this signal, Stephen threw the reins over the horse's neck, reached up, grabbed the mane, and in one fluid movement, vaulted on to his back. Gathering the reins and using only his knees and heels, he led Barabbas into a trot, canter, and finally, into a gallop. Twice around the oval, their speed creating their own headwind and with mane and tail flying, the two figures merged as one. Eventually, Stephen trotted to the first double gate, slid off, and without a word, handed the reins to the waiting Nag.

An hour later, with Barabbas bedded down and a trustworthy stable lad monitoring the CCTV, the group reassembled in Susie's kitchen.

The other horses in the yard had by now all returned to their stables. Emotionally drained, they watched the crimson ball of the setting sun drag fingers of fire over the western horizon. Peace had returned, and the contented sounds in the stables at dusk were balm to the hearts and nerves of all concerned.

Chapter 10

Susie, Julie, and Miriam set to, and in that mysterious way of women, a table of food, wine, and beer arose as if conjured by Walt Disney himself. Miriam's mother, Martha, also arrived and immediately took charge of her grandson. She had given up her attempts to get the Nag to call the child by his given name. Benjamin would forever be Benjie in the Monahan household.

The Nag and Susie were amused to observe the way Dickey Beckett had wormed his way into his in-laws' affections. There was no more talk from Burroughs of 'haunting his hole' with kicks and whips. Instead, a nice, relaxed, and respectful atmosphere existed between the parties, helped by the presence of, to them, the most beautiful and handsome baby boy in the whole world. Sarah, Julie's best friend and a constant visitor, also arrived and was made welcome.

Stephen, his well-honed cover story polished for the occasion, gave his version of his CV to his attentive audience: twenty-two years of age, single, and from Bridgetown in the parish of Kilmore, in the barony of Forth, in the county of Wexford, in the Republic of Ireland.

On a much belated gap year, he was following a different itinerary than the usual backpacking–camper van route much beloved by his fellow countrymen. He had read and heard of the unique Australian horse-racing business, and he was on the circuit on a voyage of discovery. His family back home were all involved with horses in one way or another. His own father, from whom he was taking a well-earned break, was well known in the business. Black Jack Doyle bred hunters, point-to-pointers, and the finished article for steeplechasing. Generations of Doyles were born and raised on the same 300 acres called Kiltealy after the main house on the estate.

They talked and drank the night away, Stephen nursing the same beer all evening and Julie drinking only the atmosphere of this remarkable occasion. They exchanged opinions, traded friendly insults, and speculated on the fact that every thoroughbred is listed and descended from just three Arabian stallions. They raised their glasses in a toast to the blessed trinity of the Darley Arabian, the Godolphin Arabian, and the Byerley Turk that were all imported to England from the Arab world over three centuries ago.

Stephen spurned a mixture of offers to stay over or be driven by anyone and everyone, but he and the assembled company were forcibly reminded by Julie that as she had fetched him, she would deliver him. Sarah, her blue eyes and blonde curls bobbing in adoration, also asked for a lift home, only to realize when reminded that she had brought her own car.

Again they talked and talked as they drove, and Stephen laughed when Julie remarked that from what she could see, he had won the heart of little Sarah. They pulled into the hotel car park. With the engine idling, talking stalled. He cupped her face in his hands. She looked deep into brilliant blue eyes, her heart racing, lips slightly parted. They kissed that all-important first kiss. For half a minute, they were joined, giving and receiving millions of signals from the endorphins and enzymes that power up the erogenous zones of the descendants of Adam and Eve. Not another word was spoken; Stephen disengaged, got out, closed the door, climbed the steps, and disappeared into the bustling hotel. As Julie drove away, she did not see the three orientals detach themselves from the shadows and follow Stephen into the hotel.

Later in bed, relieved to hear Julie climb the stairs humming to herself, the Nag and Susie relived the happenings of the day, especially the last magical event.

'And, Nag, not one of us boneheads had a camera—when you think of the drawers downstairs full of years of stupid snaps. I was so proud of you, Nag. It takes a real man to ask for a hand in his own yard. C'mere now, you lummox, and let your Wench give you something to smile about in your sleep.'

Chapter 11

Never a man to let matters take their own course, Bill Burroughs knocked on Stephen's door before the sun was completely over the horizon. Momentarily taken aback by Stephen's appearance, he bluntly asked what had happened. Stephen, with ripening bruises around the eyes and mouth, was doubled over in pain.

'Got into a slanging match with a couple of Brits. Thought there was two—turned out to be three.'

'Typical bloody Pommies—poofters one and all. Cowardly bastards, left us to rot under Johnny Turk in the Dardanelles. Come along, young Doyle. I'll roust my own quack, fix you up in a jiff. Things to talk about, serious things.'

True to his word, Burroughs had Stephen's wounds attended to by a kindly old doctor who looked as if he had stepped straight out of *Dr Finley's Casebook*.

'You're a fit, healthy young man. Those bruises are just that—bruises. You've a couple of cracked rips there. Come back in a week to have the bindings changed.'

The two drove in Burroughs's BMW X4 the 20-odd miles to Ballymore Estate, Stephen largely quiet and Burroughs ranting about the treacherous ways of perfidious Albion. The gravelled avenue approach to the circular drive with massive fountain setting off the ivy façade was something straight from the Home Counties. Stephen smiled at the incongruity of Burroughs's anti-English sentiments and the contrary evidence before his eyes.

Seeing Stephen's smile and recognizing the contradiction, Burroughs burst out laughing. 'Do a lot of business with the bastards. Great to see their jaws drop when they come to stay. They think we're all dirt and dust, full of sheepshaggers and kangaroo shit.'

The Barabbas syndicate were all inside, having breakfast. To forestall any more delay, Burroughs gave a quick résumé of Stephen's adventures. Then after an order for no shop talk until breakfast was finished, they sat down to tackle one of the truly great Australian institutions. Finally sated, they repaired to the teak-lined boardroom and got down to business.

Bill Burroughs took the chair and demonstrated his grasp and flair for business. Conducting in a firm but fair manner and acknowledging his minority shareholding, he ran the meeting to an equitable conclusion. Everybody had their say, and all eventually agreed to the plan they would adopt to maximize and further the career of their remarkable colt.

1. Burroughs would employ Stephen in a new position he would create in his own organization. He would second Stephen to the syndicate at no cost to them, and he would defer and liaise with the Nag.

2. The next outing for Barabbas would be in the Golden Slipper Stakes held in Sydney on the Saturday before Good Friday. This would fall on 2 April, which would give them less than a month to prepare.

3. He had formed a syndicate with wealthy friends who would assume all liabilities for a 50 per cent shareholding, and guarantee each of them one million Australian dollars the day Barabbas retired to stud.

They looked in awe at the deal-making abilities of this large, florid, deceptively jovial, rough Australian diamond.

'Lissen, mates, this is no big deal for these guys. Some of 'em don't have a clue how much they're worth. One thing they all know is they gotta be in, and preferably first in, on the next hot potato. And they're all involved with the horse industry one way or the other.'

That particular proposal was passed in record time.

But first, there was the matter of Julie's participation in the WA cross country junior trial. Just turned nineteen, she barely qualified due to the nineteen-to-twenty-one age requirement and was fiercely determined to win. To be honest, the arrival of Stephen Doyle and those new delicious feelings added an extra edge to an already highly competitive event.

'All hands on deck, me hearties. Let's get our Julie shipshape and over the horizon.'

The Nag was in terrific form and immediately enlisted Stephen in the preparations. Julie had her pick of animals, but the three of them independently came to the same conclusion. Bonbon, a 14-hand roan mainly Welsh–Cob mare with a nice nature and white blaze on her forehead, ticked all the boxes. Three days passed in a frenzy. The Ballymore and Monahan enterprises swung into action behind Julie, who was, if truth be told, an overt and covert favourite in both yards. Nice was all very well and good, but there was no substitute for talent and especially physical and mental toughness. Julie possessed all three in abundance.

The trial, set over 22 miles, required the combined skills necessary to jump, swim, and race over every imaginable obstacle in the fastest time. All the choice spots at the trickiest parts as well as the start and finish were packed. Six finalists at ten-minute intervals began at two o'clock on Friday afternoon, with Julie at No. 5.

Numbers 1 and 2 were determined to set a blistering pace and set off one after the other like proverbial rockets. Now everybody, including the contestants knew, that no horse can sustain that speed cross-country for 22 miles. They tried to pace themselves, but the lure of fame and fear of failure were their undoing. No. 2 passed No. 1 after 10 miles, blowing and sweating a storm; 2 miles later, she also pulled up, as she rightly feared the horse's heart would give out under her. Numbers 3 and 4 fared a little better; both were subsequently overtaken, while one of them eventually had to be put down.

Julie resisted the urgings of the crowd to ride like the wind and rode strictly to the plan agreed with the Nag. Georgina Naismith, her toughest competitor, was No. 6, riding a big strong bay gelding. Georgina, nearly twenty-one, was going for her last time and also for her third win in a row. After 10 miles, the route became a wilderness, crossing a treacherous stream for a 2-mile loop in a semidesert before recrossing the stream for the final 10 miles. There was no sign of Georgina as Bonbon slid down the bank into the stream for the second time. Struggling up the opposite bank on foot while pulling Bonbon by the reins, Julie was amazed to see Georgina ride past.

'What a bloomin' bitch' was as much as she could manage as she remounted Bonbon and set off in pursuit. *She must have figured I'd be a little further on and fairly blown from pushing too hard,* thought Julie as she closed the gap with her rival.

Georgina sensed rather than saw the pair behind her. Turning in her saddle to throw a backward glance, she nearly lost her stirrups at the unexpected sight hard on her heels. The look on her face was firstly comical, then enraged, and finally vicious as she lashed at Julie and Bonbon with her riding crop.

Julie slid down Bonbon's neck as her mount reared in fright. Georgina pressed her advantage and galloped ahead. The track then became too narrow and too dangerous to attempt passing a rider who would not give way.

It's going to tell over the last 4 miles, thought Julie as she rearranged her strategy. On the lookout for an ambush, she nearly missed them as she sailed over a rough stone wall guarding a deep ditch. She pulled up, trotted back, dismounted, and tied Bonbon to a small tree.

Julie slid down the grassy slope of the ditch, her fury trapped in her throat as she took in the scene below. The bay was struggling in vain to get his footing and, in the process, was trampling Georgina. Julie took hold of the reins and pulled the horse's head parallel to the bottom of the ditch and led him off. She then rushed to Georgina, who was bleeding from a large wound to her head.

Julie cradled her and heard her whisper, 'Go on and win, Julie. Send the stewards and first aid back for me. Only, please don't tell what happened. Please. My poor parents' reputation will be ruined. A boyfriend of mine is the steward at the water crossing. You've probably figured that already. You were supposed to be further along the road. I'm sorry, Julie. Please find it in your heart to forgive me.'

Just then, they heard voices calling, 'There they are! You alright down there, ladies?'

Looking up, they saw a mixed crowd of onlookers and officials.

'Go on, Julie. Go on. You've won fair and square. Don't lose it by default, for God's sake.'

Julie realized she could do nothing further here, made up her mind, bent down, kissed Georgina on the cheek, and whispered, 'Not a word will be said.'

A tired, triumphant, but a somewhat subdued Julie Dundon accepted the accolades and trophies that were her due and allowed her adoring aunt and uncle to smother her with affection and take her home. Word filtered back that Georgina Naismith had been injured. The good news was that she hadn't lost consciousness and would be okay.

Bill Burroughs smelt a rat and instructed his PR people to put a positive spin on the event. They shielded Julie from the mindless attention of some of the worst excesses of the gutter press and promised an interview with an upcoming Sunday magazine edition of the *Australian Herald*.

The media was happy with the story and delighted with their many photographs of an attractive young woman on and off an equally attractive young mare. That she was the registered owner of Barabbas was just the icing on a very delicious cake.

Before they hitched the horsebox, Julie was swept aloft in a mighty bear hug by Stephen Doyle, who shouted, 'You know what you are, Julie Dundon? Where I come from, you'd be called a dote, and that's what you are, Julie Dundon—a dote.'

Chapter 12

The massive dismantling of the infrastructure of the Bridgetown spring show began as work intensified at the Monahan stables. Barabbas was being prepared for an altogether different event than previously planned and to which they were now all fully committed. The preparations using the combined skills and knowledge of the Nag, Stephen, Bill Burroughs, Dickey, and Davey Beckett were all bearing fruit.

The question was, would a colt of Barabbas's pedigree be able to compete against colts, geldings, and fillies specially bred for short, sharp sprint-racing? If they succeeded and had back-to-back wins of the 2-mile Bridgetown Derby and the 1-mile Golden Slipper, the world status of their colt would be phenomenal. It was, in fact, a shortcut to instant international fame, a high-risk, high-reward gamble beloved of the worldwide racing fraternity.

The Golden Slipper, inaugurated in 1957, was for two-year-olds and was held annually on the Saturday before Good Friday at Rosehill Gardens Racecourse in Sydney, NSW. At over 1,200 metres, it was the premier event for two-year-olds in Australia and was the world's richest, with a purse of three million dollars. Qualified colts and geldings carried 54 kilograms, while the fillies carried 51 kilograms.

A week before the upcoming event, the Monahans, Burroughs, Becketts, Julie, Stephen, Sarah, grooms, and handlers boarded a specially charted air transport at Perth's internal terminal. Two stalls for Barabbas and Poyak, his new best friend and stable companion, were installed with all mod cons for the 3,000-mile flight.

As a special treat, Bill Burroughs arranged for the flight to circle the awesome Ayers Rock halfway across the continent at Alice Springs. They marvelled as the shifting light constantly changed this sacred place to different tones and shades of ochre red. They played cards and talked, and for those who were so inclined, a plentiful supply of beer and spirits were at hand.

As they got to know Stephen, they were naturally curious about Ireland and his life and family there. Stephen had made it his business to find out if any of them had been to Ireland or had any connections there. Relieved that none had, the nearest being a few trips to the UK, he was able to embroider his tales at will.

Stephen was a natural storyteller and possessed a fine baritone voice, which he used to good effect. As soon as he judged the conditions were right, as he did now, he initiated a singsong with a medley of all-time worldwide favourites. He sang them through Elvis, the Beatles, Everly Brothers, Roy Orbison, and Johnny Cash. Susie had them in stitches with her antics after a few glasses of anything. She loved singing, had a nice voice, refused to sing solo, but would accompany anybody and everybody using an empty bottle as a microphone.

Confusing emotions swept through Julie as they touched down at Sydney Airport. This was her first return since Susie and the Nag fetched her following the death of her parents. On the tarmac, the entire party silently hugged her. Her spirits lifted at the touch and depth of their love and concern for her.

'Thank you, each and every one, you have helped so much now and over the past few years to mend my sorrows. We have important work here. Please, let's give it one mighty effort.'

And work they did. A well-organized plan of campaign unfolded, with each member taking to his or her task with a will. To avoid the waiting press, both horses were taken to a secure location at a stud farm where Bill Burroughs had a minority shareholding. There, Barabbas was fine-tuned for his unique attempt at racing history. Stephen, Dickey, and the Nag stayed at the farm and spent every waking moment with their colt. The others were booked into the Sydney Marriott and divided their time between the farm and sightseeing.

All too soon, Saturday dawned, a crisp, sunny Autumn day at Rosehill Gardens Racecourse. A full race card of grade 1 events plus the Golden Slipper brought thousands of dedicated punters and all the 'must be seen' brigade. The advent of Good Friday the following week and the arrival of Barabbas were gifts to the colour writers of the racing and popular press.

Barabbas and Poyak were stabled at the furthest end of the owners' enclosure. Poyak now showed his true worth. According to the Nag, he was the horniest fucker he had ever seen. The fillies in a combined race were not supposed to be in season when racing. However, nothing is absolute, and with so much at stake, they were taking every precaution.

Stephen led Poyak past the stalls housing the fillies. Just as well he did, for the old campaigner made straight for the stall of Lunch Lady and started to show his amorous intentions. The stewards were called, and they in turn sent for the chief veterinarian officer. The tests showed Lunch Lady to be within permitted parameters, and the loud protests of her owner and trainer were accepted. This called for a change of plan and one for which they had prepared. The parade ring was a problem, which they solved by insisting Barabbas be first in and straight out before the other contestants arrived. Nothing in the animal world is as highly strung as a thoroughbred stallion, and even the slightest scent of oestrogen was enough to affect their attitude and performance on the track.

At three o'clock, the twelve runners and riders were in the starting gate. The crowd in full voice, the colour and glamour, excitement and sunshine providing a wonderful spectacle. Scanning the crowd below through binoculars, Julie was surprised to see Stephen in animated conversation with what appeared to be the same three oriental gentlemen from Bridgetown. Just then, a shout went up as the starter released the gates.

All twelve horses launched themselves, each successfully into an early stride. Who will make the running? Twelve different horses, twelve different strategies. Most would usually wait until the early leader set the pace and jostle for position.

Barabbas immediately powered to the front. Dickey saw the satisfied expression on the other jockeys' faces as he swept past. None of them had rated the big colt's chances at this distance. They themselves were ultra small and light compared to him. Dickey drove Barabbas ten lengths ahead and eased off, keeping the colt on the bridle. The pursuers had to quicken and soon thundered up behind. Dickey allowed the lead horse to come abreast.

Crouched in the stirrups, he leaned along his horse's neck, loosened the reins, and shouted, 'GO, Barabbas, *go!*' As if lit by an afterburner, Barabbas surged ahead, his stride a blur. Dickey drove him on, leaving his pursuers further and further behind, and he passed the winning post still running flat out.

Pandemonium, as stopwatches and cameras clicked like cricket legs, and people delirious with excitement at the sheer wonder of what they had witnessed. Almost immediately, speculation and comparisons with past champions and the future racing itinerary of this new wonder horse were being discussed in bars, tracks, and bistros up and down the country.

Australian pride at this native-born and -bred super horse prompted unfair comparisons with the legendary Phar Lap. He operated from 1928 to 1932, winning thirty-seven out of fifty-one races on ten different racetracks in three Australian states and four different countries. He won fourteen straight races. His string of five wins in the 1930 Melbourne Spring Racing Carnival, including the Melbourne Cup, had never been equalled. He died in the USA in 1932 after winning the Agua Caliente Handicap, then the richest race in North America.

But the know-alls and know-nothings all agreed that Barabbas was certainly the genuine article with the brightest future since the days of his illustrious predecessor.

'Well, shiver me timbers. We've done it, shipmates.' This was from the Nag over and over until, in good humour, they all told him to stow it or else he'd walk the plank.

His big bony face was a picture, with his Adam's apple doing a fandango up and down his throat. For safety's sake, he asked Stephen to lead Barabbas with Julie to and from the winner's enclosure, as he rightly feared the crazy antics of the media might tip the colt over the edge. And there they were, a handsome couple with a magical horse captured on TV, their images flashed around the globe.

Chapter 13

The following day, half a world away, those same images were shown on all sporting channels. In Bridgetown, Wexford, a family preparing to sit down to Sunday dinner were called to the sitting room of their late Georgian farmhouse.

'My God, so that's where he is. The bloody pup—the trouble he caused us. I hoped I'd never have to see him again. Stop blubbering, woman, for the love of the Almighty.'

'No, Jack, no. He's our son. Please don't say that. God, he looks really well. Turn up the sound, and maybe we'll find out more.'

Those were exactly the same words being spoken in the Dunmore Inn, a shabby public house in the fishing village of Dunmore East in County Waterford. A low-sized round-faced sixty-year-old man called Hugh Heffernan was rubbing his soft white hands together. The ex-teacher, smuggler, and former OC of the local Irish Republican Army (IRA) turned to his lifelong hero-worshipping companion.

'Get the lads together, Chris. We'll be reforming for one more overseas campaign.'

With that, he jumped down from his bar stool and went out the door, whistling an out-of-tune 'Waltzing Matilda' through crooked teeth.

Chapter 14

Back in Sydney, Bill Burroughs and his PR gurus arranged a lavish reception to celebrate their stunning victory. The high and mighty and, being the racing world, the low and mighty were invited to an extravaganza at the Sydney Tower. A spectacular venue with panoramic views of Sydney Harbour, the entire tower slowly revolves 360 degrees, giving the tipsy crowd a feeling of omnipotence as they survey the world spread out below at their feet.

After the buffet and with glasses charged for the umpteenth time, the major domo called for respectful silence. An expectant hush descended as Bill Boroughs approached the lectern. Behind him were arranged two rows of family, syndicate holders, and friends. Stephen was standing at the back of the second row with Julie and Sarah directly in front of him. He could not believe what was happening as he listened intently to Bill Burroughs outline their future career plans for Barabbas.

Looking down at his groin, he saw a hand fondling his testicles. Sarah—for fuck's sake, little Sarah—demurely with her hands behind her back, was now lightly holding what in an instant had become a huge erection. Rooted to the spot for half a minute, he shook himself into action before the unimaginable happened. Muttering an apology, he excused himself and made for the gents, covering his distress with the jacket he was carrying.

Later that night, the Nag and Susie gathered Julie, Sarah, and Stephen for a nightcap in their suite at the Marriott. Looking out on one of the most famous vistas in the world, they oohed and aahed at the sight of the floodlit Opera House and the Sydney Harbour Bridge.

'You kids and Susie are gonna take a little break—just ten days, mind. And then it's back on board, all hands on deck, and full steam ahead.'

There followed a chorus of 'We can't', 'We can', and everything in between.

'It's settled, shipmates. Sorted everything out with Burroughs and the others. Julie can show you around Sydney, and a top tour guide is arranging the rest. None of you have seen the Rain Forest or the Great Barrier Reef. It'll be a flavor of what we got down under. Reckon you'll be shoving Killarney up your arse when you see this lot, Doyle.'

An hour later, in his room two floors below, Stephen was in turmoil. He had been extra careful since his stroke of good fortune put him back on his feet. Except for the Chinaman and his goons, he was on top of the world. Too often he had blown what he had on a crazy nothing, but not this time. Besides he was enjoying the 'born again', sweet, innocent relationship he had with Julie. They had very strong feelings for each other, but she was young, and he really did not want to get 'offside' with her aunt and uncle.

Bill Burroughs had given him a very decent offer, with more to come if things worked out. Plus he got to work with a once-in-a-lifetime super horse. No, this time Mr Hyde was firmly under control. As he was drifting off to sleep, a slight sound barely registered on his subconscious. He wondered drowsily if it came from outside or possibly from the door to his suite.

'How on earth did you get in?' was all he could manage before a flying female form landed on his chest. Groping for the light switch, he momentarily grappled with his conscience and lost. In the time it took for the bulb to light, he was doomed.

Bathed in the soft glow of the bedside light, Sarah straddled his chest. She was on fire. Her blonde hair crackled with static electricity. Wearing only a short cotton nightdress, she transmitted molten, damp heat from her body to his.

Reaching under herself, she withdrew a moist index finger and placed it gently on his lips. 'Sshh, we don't have to say anything. All you need to know is that I've craved you the moment we met. This is just between you and me. Nobody need ever know. And I'm afraid I'm not a virgin.'

Still straddling his chest, she pulled the nightdress over her head. They looked at each other for a breathless moment. He brushed the palm of his hands across her nipples, feeling their spring-hard tautness. She felt the beat of his heart through her swollen sex. She gripped his sides with her knees and calves and climaxed.

Like history eternally repeating itself, they sealed their doomed Faustian pact. Throughout the night, they indulged their young animal passions in every imaginable way. Before the new dawn broke, Sarah stole away, leaving behind disarray and a smell of musk.

And so the next few days became a see-saw of emotions. The weather held fair, crisp mornings and evenings and was pleasantly warm in between. During the day, a very important and efficient Julie conducted them on a tour of her native city, starting with an early breakfast, then off to visit the downtown city area, then back for lunch at the outside tables of Darling Harbour.

Superlatives failed them as they walked the Botanic Gardens with their extraordinary collection of flora and fauna. Then Sydney Opera House at night for a performance of Bizet's *Carmen*. On a Harbour Cruise, they took in everything, then returned in a hired minibus for a visit to glorious Manly and its golden beach, then on to Doyles of Watson Bay for a truly memorable seafood lunch of barramundi and Morton Bay bugs.

Doyles had a direct Irish connection, but they operated a policy of non-recognition of any of the many worldwide Doyles looking for, or claiming, a link. They laughed as Stephen's renowned charming offensive fell on deaf ears. A trip to the world-class Sydney Zoo, where they saw the massive one-tusk bull elephant, was followed by a trip to Bondi Beach. There they all admired the graceful, nude male and female volleyball players.

Susie hooted with laughter at their antics. 'Oh my god! Would you look at them and their ol' willies flopping up and down like headless chickens?'   .

The day before departing this magical city, they visited the Sydney Aquarium. They gazed in wonder at the creatures of the deep as they walked through glass tunnels with water on three sides. Sharks of every hue, including great whites, giant manta rays trailing their tails of venom, and multicoloured shoals of smaller fish darting and swarming and reforming filled them with awe. Their final treat was an organized climb and walk along the top of Sydney Harbour Bridge. Breathless and with hair standing on end, they staggered out, clutching official certificates confirming their adventure.

Stephen and Julie's relationship blossomed during those few magical days. Under the watchful but benevolent eye of her aunt, they were constant companions, hands sometimes accidentally brushing, causing goosebumps of delight tingling up Julie's arms. Sometimes they were able to seize a moment to embrace and kiss and hug and hold. Like lovers the world over, they only had eyes for each other and couldn't imagine that anyone else would notice.

Sarah, of course, noticed, and her nightly visits became a form of punishment, jealousy, and revenge. Lovemaking did not describe their coupling. It became coarse and brutal, with barely a word exchanged. Like an addictive narcotic, he hungered for the sound of Sarah slipping into his room.

The next morning, with black rings under his eyes, he suffered the shame, regret, and suffering of the damned. Then Julie's eyes would light up across the breakfast table at her first sight of him, and with that, the cycle of ecstasy and deceit would begin again. A soul in torment, Stephen lived for the day and longed for the night.

Matters came to a head the night before they were to depart for the north-east. After a particularly intense bout of sex, Sarah expressed a wish to spend the night and 'wake up beside her man like any normal couple'.

With those ill-chosen words hanging mid-air, something snapped in Stephen.

'We are not a fucking couple—no, no, correction. That's exactly what we are—a fucking couple. I don't love you. I don't even like you. Don't you even think of going down that road—not now, not ever.'

'You think you'll last a second if the Monahans and Burroughs find out what their precious Stephen Doyle is up to? Shagging their darling Julie Dundon's best friend behind their backs? Yeah, that would do it. Send those hypocrites right up the wall and you back to the gutter.'

Stephen pounced, caught Sarah in a vice-like grip around her throat, and started to squeeze. Sarah stumbled back, terrified at the murderous hatred in Stephen's eyes. In doing so, she fell over the spindly armchair on which Stephen had thrown his ripped-off clothes. Something hard and metallic fell to the tiled floor. They both instinctively looked down to see a large black revolver spinning on the tiles. Stephen snatched it up and pressed the barrel up under Sarah's chin.

'You get the hell out of my life right now. One peep out of you, and you're history. If you imagine for one solitary moment I'd let a slut like you ruin my life—look at me Sarah. Take a good look, and know I mean it. After all, as you say, I've nothing to lose. Tell the others you have to cancel the rest of the trip. Use any damn excuse you like, but you're outta here one way or another. Up to you, Sarah.'

The fight and defiance went out of Sarah like air from a child's balloon. She realized she was an eighteen-year-old out of her depth. And she was scared—scared and frightened of what she knew to be true—that this man, this person, would snuff out her life in an instant.

She blinked back tears and nodded. He knew then he had complete control. Handing her a tissue to dry her eyes, he sat her down and rehearsed over and over the steps she would take in the morning.

With much sobbing and clinging, Julie and Susie accepted that Sarah's parents really needed her. Apparently, her father had taken a slight 'turn' and was asking for his favourite daughter. Stephen had cleverly suggested that Sarah confide to her mother that he (Stephen), Julie's boyfriend, was coming on to her. As a notorious social climber, her mother would not dare risk a rift with the wealthy Monahan and Burroughs families.

Chapter 15

The next morning, they parted at Sydney Airport—Sarah for Perth, and Stephen, Julie, and Susie on a Qantas flight to Queensland and the tropical city of Cairns. There they embarked by coach for the nearby town of Port Douglas. As a wanderer, Stephen for the first time felt an instant bond with a particular place. Their guide was one of those rarities who loved people and her job, and it showed. The town, laid out in a simple grid pattern, allowed no high-rise buildings whatsoever. The abundance of lush vegetation, the eye-catching colour and variety of growth, the sight and sound of exotic birds, and the unforgettable smell of the tropics were overwhelming. Rosita, their guide of Brazilian extraction, had her own affinity with the place.

'Your boss pay me big money to show you. Very good for me because if I have no family and no have to work, I would show you for nothing—for the love I have for this wonderful place. It is very special for Australia and for the world.'

She booked them into luxurious apartments on Macrossan Street rather than in any of the many five-star hotels with obligatory golf courses that surround the town. They settled in, with Susie and Julie in one apartment and Stephen across the street in another.

Like any true professional, Rosita seemed to know everybody they met. She brought them to bars, clubs, pubs, restaurants, and out to the Great Barrier Reef for a day of snorkelling, diving, and swimming amongst the myriad forms of fish life inhabiting this remarkable place. Another day was spent going over the rainforest in a Skyrail gondola, which looked for all the world like a ski lift in the tropics. They looked down on the forest canopy as they soared up to the little town of Kuranda. Rosita brought them on foot through the rainforest, where they saw the majestic kauri pine and the graceful maple silkwood towering way above them.

Stephen and Julie had by now graduated to publicly holding hands. Susie often almost blurted some words of objection but, in all conscience, could not deny the loving tenderness between them. Julie had a glow about her, while Stephen exhibited the manly qualities she so admired. He was mannerly, polite, and obviously a complete gentleman. However, Susie knew well the pull of nature and subtly made sure opportunities did not exist.

That afternoon, they left Kuranda's charming old-world railway station in a steam train on a narrow-gauge track and descended the 4.7 miles in the most exhilarating free-fall train journey in the world.

Chapter 16

Back in Ireland, Hugh Heffernan had been busy. The IRA Army Council, the supreme body of the provisional movement, granted him an interview. He had some sympathetic support there even though he had in their parlance been stood down. He again outlined the sequence of events leading to his 'difficulties'. The fact that Stephen Doyle had resurfaced in such a prominent way was significant. They agreed to his request for the use of their considerable intelligence resources plus the secondment of one of their experienced hit-and-grab teams.

Well satisfied, Heffernan began casting his net, his mind fixed on the prize—rehabilitation for him and curtains for Doyle. His first move was to alert a buried asset in the federal police in Canberra, the federal capital of Australia. Police forces were always a prime source of intelligence for the IRA.

The Irish Diaspora beginning in 1847 had scattered Irishmen and -women across the world. A significant number had found successful careers in various police forces and armies. Succeeding generations had retained a sentimental affection for the 'old sod'. This was fertile recruiting ground for the Provisional IRA, whose clever propaganda touched a nerve in all Irishmen who aspired for a united thirty-two-county Irish republic.

Chapter 17

Rosita, like a mother hen, was on hand to make sure nothing was missed. She believed that although people could return, nothing would ever match the wonder of first impressions. They swam and walked on splendid beaches, the tropical sun giving them healthy glowing suntans.

A trip on a converted deep-sea trawler up the Daintree River, with food, wine, music, and a bunch of wild young holidaymakers was terrific fun with a scary ending. The organizers promised a sighting of crocodiles in their natural element. The wine and other booze flowed. The skipper brought the vessel as close as he could to a sandbar, where he pointed to several crocs sunning themselves.

After viewing the unmoving forms for several minutes, a brash, drunken young man offered his opinion. 'Not a bloody sign of life, mates. It's all a bloody con. I'll show the lot of ya. They're only carved logs, I'm telling ya.'

With that, he jumped off the transom into the water. When he surfaced and struck out for the bar, he didn't see the largest 'log' react to the splash. The giant saltwater croc ran with amazing agility on short bowed legs and slid into the river. Instantaneously, the skipper fired the already idling engines, and Stephen dived into the water. In a few strokes, he reached the spluttering youth, and the skipper interposed the vessel between them and the croc. Willing hands hauled the dripping pair aboard.

The skipper jumped from the bridge, ran down to the unfortunate young man, gave him an open-handed left and right smack to the head, turned him round, and delivered an unmerciful kick to his behind.

'Sue me if you like, you little asshole. Now get below and stay there till we tie up in Douglas.' He turned to Stephen and looked him up and down. 'You're a bloody idiot, mate, riskin' your life for a fool. No, no, don't say nothin'. I'd like to shake your hand, and thanks for doin' Gawd's

46

truth, what I for one couldn't do. Now get down to my cabin. You need a quick shower and a change of clobber.'

Stephen turned to find Susie gaping and Julie white-faced and pale.

'Please, please forgive me. I'm sorry, that was stupid. I don't know what I was thinking. I'm really sorry.'

The two women ran up and, without a word, hugged and hugged and hugged the sopping, contrite Irishman.

Word via mobile phone had gone before them. When they reached the dock, a mob of well-wishers, rubberneckers, and the local press awaited. Stephen, Julie, and Susie had agreed to say absolutely nothing. Apart from being snapped a hundred times, they escaped through the dockside patio of Fiorelli's, through the restaurant, and out on to Wharf Street. Looking back, they saw the skipper displaying no such qualms as he posed for the photographers with his arm draped around the shoulder of the abashed young man now nicknamed Crocodile Douglas for his trouble.

Modern technology meant their images and story were being picked up from the wire services within hours. A sharp-eyed subeditor made the connection between the trio and the fame surrounding Barabbas. Next morning, the _Sydney Herald_ ran with the story 'Famous Horse, the Beautiful People, and the Mystery Hero' complete with pictures from Bridgetown, Sydney, and Port Douglas.

Rosita whisked them away from their apartments, and they laughed their heads off at her next surprise on their itinerary. A visit to the renowned Hartley's Creek Crocodile Farm left them speechless. The most talkative, enthusiastic wildlife ranger in the entire state of Queensland gave them the A-list treatment.

They saw the breeding pens and the separate pools for the bulls and females. At feeding time, the reptiles were allowed to feed together. As the rangers held out raw, rotting meat on the end of metal poles, the crocodiles leapt and grabbed, tearing and rolling with frightening speed. Then came the highlight of the day. The biggest, scariest, and meanest old bull had been bellowing in his pen. The gates slid up, and a 15-feet monster straight out of _Jurassic Park_ shot into the pool. He crashed into the reed beds, flushing out the other crocs, who quickly made their escape down a submerged tunnel.

As the last one escaped, the ranger closed the gate, leaving just him and the very large, very angry, and very hungry crocodile. The ranger then proceeded to feed and goad the terrible beast. The audience shrieked with terror as the ranger went through his paces, culminating with the man leaning over the water with a lump of meat dangling from a rope in his outstretched hand. A relieved round of applause after the hideous reptile leapt 6 feet to grab the food brought the show to an end.

Susie could not help but notice Julie clinging to Stephen as she shrieked along with the rest of the audience and Stephen with a protective arm around her shoulder.

On their way back to Port Douglas, Stephen asked Rosita to stop at a store he had noticed on the way to Hartley's.

'Ladies, there's no way I can manage what I want to do behind your backs. Now, no arguing. I intend to buy a little token of my esteem—a small thank you from a guy who is having the most fantastic time of his life. Now what did I say? Not a word, not a peep.'

There were times Stephen felt he could talk the Pope out of Rome, and this was one of them. He ushered the three women to an adjoining café and told them to wait. He crossed the sunny parking lot and entered the cool interior of Australia's leading opal and semi-precious stone emporium.

Adjusting to the dim lighting, he surveyed the vast room. What he needed was not just help but enthusiastic assistance. Eventually, he spotted her, an attractive middle-aged smartly dressed woman. She seemed like a woman who had looked at life, liked what she saw, and lived it to the full. Stephen approached and made eye contact.

Her name tag said 'Kate'. He introduced himself, and that certain signal from man to woman as old as time was exchanged. Quickly he explained. Asking him to wait, she slipped on a light work coat, left the building, and crossed to the café. There she made a minor purchase, inspected the three women, and returned to the showroom.

'One each but different, but not too different—but one subtly different so that the special one will feel the difference? How am I doing so far?'

'Spot on, Kate. Can you do it without the option of the poorhouse for yours truly?'

'Trust me, young Stephen. How can any woman resist those blue Irish eyes?'

Twenty minutes later, he emerged and handed each of them a beautifully wrapped package.

'One condition—open them only in the privacy of your own room. I couldn't bear to see three gorgeous girls stutter for words of thanks for something they don't really like. I feel great now that's done. Let's go, girls, I'm starving.'

Back at Port Douglas, they washed, combed, and primped themselves for dinner. That night, Rosita brought them to the outdoor section of Menolla's, an exquisite Catalan-themed restaurant specializing in lamb dishes. The three ladies sported their opal jewellery. Stephen was relieved at their genuine delight at his gesture and choices—a brooch for Rosita, a bracelet for Susie, and a pendant for Julie.

He silenced them with a simple 'It was my pleasure. Now, ladies, please, no more. You know, I can't cope. Thank you.'

With girly grins lighting their beautiful made-up faces, they continued to tease him as the house specialty was ordered, which was in turn washed down by copious glasses of the finest Spanish and Australian wines.

Susie had to be soothed and reassured when she thought the wine was making her see rats running up and down the decorative palm trees. Menolla was summoned. He explained they were a rare, endangered, protected species related to the marsupials and were most definitely not rodents. He bowed and kissed Susie's hand and left them with a Department of Parks and Wildlife leaflet on the subject.

Following a gargantuan feast overseen by the proprietor himself, they wobbled up the street to their apartments in the early hours of the morning. Going up a short flight of steps, Susie stumbled and turned her ankle.

Chapter 18

Two separate groups were now acting on the same information. Heffernan with his minder Chris Murphy, were met at Perth Airport international terminal by a minor functionary in the federal police. He informed them of the latest events at Port Douglas, including addresses and photographs. As the last connection between Perth and Cairns had recently departed, he had booked them on the first available morning flight. They were also booked overnight in the nearby Holiday Inn, where Heffernan met up with the four-man hit-and-grab team already in place from the previous day.

Their contact had already supplied the team with a selection of untraceable handguns and ammunition. Two of the team would travel to Cairns to reconnoitre, while the others would stake out Perth Airport and Bill Burroughs's Ballymore Stud in Bridgetown. They agreed with Heffernan's assessment that logically the trio were on holiday and had to return to where they lived and worked.

Meanwhile, the Chinaman and his henchmen were aboard the flight missed by Heffernan and were bound for Cairns.

Chapter 19

In Port Douglas, another heavenly tropical day dawned. The sun quickly burned off the morning mists and opened the petals of millions of plants, flowers, and shrubs, filling the air with nature's heady perfume. Susie's ankle was slightly swollen and tender to the touch. Rosita summoned a young doctor from a nearby clinic, who diagnosed a slight sprain. As they were to return to Perth the following day, he prescribed anti-inflammatory tablets and bed rest.

With the change of circumstances, an argument grew as to how they would spend their final day. Susie was adamant the others would not spend it moping around, and being a forceful woman, she had her way. Julie, while initially determined to stay with her aunt, was persuaded to compromise. They would spend the morning shopping locally and the afternoon on the fabulous nearby Four Mile Beach.

Leaving Susie comfortably propped up with magazines and chocolate, they left to enjoy their final day in what they now firmly believed to be their personal Garden of Eden. Shopping in the many boutiques with international brands was naturally a delight for Julie; guided by Rosita, she made her purchases in record time. Storing the packages in Rosita's Land Cruiser and picking up Stephen and a packed hamper, they drove down a couple of streets and emerged on golden sands stretching as far as eye could see.

The first thing to greet them was a nearly deserted beach. The red 'No swimming' flags were fluttering from the lifeguard station. When they enquired from the bronzed pair on the upper deck of the station, they were told an unseasonable onshore breeze had overnight brought an infestation of venomous jellyfish. Word had already reached them that a male swimmer down the coast near Brisbane had ignored local warnings and had died a horrible death.

This news required a change of plan. Rosita had some errands she could do. She also wanted to check in on Susie to make sure she had taken her lunch. The other two would sunbathe, walk, throw a Frisbee, have the picnic lunch, and meet back at the lifeguard station in three hours' time.

'Right, Mr Muscles, pick up that picnic basket and follow me.' Julie set off at a brisk pace, taking off her wrap and leaving Stephen to follow her gorgeous undulating behind, juggling like two puppies in the bottom half of a lemon bikini.

After a mile, she veered sharp right into a gap in the towering dunes. Five minutes later, they came to a natural grassy hollow sheltered from the breeze. Julie, out of breath and her bosom heaving, turned to Stephen, who was gasping from the weight of the hamper and the pace of the forced march.

'Catch your breath, mister, while I spread the blanket and get you a drink.' She laid the blanket and unscrewed the cap from a bottle of chilled water.

She watched his Adam's apple bob up and down as he gulped the sparkling liquid. A tiny rivulet stole from his mouth and trickled down his chest. Fascinated for some reason, she stared as the trickle disappeared down the front of his shorts. She held out her hand for her share of the drink.

Wordlessly he handed it over and watched as she tilted her head and, holding the bottle above her open mouth, poured the remaining contents down her throat. Wiping her mouth with the back of her hand, she tossed the empty bottle back in the hamper. For a minute, without moving or speaking, they stood gazing intently at one another.

'Now don't feel badly, Stephen. I knew about the jellyfish before we arrived here. As soon as I knew my aunt's sprain wasn't serious, I made my plans. We are here together because I wanted to, and I think you feel the same. Now kindly remove your shirt.'

Dumbfounded, Stephen shrugged off his shirt, barely believing what he was hearing. Then slipping off her top, Julie stood on tiptoe, slid her arms around his neck, and kissed him long and deep. Stepping back, she smiled, and noting with satisfaction the effect she was having, she kicked off her bottoms with a flick of a dainty ankle. Putting her hands on his shoulders, she pressed him down so that they were kneeling facing each other.

'Now, Mr Doyle, I am a first time virgin, probably with a torn hymen from a lifetime on horses. I have chosen you, and I hope you will choose me. We both felt something for each other when first we met. Who knows what lies ahead? Let's live for the moment just this once. Please show me the ways of love. I know that sounds corny, but what do I know? And, Stephen, I hope what's happening to me is normal because I'm drenched, and something moist is running down my thighs.'

Stephen, not usually stuck for words, knelt there with his mouth occasionally opening and closing, drinking in the sight of this fabulous naked girl wearing only an opal pendant. So far he had not uttered a single word. He could sense she was nervous, but he had come to learn she possessed strong, implacable willpower.

Mr Hyde was in overdrive. *Yes, yes, yes.* His best intentions, including his fear of the consequences and his future, were screaming, *No, no, no.* Julie was grinning at his discomfort, and for some reason, he noticed her teeth were sparkling whiter and whiter.

She reached down and unbuckled the belt of his shorts. 'Ah, Mr Doyle, where's the blarney when you need it most? Now you're not to be worried about a thing. I was always determined to make love for the first time without drink or drugs, in the broad daylight, with the sun on my back. I've even bought a pack of rubbers this morning. Now what do we have here?'

With that, she peeled down his shorts. She took a second to observe the bulge in his briefs. Hooking her fingers into the waistband, she yanked them down. They snagged, and she had to ease them over the offending obstacle. The erection, free at last, sprang to throbbing attention in all its glory.

'Wow.'

'Don't be frightened, Julie. I promise I won't hurt you.'

'I'm not one bit frightened, Stephen. I just wonder if it will fit. Is it an unusually big one? Can I just hold it for a second?'

In a comedy of errors, with Julie still holding him, Stephen tried to slip out of his shorts and briefs. In the process of hopping on one leg, he fell over on the blanket. Julie shrieked with laughter, and Stephen could do nothing else but join in. By the time they stopped, Stephen had quite deflated. The nervous release of laughter calmed them.

They looked deep into each other's eyes and began kissing and nibbling and touching and fondling. Under Stephen's guidance and Julie's natural reactions, they joined together at the height of their arousal. After a few moments, he withdrew, quickly fitted the condom, re-entered, and paused. Then he began the slow rhythmic motion of instinctive lovemaking. With shocks of pleasure, they soared to a peak where, for microseconds, time was suspended in exquisite delight. With all the senses at full throttle, every detail of sound, feel, touch, and smell are fully engaged. Then after ecstatic release came the languid descent from Olympus to a blanket on a beach on the north-eastern coast of Australia.

Back at the apartment, Susie was mulling over the news from Rosita. *Three hours, plenty of time, but it's broad daylight, and there's bound to be some people around.* Still she was uneasy.

She was more than uneasy when Rosita brought them back. The sight of a flustered Rosita, who herself was an earthy woman of the world and had read the obvious signs, was enough to confirm her own worst fears. Far from looking shifty or guilty, they both looked her straight in the eye as they asked about her sprain and the final treat arranged by Rosita for later on that evening.

The dress code was the usual smart casual, and at 7 p.m., they arrived for the twice-a-week barbecue at the famous Iron House bar and restaurant extraordinaire. Besides the complete spread of barbecue fare, the Iron House promised a night of never-to-be-forgotten fun. They ate heartily, enjoying the delicious food. Copious cans or stubbies of Foster's and Black Swan were consumed, leaving them in sparkling form for the main attraction.

Susie and Rosita, being pragmatic women, knew that what was done could not be undone. They nodded wordlessly to each other with that worldwide Gallic gesture of raised shoulders and open palms. And clearly it wasn't as if a big bad wolf had seduced their little innocent, shrinking violet. Julie was obviously in charge, and in that subtle way, she had already crossed her threshold to women's estate.

Going inside, they were greeted by one of the world's greatest flimflam artists. Using the patter of a Virginia tobacco auctioneer, he sold the merits of five enormous cane toads. These vile creatures were deliberately introduced to the Australian cane fields from Sri Lanka to eat harmful insects. They were absolutely useless at this and have bred and spread alarmingly across Australia like the proverbial biblical plague.

Dressed in jockeys' colours, the horrible, slimy, warty creatures were induced to race along a table. The propellant was a drinking straw used by the owners to blow air up their behinds. If one fell or jumped off the table, the owner had to pick it up from the floor or from some hysterical female's lap. They each bid and bought the racing rights of three of the toads. The competition between them and their toads had them shrieking and cheering with the rest. The balmy tropical night, the good food and wine, the raucous crowd, and their own altered lives became one of those special life-enhancing occasions.

Susie had been rehearsing with herself how to broach her suspicions with the Nag when she phoned him later. They returned to their respective apartments in fine form, having confirmed arrangements with Rosita for their departure the following morning. Fully rested and restored after their ten-day break, they were now eager to return to Bridgetown. The next instalment of Barabbas's career promised as much excitement as the first.

That night, Julie Dundon disappeared.

Chapter 20

The Chinaman and his crew had stalked Stephen and his three female companions all evening. It was easy for them to keep an eye on the Iron House from a distance. While they were competent at surveillance, they were clueless at counter-surveillance. On the other hand, Heffernan's newly arrived henchmen, Brody and Moran, were extremely competent. As soon as they arrived from Cairns in a hired van, they rented a small house on a run-down property on Grant Street.

With the addresses of both apartments in hand, they immediately reconnoitred the surrounding area. They had easily established that Stephen and co. were being watched. Under orders to shadow their prey back to Bridgetown, they decided to watch and wait. As the two apartments were literally across the street from each other, though not fronting the street, they were able to keep an eye on both. Parked discreetly behind smoked glass, they settled down in a well-rehearsed routine.

Brody nudged Moran at 3.30 a.m. 'Somebody's trying to get into Doyle's apartment.'

'Yeah, got him. He might be good. Nearly didn't cop him.'

'Let's see what he's up to. Hope he ain't going to pop Doyle. Heffernan would have our guts.'

They slid from the van, having unscrewed the bulb from the vanity light, soundlessly closing the door.

Up the steps, using well-practiced hand signals, Brody nudged the open door with an extended foot. A quick glance inside showed a shadowy figure bending over a bedside locker. The sleeping form woke up with a start and turned on the light. Stephen and the intruder froze for a second. In an instant, Stephen reared up, attempting to headbutt his assailant. About to shout, Stephen was smashed over the head with the butt of a compact Uzi sub-machine gun.

Fearing that Doyle was about to be shot, Moran jumped through the door, assuming the classic shooter's pose. 'Drop it, or you're fucking dead.'

The intruder, wearing a ski mask, whipped around, bringing up the barrel of his weapon. Moran shot him through the left eye with a silenced Beretta. All hope of caution was dashed as the death throes of the masked man caused his finger to convulsively pull the trigger. Brody and Moran dived to the floor as the lethal contents of the Uzi were sprayed in all directions, creating a deafening noise in the confined space.

As the intruder slumped to the floor, the magazine was emptied, followed by an abrupt silence. The reek of cordite filled the air, and they first checked themselves and then whether Stephen was still breathing. They pulled the ski mask from the dead man and saw he was oriental. Pulling up both sleeves, they noticed the heavy tattoos depicting black and red dragons entwined.

'The fucking Kowloon triads—now what is Stephie boy doing mixed up with that crazy crowd?'

'He was leaving a note. Look, Moran, they say they've got the girl. Go back to Bridgetown and wait for instructions. Well, well, well . . . Okay, quick now, over the street. Maybe we can grab the girl ourselves.'

'No, Brody, we've got to be invisible. All sorts of shit will hit the fan in minutes.'

'Okay then, but a quick look to see the state of play across the street.'

Lights were coming on up and down the street. Shouts of alarm and confusion were ringing out. Pocketing the note, they ran across Macrossan Street and up the steps to where the light was spilling from an open door. A middle-aged woman was sitting gagged and trussed to a chair. She had a cut to her forehead, and her eyes blazed with fury. Running back outside, they heard a car roaring up from the underground car park. Again they dived for cover as a figure standing in the sunroof blazed at them with an assault rifle. The car careened around the corner, heading for the marina. By the time Brody and Moran's van reached the dock, the car was empty, with all doors swinging open. In the distance, the sound of a high-powered pleasure craft disappeared in the mist.

'Ten to one, Moran, they were renting an apartment in the same block, down the estuary, on to a bigger boat or a seaplane, and away. Not bad, not bad at all. I might be completely wrong, but it fits. They've got the girl. We've got Doyle. It's all about the horse, Moran, and the horse is in Bridgetown. That's where the next move will be. We'll get Hennessy on the blower and compare notes.'

Back in their safe house, Brody used a satellite phone to contact Heffernan. Their professional experience, long used to improvisation, helped them quickly agree to a plan. Their federal police contacts, quoting 'confidential classified information', would immediately contact Bridgetown and recommend a news blackout. Assuming a positive response, they would already have gotten the federal police to relay the order to the local police in Cairns and Port Douglas. Then the equivalent to the British D notice would simultaneously be served on all elements of the Australian media. This could only work temporarily, as the media, like a pack of hounds smelling blood, hated to be muzzled, especially one with a juicy story and international implications.

Stephen was taken into custody. He was still unconscious when the local police arrived. However, he was unconscious in a bullet-shattered apartment with a dead man. Then there was the small matter of the Webley revolver, admittedly loaded but apparently not recently fired, which they discovered at the bottom of a wardrobe. All that was put on hold until he was released from the hospital where he was under observation for suspected concussion.

Susie, hospitalized briefly, couldn't be contained. She was like a demented madwoman overcome with fear and guilt. Her Julie, their Julie was taken from them by brutes. Who were they? What did they want? Was she safe? Why were they attacked?

Stephen decided to keep his mouth shut concerning the Chinaman when told the ethnic origin of his attacker. He could not imagine them going this far, and if by any chance, they had, then he, Stephen, would concoct whatever plan was necessary to secure Julie's safe return.

In the meantime, the Nag and Bill Burroughs, together with a team of lawyers, had arrived. Having made a statement to the police to the effect that he had no idea why Julie might be kidnapped, Stephen was released. Burroughs convinced the police that Stephen's presence was vital to the quest to find Julie. The matter of an illegally held firearm would remain on file for further consideration.

The police summarized the situation as they saw it. First of all, they had a kidnapped wealthy young woman. Secondly, a dead person of Chinese extraction bearing the trademark tattoos of a notorious criminal fraternity was shot and killed by a person or persons with unknown motives. Thirdly, a male companion of the kidnapped girl was found unconscious in a separate apartment containing the body of the deceased.

Forensics found no evidence of Julie in Stephen's apartment or of Stephen in Julie's apartment. The one matter on which they all agreed was that the motive had to be money, and subsequently, a ransom demand would appear. At the end of a fruitless week of searching by land, sea, and air, they returned to Bridgetown to await contact and confirmation that their Julie was alive.

Chapter 21

During their absence, the other members of Heffernan's squad used the opportunity to 'visit' the Monahan and Burroughs homesteads. There they planted an array of sophisticated listening devices otherwise known as bugs. Not an easy task, but not difficult either for the dedicated members of one of the world's most ruthless organizations.

Federal and local police, plus specialist hostage negotiators, set up their command and control centre in Bridgetown. The phone call when it came unleashed a tidal wave of consequences.

'I wish to speak to Stephen Doyle. Tell him it's the Song, not the Singer. If he is not there, I will call again in exactly four hours. In the meantime, my guest wishes to say a brief hello.'

Everybody stared in fascinated horror at the whirring recording devices and immediately put on their headphones.

They heard Julie say, 'I am reading this. I am okay. Do exactly as they say. Love you all.'

At the click of the disconnection, Susie shrieked and collapsed.

On his return to Bridgetown, Stephen spent every waking moment with Barabbas. This in turn was counterproductive, as such a highly intelligent animal immediately sensed something amiss. Stephen countered this by bringing one of Julie's hacking jackets to the stall. Barabbas snorted and sniffed the jacket and allowed himself to be soothed and lulled by the touch of the maestro. Dickey Bennett brought him up to date regarding the preparations for their next big event. Dickey was devastated at the news concerning Julie's disappearance. He, like everybody else, had been sworn to secrecy and told to avoid gossip and the press like the plague.

Stephen, taking Barabbas through his paces on the gallops, let his tensions go as they flew over the misted early morning ground. Here he felt spiritually closer to the beautiful young woman who had become the love of his life. Stephen had hoped against hope that he would be contacted indirectly. Already the seeds of a plan were forming. Given his history, he was accomplished in the devious and cunning arts and was well versed in the ducking, diving, and dodging departments.

Summoned from a deep sleep, he faced the hardened, suspicious faces of those he had hoped to consider as friends and, for want of a different word, as *family*.

Susie took both of his hands in hers and looked him in the eye. 'Stephen, there's something going on you need to share with us. Now don't lie to me. I know you two are in love—shut up, Nag, we'll talk later. Stephen, she's all we have, so help us please.'

Keeping direct eye contact, Stephen, against his nature, started to tell selected versions of the truth, 'I won't and I can't deny that I love Julie. You know how we met. It wasn't planned or connived. I haven't told her in so many words, but it's true. And I cannot bear to think that my past has put her in harm's way.' Stephen's voice shook and trembled with emotion as he began to relate how Quan Song Li and he had first met.

Ten years ago, Wexford in Southern Ireland was a very different place. It was a time of change. A new economic phenomenon christened the Celtic Tiger was in gestation. A unique combination of factors converged—record low interest rates, low inflation, a young well-educated population, and very low rates of corporation tax. Also, membership in the EU and the eurozone and the advent of the multinationals in the new global economy completed the rosy picture.

Money became supreme; the new god was Mammon, and Ireland, kicking out the old values and traditions, became its devoted slave. Yet those very traditions were everywhere to be seen. Wexford, on the harbour of the mighty River Slaney, has recorded human habitation before the Stone Age. The Vikings, long a scourge of the native Celtic people, were gradually assimilated and established the first permanent settlement, which they called Weis Forde. The town strung along the harbour rises in tiers from the water with narrow, winding streets, and the skyline dominated by the spires of magnificent twin churches. Visitors strolling along the boardwalk on the quay front must give way four times daily as the Dublin train en route to Rosslare Harbour creeps slowly along the waterfront.

Subsequent history is littered with references to Wexford. The Normans, who eventually conquered Ireland, landed in South Wexford at Baginbun near Bridgetown. The king of Leinster (one of the four provinces of Ireland) lost his wife to a local chieftain. Unable to sort matters himself, the king appealed to the Norman king of England. He had a bunch of battle-hardened nobles and knights hanging around with idle hands. He dispatched them to Ireland in 1169, and the Irish spent the next 753 years trying to get them to leave.

In 1170 the Normans built their first permanent castle in Ireland on the River Slaney above Wexford. The previous year, the first treaty between England and Ireland was signed at the historic Selskar Abbey located in the town of Wexford. Both are preserved and still standing. The Abbey has the historical distinction as the place where England's Henry II did his penance for the murder of St Thomas, a Becket, the troublesome archbishop of Canterbury.

Others followed down the centuries (Tudors, Elizabethans, Jacobites, Williamites, and Cromwellians), each leaving their mark before being absorbed into the glue pot of Ireland. In more recent times, a fine statue was erected by the American government on Crescent Quay to honour Commodore John Barry, the founder of the United States Navy, who was born near Bridgetown. President John F. Kennedy visited Wexford Town and New Ross, County Wexford, from where his great grandfather emigrated to the USA. Four months later, he was assassinated, and the light of Wexford's pride and joy was extinguished. A magnificent arboretum and park outside New Ross was dedicated to his name and memory.

A polyglot of invaders arrived and stayed principally for the land. The land of Wexford was the richest arable land in Ireland, particularly the limestone land around Bridgetown, 7 miles south of Wexford Town, and especially suited to raising horses. The Doyles arrived in the 1640s as mercenaries with Oliver Cromwell, the butcher of Ireland, and were granted confiscated land in lieu of pay.

The Doyles prospered as farmers and bloodstock owners, but Stephen and Black Jack, his father, were on a collision course. Stephen, in his sixth and last year in secondary school, dropped out, and beatings and pleadings could not get him to return. A brilliant student with an uncanny affinity for figures and finance, he had at times been a great help to the school board by helping prepare the annual accounts.

His mother pleaded with his father to give him space and time. 'He'll come round, Jack, you'll see. He's a good lad. Sure, he's not yet eighteen. Give him a chance. A year with you in the yard should do the trick.'

What they all suspected swiftly came to pass. Born and raised with horses, it was easy to see his natural affinity. But given responsibility and with the passion to impress his father, he was soon at a different level. Stephen was in his element. His siblings, who should have been jealous, were not. The stable lads and his contemporaries affectionately nicknamed him the Horse Whisperer after Robert Redford's movie character of the same name.

Going to race meetings with their own or their client's horses had a special excitement. Stephen didn't seem to need sleep; he was up late preparing and up early loading the horseboxes. The sound and smell of horses were in his soul and coursed like blood through his veins. Like any young lad, especially one with a head for figures, having a flutter was a natural progression.

Unfortunately, unknown to him or his family, he possessed the seeds of destruction, and these seeds were about to sprout. Gambling addiction, like alcoholism, is all-consuming, with the difference that the drinker will eventually fall down, while the gambler is only constrained by the amount of money he could beg, borrow, or steal.

Chapter 22

The arrival of the Chinese restaurant and takeaway phenomenon years before the Celtic Tiger, meant that the Chinese were embedded in the cuisine and landscape of Ireland. No town, city, village, or hamlet was without one. They worked hard, kept to themselves, and didn't make claims on the state's resources. The authorities left them alone. They bought their ingredients locally, except for the sauces, and paid their taxes. They were invisible. They all looked the same to the locals, and this had enabled them to lead parallel lives. They all retained strong links with their old country. Some of these links were good, and some were definitely not so good.

One thing they excelled at was their 'underground railway'. They unobtrusively moved their people around the world through their restaurants and other business. And so, an errant son of a distinguished Hong Kong triad family found himself exiled to Wexford. There he would redeem himself through hard work and also keep an eye on the family investments spread over the entire south-east of Ireland.

Two facts define both peoples. If the Irish as a nation like to drink, then the Chinese as a people love to gamble.

One evening, on his way back from a race meeting in Clonmel, Stephen and some friends stopped for a meal at the Yellow Wall, a Chinese restaurant on the quay front in New Ross. The young waiter was particularly attentive. As Stephen paid the bill, the waiter in perfect English addressed him by name. Explaining that he had often seen Stephen at the track, he wondered if he had any tips for the next meeting at Bettyville, Wexford Town's racecourse. Like addicts of every stripe the world over, Stephen recognized the smiling young man as a kindred soul. The waiter introduced himself as Quan Song Li and said he would be working in the Red Dragon, their Wexford restaurant, on race day.

Without thinking, Stephen said he might pop in for a quick bite of lunch on his way to the meeting.

A firm friendship began that Thursday. They had a lot in common, being younger sons in large families and perpetually at war with dominant fathers. Both had a mischievous sense of fun bordering on the reckless. His parents gave Stephen a fair amount of latitude due to his aptitude for hard work and the fact he had no interest in alcohol. Quan was equally hard-working and had adapted remarkably to working and living in such an alien environment.

Soon they became familiar and inseparable all over the south-east. Race meetings, dog tracks, card games, darts, and snooker—any place people gathered and were prepared to wager on a particular outcome were sure to attract Butch and Sundance, as they were affectionately named. Sometimes, for fun and fuelled by excessive testosterone, they would mingle with the guests at large country weddings held in Whites or the Talbot Hotel. This gave them a shot at the bridesmaids, with bets between them as to who would be the first to lure one 'upstairs'. When that failed, they singled out a wallflower for half the bet. With the simple expedience of sticking a carnation into the buttonhole of a decent jacket, they would enjoy bluffing the bride's and/or the groom's families that they were with the other side. Stephen instructed a nervous Quan that a bluff often worked best when it was done openly. The fact that Quan was obviously not Irish further insulated them from challenge.

Other times they might turn up at a funeral in the town where the deceased was waked out at home. With the simple expedience of knocking on the door with a black crepe, with half a dozen Guinness in hand and the immortal words 'Friend of the corpse. Sorry for your trouble, missus', they were off on another adventure of singing and bluffing and opportunity. Stephen had a theory that females were most vulnerable at weddings and funerals, and he expended enormous time and energy to prove that point.

Quan was amused at all this frantic bother. In his culture, that degree of effort was saved for the pursuit of a wife, but that was unless you had parents of the old stock still implacably believing in arranged marriages. For him, sex was an itch that occasionally had to be scratched. He felt it was pointless mooning after an unattainable girl, especially for him, here in Ireland.

Their gambling was entering a serious stage, so Quan proposed a novel solution to quench Stephen's insatiable sex drive. Quan looked after six restaurants and takeaways spread over three counties. Each one would employ approximately ten females, mostly young and were in the country illegally. Quan's job was to get the maximum productivity out of these girls, who were in turn paying off large debts on loans incurred by their impoverished parents. These loans were with the same loan sharks run by the triads, who indirectly owned restaurants spread all over the Western world.

This practice, a modern version of indentured slavery and so ingrained in oriental culture, did not register on the social conscience of local managers. As a good manager, Quan realized that contentment rather than fear was more likely to achieve his objectives. Reinstatement into his father's affections and a recall home were his ultimate goals, and healthy profits from their Irish enterprise were the means.

One evening, on the way back from a successful race meeting at Gowran Park, Quan made his pitch.

'Stephen, this is a beautiful land—all green, sometimes all seasons in one day, rivers and roads winding like ribbons, nothing straight, warrior people easily fooled by priests and politicians. The world outside is a glorious place, with riches and new experiences waiting for those who dare. By now, you know me. Some business colleagues from home will arrive soon. They are interested in us and might be prepared to help us get to the back rooms, where we know all the big action takes place. But first, I have a special treat, which will be good for you and for me.'

Quan then went on to explain how, far from home and uninitiated in these matters, lonely Chinese girls had the same desires and longings as anybody else. He had a penthouse apartment at the Red Dragon overlooking the Crescent Harbour in Wexford. There he would introduce Stephen to his Chinese ladies, starting with his senior assistant, who was experienced in sexual practices. Quan was astonished at how reluctant Stephen appeared at the suggestion. The Stephen he knew was game for anything, but it took all his powers of persuasion to get him to agree.

Ming Tai was a revelation. Playing the submissive, she instigated and orchestrated events to their mutual satisfaction. The wham-bam of the after-pub knee-trembler was an anathema to the oriental notion of lovemaking. To them, it was something to be tantalizingly experienced at leisure.

And so a grateful Stephen confided to Quan, 'Got to tell the truth, buddy, that's the first proper time for me. I didn't know if I could. Never mind all the other stuff—all hit and hope. That's just me spoofing to beat you to those other birds and win our bets. Thanks, pal. I owe you big time. What a woman.'

Now that he was sorted, Stephen quickly entered the spirit of Quan's proposal. Stephen had to agree to treat all the ladies equally. Otherwise, the plan would backfire, and Quan would face a ferocious female rebellion with a subsequent hit to the bottom line. The ladies were guaranteed to be 'clean' and fully understood the nature of their involvement in Quan's incentive scheme.

What could have been a disaster instead became a brilliant success. The first time for all of them was a little shaky, but Ming Tai was superb at putting everybody at ease. She provided the perfect little touches of soft lights, music, scented candles, and trays of delicious nibbles with wine or soft drinks.

Stephen sharpened his understanding of human nature during these times. He was naturally alert to the different nuances and characteristics of each lady and quickly found that no two were the same. Exactly like his horses, they each had their own little way, and his understanding of this led to their increased pleasure. Also, nature had endowed him with a superb set of equipment, which drew gasps of wonder and squeals of delight at first encounter.

Each Monday night, a different lady ascended the backstairs to what Ming Tai called her heavenly kingdom and where, at the end of the evening, she sometimes slyly helped herself to her own portion of pleasure.

Chapter 23

Stephen was a naturally well-organized person. All activities away from the yard took place in the early evening. As far as humanely possible, except for special occasions, he was in his bed in Bridgetown at a respectable hour. Another priority was the Doyle Sunday lunch, a gargantuan after-Mass family affair. His mother and sisters, who had awards for food and cooking from every showground in Ireland, prepared this weekly feast. All were welcome, and each family member could bring whomever they liked.

The Doyles, in the best Irish tradition, operated an open, revolving-door style of hospitality. Black Jack presided, and his ramrod back, at 6 feet 2 inches with thumbs in his waistcoat, was the undisputed head of the clan. Brought up in hard times, he was a stickler for professionalism and would not tolerate slackers or slackness in any form. Theirs was a business totally dependent on results. As he often reminded them, reputations that took years to build could be destroyed in an instant.

Stephen contemplated his world as he prepared the Diddler, a sleek, stamina-stacked grey mare. The angle of a shaft of sunlight over the half door, the swirling golden dust motes in its beam, the stamping hooves, the occasional whinny up and down the yard, and the smell of oats and hay were embedded in his subconscious. Down the years, whenever he thought or spoke of home on his travels, this was the image that leapt to mind.

Then through a phone call to the yard, Quan invited Stephen to a meal in Whites to meet his 'uncles' from Macao.

Chapter 24

The meeting and meal went very well. The venue was well chosen, the newly renovated Whites Hotel stood on the same site as the original White's Coaching Inn established in 1779. Light from the soaring atrium illuminated the little tableau. Two bright, eager young men and two sleek, well-groomed middle-aged men sat down to enjoy a sumptuous meal. The two 'uncles' called Chou and Ling were urbane men of the world. They understood and appreciated fine wines, fine food, and fine living. They were particularly impressed by Stephen's indifference to alcohol, given their stereotypical image of the wild Irishman. Quan laughingly told them their perceptions were bang on except that Stephen was different.

Getting down to business, they explained they were responsible for large sums of their family's wealth. Their mission was to safeguard that wealth and to make it grow. Quan, in his reports to Macao, had mentioned Stephen's friendship with him, his affinity with horses, and his access to the racing world through the yard.

'Let us explain. We are not interested in anything illegal, just information based on sound judgment. You will not be asked to dope or injure any animal, which I believe would be completely repugnant to you. We control vast gambling enterprises, which is like a huge shark that can never rest. Nothing in business can stand still. To stand still is to go backwards. Ireland is a small but profitable market for us. We have decided to invest our Irish profits here in local racing for the time being. Eventually, we would like to buy or control some element of Irish bookmaking. We believe you would be well placed to assist us in this endeavour. Quan tells us you have been, shall we say, uniquely helpful to him in the running of the business. You will be suitably rewarded.'

At this, Stephen stared at Quan, who had assumed his inscrutable oriental look.

'Quan, you bastard, how could you? Is it true? The truth now, Quan, or I'm out the door.'

Quan in turn looked over at Uncle Ling, who gave an imperceptible nod.

'For no other reason except habit, with no ulterior motive, I did film your Monday visits to the Red Dragon, and in boasting to my uncles, I did let it slip. You shall have the one and only tape and my heartfelt apologies. Please forgive me, dear friend.'

Stephen thought for a moment. They weren't here in Ireland all the way from Macao to simply blackmail a young chap in a minor racing yard. What could they do? He had done nothing illegal—immoral maybe, but not illegal. He wasn't married or even engaged. So how could he turn this to his advantage? Knowledge was power, and the realization of how subservient Quan was to his family hierarchy was a surprise. He, on the other hand, was a free agent, and they needed his contacts and expertise. On the other-other hand, Ling had intended Stephen to know they had him taped. A little matter of intimidation perhaps? A touch of the old steel hand in the velvet glove? Interesting!

'Quan, I'm really disappointed. No good saying I'm not. Next Monday night, show me the set-up and give me the tape. Shall we get down to business, gentlemen? How exactly do you intend to go about this? And where do I fit in?'

The following two years were a roller coaster. Stephen drew up a master plan. Initially, they divided the south-east into areas where Quan's six restaurants were located. Using the restaurants as cover and their profits as stake money, the local manager would place bets with local bookmakers. Stephen and Quan would place other bets at the track and Tote.

Starting small, they were soon up and running as an efficient gambling machine. Sometimes, for bigger wagers, they tapped into the wider Chinese communities located in the larger urban areas of Dublin, Cork, Belfast, Waterford, Limerick, and Galway. Being the most adept with figures, Stephen insisted on keeping his own encrypted set of accounts. He had made this point at the original meeting, insisting he had to have this information to calculate how much commission he was earning. This, plus his cut of 5 per cent, was non-negotiable. The impasse was a deal breaker. Stephen, the master bluffer, held his nerve, and eventually they agreed.

Carmel, Stephen's youngest sister, worked for an offshore bank in Jersey. Another sister, Betty, worked in a local clearing bank in

Wexford. Between them and using the easily acquired birth certificate of a long-dead infant as ID, an account was opened, and the funds were electronically transferred on a regular basis.

The nerve centre was the apartment over the Red Dragon. They installed TVs, monitors, and high-speed broadband Internet connection. The era of Internet-spread betting had arrived and, with it, the new attraction of 'lay betting', where horses were backed not only to win but also to lose. Quan and Stephen had until now operated the enterprise strictly as a business.

Gradually, the lure of the gamble for its own sake started to take its toll. They began setting aside restaurant money as well as profits on a series of bets that doubled in wins or losses as the bet progressed. This bet involved five horses of their choice over a two-month period. As each race approached, they had to decide whether to bet on the horse to win or to lose.

They were completely out of their depth, betting on races taking place all over the world. Initially, they had great success with this bet using Irish horses running in Ireland. Stephen's very own Diddler winning in style at Leopardstown successfully concluded their last major coup. Congratulations were showered on them from Macao, and they had a special invitation to visit by Quan's father. They planned to travel after the finish of the flat season, and before the beginning of the jump season.

Now two wrong calls had them staring into the abyss. This was the narcotic of the gambler. They were both thrilled and terrified at the same time.

'Quan, for fuck's sake, calm down. Trust me. The next race is on a dirt track in Syracuse. I've good information on this one. Only thing is, the position we're in means we'll have to go for a win. The odds for a loss would wipe us out.'

Syracuse did not oblige, and they needed to get their hands on 200,000 pounds to stay in the ring. They had to pick a winner or a loser at tremendous odds to survive. Again, the likelihood was that only a winner would deliver. The tension between Stephen and Quan was palpable. Both were hanging in but looking for a way out.

Stephen's mathematical brain was in conflict with his gambler's brain. His head and his gut were completely at odds. An unwelcome visitor at lunch the following Sunday helped him make an irrevocable decision.

Chapter 25

His mother, Elizabeth—or Becky, as his father preferred—called up the stairs, 'Stephen, you have a visitor. I've put him in the front parlour. Ask him to stay for lunch.'

On his way downstairs, Stephen wondered who it could be. If it were Quan or any of his usual friends, she would have said so.

A short middle-aged man looking out the window turned at Stephen's approach. 'And how is my favourite pupil? Brother Superior sends his regards and wonders if you could straight away assist preparing the annual accounts. I would be particularly grateful. I know you must be extremely busy, but I really must insist.'

The blood in Stephen's veins turned to ice. He felt faint, sick, and murderous at the same time. Hugh Heffernan, his former maths teacher, stood there with soft white hands clasped together. He was the last person on earth he wanted to see.

'We haven't time for pleasantries, Stephen. This really is urgent. I've been instructed to move our funds. The side effects from the Belfast business have changed a lot of things. You've been out of the loop a while. Need I remind you of your oath or the danger for everyone if you disobey? Your skills are required to resurrect the funds you so skilfully buried on our behalf.'

Stephen's face reddened as he remembered the honeyed words, the siren song of romantic Irish nationalist fervour, and the recruitment at sixteen to serve the cause that, from the cradle, all Irish people are encouraged to embrace. The cost to family, business, home, or religion is irrelevant to the fanatics of the Provisional IRA. The whole approach was skilfully executed when Brother Superior, during Stephen's induction, massaged his pride and vanity. That skill was necessary when Stephen learned that Hugh Heffernan was to be his OC and would in fact administer the oath of allegiance.

Brother Superior realized there was bad blood between the teacher and pupil. He decided not to interfere. He pulled rank on both and would not tolerate dissent. Stephen's last active role was in transferring arms and ammunition from a deep-sea vessel to a trawler. This cargo was landed in the dead of night at the small harbours at Ballyhack, Cheekpoint, and Passage East. However, with the advent of the Good Friday Agreement (Belfast Agreement), he loosened his hold on Stephen with the warning that he was to be available whenever required.

Stephen's brain raced with mixed emotions see-sawing from his gambling problems to his oath and to the physical safety of his family. He had no illusions as to the displeasure of the Chinese when they discovered the restaurant business had been plundered. He certainly had no illusions as to the reaction of the IRA if any of their funds went missing. Stephen had used the diverse locations and bank accounts of the religious order to launder and hide the fighting funds of the southern brigade of the IRA. These were the proceeds of bank robberies, blackmail, extortion, and protection rackets. Some of these proceeds were in the form of gold, precious stones, art, bearer bonds, and currency.

'Tell Brother Superior I'll call to the monastery at eleven o'clock tomorrow morning to start the procedures. On no account are you to be there. If I ever see you again, I'll stick a fucking knife in you. Now get out of here, and don't ever come near my home or family again.'

The two stared with mutual hatred blazing at each other.

'tut-tut, dear boy. No need for such strong language after all we meant to each other. Just obey orders, and sleeping dogs will stay sleeping.'

The next few days were frantic as Stephen began to burn his boats. To protect his family, he emptied their current and savings accounts. It was essential for them to be visibly and publicly outraged at the betrayal of their own flesh and blood. Not willing to throw good money after bad, Stephen persuaded Quan to raise 100,000 pounds by any means possible with the promise that he would raise the rest.

Then he disappeared, taking 60,000 pounds from his family, 100,000 pounds from Quan, and 500,000 pounds from the IRA.

Chapter 26

Stephen slipped out of Ireland knowing he could never return. By way of London, Jersey, and Luxemburg, he arranged for his funds to be liquid anywhere in the civilized world. After that, he zigzagged around Europe, then to South East Asia, making curious friendships amongst the low and mighty he encountered along the way. Within three years, his stash was considerably reduced. Again, the turn of a card or the false fancy of a well-presented lump of horseflesh were his undoing.

Never afraid to get his hands dirty, he would take to anything to turn a shilling. Usually, he gravitated to studs and stables, where his gifts and love of these magnificent animals were an obvious advantage. Acquiring false papers was not a major problem if a person had money and contacts. Eventually, he reached Australia and began following the big racing festivals around the continent.

Last March, he arrived in Balingup for the Bridgetown Derby and met Julie by absolute chance. It was while staying at the Coachman's that Quan Song Li re-entered his life. Somewhere along the way, he had brushed against the vast spider's web of the worldwide Chinese presence.

Susie, the Nag, the Burroughs, and the Becketts listened in stunned amazement to the abridged version of the life and times of Stephen Doyle. He told them practically everything, with the exception of his role in Quan's incentive scheme at the Red Dragon. Having matured considerably since then, he was not particularly proud of that particular episode.

Susie, still shaking her head, asked, 'What did Quan want, Stephen? Obviously, money. Did he tell you to worm your way into our lives and our racing business?'

'No, Susie, they had no interest in you at that time. It was always going to be a matter of 'face' with the Chinese. They still had great faith in my abilities. They wanted me to voluntarily go to Macau and work for them until the debt to their purse and honour was repaid. If it was a matter of revenge, they could have killed me at any time. I brushed them off once too often. I never thought in a million years they would grab Julie. When he calls again, I will agree to everything, do whatever they want to get Julie back, then I'll get out of your lives forever.'

The Nag, on a tight leash held by Susie, could not contain himself. 'Struth, Matey, you are one fucking Jonah. Too right, you'll walk the plank when our Julie comes back. And if one hair on her head is damaged, you'll wish you were never born.'

Bill Burroughs, ever the practical businessman, spoke up, 'Obviously, they were the crowd who did you over at the Coachman's the night before I called for you. We must keep calm and focused, see what they want, and use whatever it takes to get Julie back.'

Just then the phone rang.

'I wish to speak to Stephen Doyle. I know the police are listening. Ask Mr Burroughs to text his private number to this disposable mobile phone. We'll be done by the time the authorities can interfere.'

Five minutes later, Bill Burroughs's cell phone rang. He put it on speaker mode.

'I'll be brief. You listen, I'll talk. Our guest has been most informative. She is well and completely unharmed. She is staying in a place far from Australia, with no prospect of escape or rescue. You may speak with her in a moment. Our new information has raised the stakes. She says she loves you, Stephen. How delicious. And when we threatened to kill you, she said she would do anything to save you. All she wants is for you to be together. She's young, Stephen, but she'll learn. In the meantime, I don't wish to have to start sending bits of her body parts to encourage you. As you probably know, Stephen, your actions have destroyed my life. With us, it is all about respect and family. I am an outcast until and unless I redeem myself. We lost a good man in Port Douglas. Our contacts tell me you did not shoot him, but somebody did. All he was trying to do was leave a note to say we had Miss Dundon and to await contact. This is an unexpected and unwelcome complication. We are putting a lot of resources to find their identity, and I presume the police are doing likewise. Now here are my demands. I know Barabbas is to run at Belmont Park in Perth next month. The syndicate is to transfer ownership of the horse after the race to you, Stephen. Make sure he wins. Miss Dundon's will be the final signature when you bring the horse and papers to us. You will, of course, transfer ownership to my father for an amount equal to what you stole from us. Please make arrangements immediately to have the animal shipped to the equestrian quarantine facility in Hong Kong.'

In stunned silence, they looked at each other, and in unison, they turned and looked at Stephen, incomprehension on every face.

Before the inevitable recriminations flew, Susie broke the silence, 'I want to speak to my niece, Mr Quan, if you please. She's the only one worth anything in all of this. We'll work everything out. I'll make sure nothing happens to harm our Julie.'

'Very well, madam. Now I beg you not to attempt to influence Miss Dundon. You may put her life in jeopardy trying to be too clever.'

'Hi, everybody. I'm holding up. What a mess. I've agreed to Mr Quan's demands, and I really hope you can go along with it. See you in Hong Kong after the Perth meeting. That's all I'm allowed to say.'

'I have devised a secure means to contact you through Mr Burroughs. Do not attempt to frustrate me. Many lives are at stake.'

As the connection cut, they could hear the sound of sirens as the police raced up the drive. They all suffered conflicting emotions as to what they should or could say.

Again, the practical Bill Burroughs stepped in. 'We can't all keep a convincing lie going. The police will be furious at being outsmarted. They didn't think they had to be physically with us with all the phone lines tapped and recorded. They'll ask us to hand over our mobiles probably to attach some tracking software. Cooperate fully. Just don't mention Hong Kong or Barabbas. Tell them Quan wanted to show us and the police how clever he is. I have some very important contacts there. Something might be possible. Now before you claw me, Susie, nothing, absolutely nothing, will happen until Julie is back in Bridgetown.'

The police duly arrived, led by an infuriated Commander Wakefield. His neat military moustache bristled as he barked out orders and requests. He calmed down when their corroborating stories matched the facts. He agreed he didn't have the resources to put a cordon around such vast sprawling properties. He accepted their pledges to be fully compliant and cooperative. He would not discuss his plans or intentions. Slapping his hand on the kitchen table, he laid out the dire consequences of any attempt to obstruct or pervert the course of justice.

Turning to Stephen, he said, 'I'll need a further statement from you. In light of what we've discussed, it appears, with all your other troubles, you are also an illegal immigrant.'

Chapter 27

In their suite at the nearby Coachman's, Heffernan, Brody, Moran, and the other members were mulling over this transmitted information. Scenarios and possibilities swirled around for an hour.

Heffernan, taking the lead as the Senior Officer, summed up, 'I'd love to hit them now while they're still like headless chickens, but we can't tip our hand, especially if our contact in the Federals could be compromised. Gentlemen, the facts are that this horse is extremely valuable and will be worth millions at stud. Complete ownership will be vested in Doyle in Hong Kong for a short period after the girl signs the papers. I have the bones of a plan, but I need to go back to Ireland to sell it to the Army Council. Hong Kong will be a madhouse with the Olympic equestrian events going on there. That's what the Chinks are banking on. Chaos and confusion on their own ground will give them the advantage. They will expect a move from somewhere, but hopefully not from us.'

Chapter 28

Quan kept in touch by the simple expedience of mailing a pre-paid mobile phone to Bill Burroughs's office the day before he called. He would only call that phone once from a similar prepaid phone. To keep the police wrong-footed, Quan occasionally called the house phones and, in effect, conducted parallel negotiations.

Events were moving inexorably to a conclusion. Dickey Beckett and Susie were the only ones throwing a kind word in Stephen's direction. The Syndicate had met and agreed to sign over their shares. The Nag and Burroughs promised to indemnify the others as best they could, although the eventual value of stud fees was unimaginable.

Chapter 29

Two weeks later, Heffernan was back. He called a meeting and, rubbing his hands, filled them in, 'We're going to hit them just before the race. Our Federal contact is safely out of the loop. Scare them shitless so's they jump to our tune. Got to have them singing from our hymn sheet. Friends in Hong Kong will have all the hardware we need.'

Chapter 30

Stephen lost himself in preparing Barabbas. He practically lived in the stables and on the gallops. He refused to go into the house except when summoned by a call from Quan. Susie fretted and worried as she saw the weight drop from him at an alarming rate. She made him sit down and promise to eat, reasoning that he would fall ill and be useless to his vow to do everything to rescue Julie. He agreed on the condition that he moved to the stable lads' quarters over the yard.

Late at night, as he lay in his bunk, praying for sleep, the events of the past few months hammered his brain to bursting point. Bits and pieces from his conversations with Quan began to form. Quan delighted in tormenting and goading him about Julie and Barabbas. His instincts convinced him Quan had another scheme on the boil. Like a bulb going off, he figured it out. Getting dressed, he immediately went to look for Bill Burroughs.

'Quan can't help himself, Mr Burroughs. He cannot leave well enough alone. The Australian Royal Cup at 1.5 miles would have been tough with the standard of declared runners, but that was before we learned Barabbas's true potential. Now he will be a sky-high favourite with no odds. When we started playing the exchanges back in Ireland, he was like a madman. Even though it won't be in his family's best interest, his mind will be locked into a coup. He'll try something, look for any suspicious changes in the runners and riders. He'll bet for Barabbas to lose. When his money goes down—and this will be at the last minute—the odds will change dramatically. Stand by and hit him in the last half minute.'

Bill Burroughs contemplated the young man standing before his desk. He admired so much about him but had to admit he was like a lightning rod. He seemed to attract trouble and expense to those standing too close. And yet, with what they knew of Quan and his weakness, there just might be something in what Stephen proposed.

Chapter 31

The day before the Perth Royal Cup, police commander Wakefield received a visitor. As a fellow officer of the law, he extended the usual courtesies.

Refilling his guest with a universally revolting cup of police canteen tea, he asked, 'Superintendent Deegan, please let me know if I can be of service. Quite frankly, I'm intrigued. I'm told you've flown directly from Ireland.'

A slight, intense, middle-aged man with greying hair swept back to match a gray complexion sat there longing for a cigarette.

'Thanks for seeing me, Commander. As my warrant card shows, I'm from Irish Special Branch attached to Interpol. Amongst other things, we try to match people to criminal events. We saw on the wires that you have a situation originating in Port Douglas and that you still have it under wraps. The first interesting thing for us was the MO of the shooter. It matches an IRA hitman called Joe Moran. Brilliant marksman, left eye with a Beretta his specialty. Anyway, we looked him up. Dropped out of sight with Ray Brody, his right-hand man. Ditto their former CO, Hugh Heffernan and his buddy Chris Murphy, plus two others from the old days. They're all supposed to be stood down and decommissioned, but old dogs and new tricks come to mind. Since the so-called peace process, we've learned the identity of their political master. They call him Brother Superior. We thought it was a code name, but that's exactly what he is— brother superior of the Palladine Brothers. And as you may know, they have houses all over the world, including Australia. They may be holed up in the local monastery here in Perth. What I would like to know is what interest would former IRA terrorists have in an Australian heiress? Also, the dead triad member is another intriguing fly in the muddy water. The IRA are ruthless and opportunistic, Commander. They have a global network of members, contacts, and sympathizers. Underestimate them at your peril.'

Commander Wakefield closed the door, opened the window, and lit up a stinking black briar pipe. A relieved Deegan did likewise with an unfiltered John Player. As they contentedly puffed away, Wakefield opened his safe and slapped a file on his desk.

Chapter 32

About 10 miles away, Stephen, Bill Burroughs, Martha Burroughs, the Nag, Susie, and Davey Beckett gathered in the outsized kitchen of Burroughs's Ballymore Estate. They had finished supper an hour ago, and the staff had long departed. Davey, the only one availing of the drink's cabinet, helped himself to another large Scotch. They were discussing tomorrow's afternoon race meeting and their lack of options with Quan. Barabbas and Poyak, his stable companion, along with four grooms and Dickey Beckett were already at the track.

Burroughs took Stephen aside. 'You were right. Last minute change of jockey for Seabreeze. Silkie Scott got the ride. Just back from suspension, always a cloud over that tulip, wouldn't trust him an inch. Word is, he's up for anything. I've had a think. Roped in some good mates. We're standing by with the kitchen sink if the price changes on Barabbas. Now don't add this to your worries. We're all big boys who love a flutter. If this pays off, I'll have a decent wedge to help pay off the syndicate.'

With that, the door burst open. Six armed men wearing dark boiler suits and balaclavas raced across the marble-tiled floor. Suppressed weapons cocked, roaring and shouting, 'Down, down now! Do it now! Don't move—not a fucking breath!'

As they each stood, mouths agape in stunned astonishment, one of the raiders struck Bill Burroughs left and right around the head and forced him to his knees. At more roaring and ranting, they all dropped to the floor—except Davey Beckett, who dropped his Scotch and reached for a Kitchen Devil knife on the counter behind him. At the sound of the knife leaving the scabbard, one of the raiders looked up and, in an instant, shot Davey through the left eye.

An excruciating second of disbelief was followed by cries of terror and anguish. The Nag, obeying a natural instinct, struggled to his feet, with Susie hanging from his arm. One of the other raiders punched her in the face and shot the Nag above the right knee. With a scream of pain, he fell to the ground. Susie leapt across, attempting to shield him from further harm.

Stephen struggled to sit up. As he did, his hair was grabbed from behind and his head forced in the direction of Davey Beckett's body. Davey lay slumped and unmoving, one eye staring sightlessly and the other a red open wound with blood trickling down his cheek.

'Get the picture, Stevie boy? Tell these good folks we mean business. Cooperate, and you have a chance. Otherwise, I don't give a fuck.'

The speaker whipped off the balaclava and was rewarded at the look of utter astonishment on Stephen's face.

'Heffernan!'

'Didn't think we could forget or forgive our old comrade then, did you, Stevie boy? Now stop snivelling, missus. This dumbfuck didn't have to act the hero. He's dead, but on the other hand, your husband won't die of the little kneecapping job, one of our specialties. Only a bit of a flesh wound. In and out, sweet as a nut. Maybe a little limp as a memento.'

Heffernan surveyed the scene of devastation as his henchmen removed their masks and took up positions around the room.

'Now, here's the way it is. We know everything that was said in both houses since your return from Port Douglas. Yes, folks, bugged by the best in the business. Not very clever of the good commander not to have swept for bugs, but there you are. Two of my men will accompany Mr and Mrs Monahan back to their house. One of the lads is a trained paramedic. He'll sort out the leg. Two more will stay here with Mrs Burroughs and clear up the mess. The story for any nosey parker is the boys are extra security. Myself and Chris—you remember Chris, don't you, Stevie?—will dispose of the stiff.'

'Your quarrel is with me, Heffernan. There's no need to involve these innocent people. You can't do any worse to me. You don't need to harm them.'

Heffernan looked with loathing at the pale, frightened young man, hands trembling with delayed shock. 'You know what you meant to me as your CO, Stevie boy, and to the movement. But, no, you turned your back on us, took what was ours, and threw me to the wolves. Now you'll pay, but you know that. As for the others, they'll do what I say. All of you, cell phones on the table, if you please.'

Heffernan, pleased with his efforts, took stock. He was used to his handiwork altering forever the lives of innocent bystanders. He draped his arm around Stephen's shoulder and shoved the Walther PPK under his chin. Stephen jumped as if jolted by an electrical current, his face a mixture of fear and revulsion. Heffernan backhanded him with the pistol. Blinded by blood pouring from a cut over the eye, Stephen tripped and fell to the floor. Heffernan, in fury, raised his boot to stomp on Stephen's head.

'Hold it, Hughie. We have our orders. We can't complete the mission without Doyle.'

Heffernan stopped, and his heart skipped a beat as he looked into the merciless eyes of the cold-blooded killer. Moran held the Beretta loosely, his right hand down by his side. A flawed human being without the normal moral compass, Moran's unshakable belief in 'the struggle' sustained and nourished him. The only person Moran ever acknowledged was Brother Superior. With his life now on a thread, Heffernan realized he was dispensable. A wrong move now would be his last. He took a long shuddering breath and shook himself as if waking from a sleep. He dropped his arm and tossed the pistol on to a chintz-covered couch.

'Tomorrow's the big day, Burroughs. You and Doyle will go to the track. After the race, stay over in Perth and bring the horse as arranged to the airport. He is already booked into quarantine in Hong Kong. Do everything the Chink tells you. If he suspects anything, they'll kill the girl, and we'll have to provide the same service to you. And, Burroughs, we're keeping a friendly eye on your Miriam and little Benjamin. Wouldn't want the little tyke to lose a second relation so soon now, would we? This is not idle pub talk, folks, but I'm sure you realize that by now.'

Heffernan then organized sleeping bags for the captives and told them to settle down for the night in the living room. He ordered, watched, and listened to Burroughs phone Commander Wakefield to ask for any news. Susie and Martha had to endure the indignity of going to the bathroom with the light on and door open.

Susie brought a damp facecloth and wiped the blood from Stephen's face. 'He was your teacher from a young age?'

Stephen nodded with eyes closed. 'Did he abuse you as a child?'

Another nod—this time, barely perceptible. Tears welled up and silently stole down his cheeks.

'You poor, poor boy, what's that monster done to you and now to us? God bless and keep you. I'll pray till heaven cracks open to save us all.'

Stephen watched as Susie led the way out, followed by the two terrorists supporting a struggling Nag. Heffernan had found the massive walk-in cold room at the rear of the kitchen and decided to keep Davey Beckett's remains hidden there overnight. The three of them settled down on the Persian carpet to try to get what sleep they could.

Chapter 33

The morning which they felt should have dawned gray and weeping to match their mood was instead glorious. By the time the early staff arrived, they were all showered and suitably dressed for the day ahead. A storm of activity before daybreak removed all signs of the previous night's events. The four intruders adopted their role as extra security personnel. Burroughs's own staff with years of inherited family service had been sworn to secrecy. They were only mildly surprised at this latest development. All the activity surrounding Julie's disappearance had put a huge strain on everybody, but their devotion and loyalty endured.

Heffernan visited the corpse, decided to leave it for now, stacked two more crates over it, and left. Lying on the back seat of Burroughs's BMW on the way to the racecourse, he gave last-minute instructions, 'Keep to your normal routine. We'll be watching. If the Chink approaches you, which I doubt, we won't react. The police will probably contact you to show they're on the job—again, no problem. If you or somebody really clever nabs us, and we don't contact the others when we should, then Moran will kill them all, and that includes the kid. I don't make idle threats. I don't have to. Today is the 10th of August. When the Chink next contacts you, tell him the horse will be in Hong Kong's quarantine station on the 14th, not a day before or after. This is vital, non-negotiable. Now clip these voice-activated transmitter/receivers inside your shirts—the best that CIA money can buy. If you turn them off or take them off, I'll know. Turn them off only going through security at both airports. They'll pass for the latest iPods. Use your loaf and ditch them after you meet the Chink. You'll be searched and best not be caught with this gear, but it's vital we have some idea of his plans. Be inventive, gentlemen. Otherwise, we'll eliminate you and your families, then we'll disappear, and the triads will get blamed. What of your bitch then, Stevie boy? The Chinks will have to waste her to cover their tracks. I guess that's plenty of incentive for the moment.'

Chapter 34

Stephen settled back in the passenger seat and could not help but admire the lush countryside of the month of August, the spring of the year in this most beautiful part of Western Australia.

Soon they reached the well-planned outskirts of Perth and, following the race day signposts, approached the world-famous Belmont Park. Set on an isthmus on the bend of a river overlooked by two world championship golf courses, the racecourse was a salute to modern gracious living. Every conceivable amenity was at hand to pamper the sophisticates. Members' boxes, pavilions, bars, and restaurants competed for business and attention. Great expanses of glass shielded the golden people from the common people. However, the management were far too clever to be usurped by snobbery. The facilities for the real people of the real world were second to none. Their amenities matched the others in every respect except for a few frills, and they had far better fun.

The Australian Royal Cup ran over 1.5 miles and was the last group 1 meeting in Perth before Western Australia's highlight, the Perth Cup, held in midsummer on New Year's Day at the nearby Ascot Racecourse. Most people preferred the Royal Australian, which was held without the formality of extravagant ladies' hats and gentlemen's morning wear.

Stephen conferred with Dickey Beckett, who was concerned at the haunted, haggard look of the young Irishman.

'Stephen, don't fret. You look like shit. Barabbas is up for it, trust me. Leave this part to us. You concentrate on getting Julie back.'

Tears sprang to Stephen's eyes. He agonized over telling Dickey his uncle had been brutally murdered. He realized he couldn't, as any public drama now would alert Quan and put them all in jeopardy. He made up a yarn explaining why the Nag and Susie were delayed but on their way.

He contented with passing on the information concerning Silkie Scott getting the ride on Seabreeze.

'Had that spotted, Stephen. He's the sort who'd prefer to be crooked and lose rather than straight and win. So now you think the Chinese have him bribed to pull some stunt on us? Well, bugger that.'

With the preliminary races concluded, the massive crowd buzzed like a swarm of bees in a disturbed hive.

3.30 p.m. and the final prospect of seeing Australia's own wonder horse before he goes on to compete overseas. In agreement with Quan and with no choice, Bill Burroughs held a press conference outlining a two-year itinerary—first to Hong Kong to compete at Happy Valley, then Dubai for the World Cup, England for the Epsom Derby, Paris for the Prix de l'Arc de Triomphe, the Curragh for the Irish Derby, Churchill Downs for the Kentucky Derby, and hopefully, twice in that time for the Melbourne Cup before retiring to stud. He had, of course, cautioned of the many slips between cup and lip, but horse-mad, sports-crazy Australians had enthusiastically signed on for the whole ten yards.

The parade ring at a remove from the stands and bookmakers' stalls was under siege. The crowd, though excited, was hushed. Eight magnificent animals being led on a circuit of the shaded arena was as close as most of the fans would ever get to such quality horseflesh. Stephen, feeling many eyes—mostly friendly, some hostile—led Barabbas on a short rein. Shutting down the outside world, he talked continuously to his black-coated charge.

Bill Burroughs, in his trademark tweeds and Panama hat, in the centre circle talking to the stewards, owners, and trainers. Last-minute check with Dickey Beckett, then the bell to signal mount-up and canter to the starting gates. The crowds break away and rush to their favourite viewing spots. Stephen joined Bill Burroughs, who was on the phone in the owners' suite. Even with so much on his mind, Stephen took in the stunning panoramic view of track, river, golf course, and the multi-coloured mass of humanity.

'Just got word, Stephen. Massive lay on Barabbas on the exchanges. He's now gone from 4 to 1 against to 3 to 1 on—that's a spread of 7—we're in, and we're on. This will be some roller coaster. Hope we'll get to score on that bloody Chinaman.'

Dickey is talking his own talk to Barabbas, who is bunched like a coiled spring beneath him. They have drawn gate 8 at the very outside.

This would be the kiss of death for any but the very best in a race at this level. Today, in view of the word on Silkie Scott and the outside draw, he decided to play a waiting game.

The starter dropped the flag, and the field surge from the gates past the stands in a blur of coloured silks and up the hill on this long, curving, left-handed track. The blare from the overexcited commentator blasted at a million decibels. The pace fast, but not blistering at this early stage. Dickey, coming in from the outside, is surprised to see Silkie, who had been drawn No. 2, at the outside of the bunch. The field now strung out wider than normal at this point in a 1.5-mile race.

Seabreeze, a compact grey, is not struggling but hanging back as the field now power ahead. Barabbas straining at the bit, and Dickey with a split second to decide his next move. Just then, a gap opens up inside the grey. At that instant, Dickey sees the jockey on the lead horse give a quick look behind. Nothing unusual in that except he looks directly to where he expects Seabreeze to be. Silkie taps the peak of his cap with his whip.

Dickey spots the play—not one, but two bastards involved—as the lead horse at the half-mile marker now makes his move. Silkie swerves to close the gap on his left. Seabreeze, a magnificent, well-trained thoroughbred, thinks this is his signal to go. They pass the next horse, a deep chestnut, also lengthening his stride. Seabreeze, trying to accelerate, is being hauled back by Silkie, who is looking back over his shoulder.

They are now tacking left at an alarming rate. Then contact. The grey and chestnut tangle, their speed, angle, and weight bringing them down. The sound of a leg bone shattering rings out like a pistol shot. Dickey already, committed to the gap, has kicked Barabbas into top gear. With a millisecond to decide, Dickey is faced with the prospect of adding to the wreckage.

Without breaking stride, he grips Barabbas with his knees, gathers the reins, and shouts, 'Up, Barabbas! Up, you beauty!'

As if in slow motion, every eye back at the Stands swivel to the huge TV monitors. The commentator's voice stilled as, without falter, Barabbas gathered and soared over the two stricken animals, landing like a cat, with Dickey leaning along his neck, roaring, 'Go, Barabbas! Go!' The sight of the glorious black thoroughbred eating up the ground to catch the leader and pass the post with a length in hand was something which would never ever be forgotten by racegoers the world over.

Leading Barabbas to the unsaddling enclosure through hysterical fans and mobs of press, Stephen had a momentary twinge of conscience. What if their win unhinged Quan and Julie suffered? No, that was madness; whatever Quan's reaction, his father and the triad hierarchy would be rubbing their hands at the increased value of the prize about to fall into their laps.

Chapter 35

Far across the Indian Ocean, Julie's captors allowed her to watch the race on their racing TV channel. She was being held in a closely guarded luxury penthouse suite above their gambling casino in Macau. CCTV, twenty-four-hour armed guards, infrared and pressure pad alarms—all were employed to keep her in a gilded cage. After the initial terrifying shock of being abducted, she was treated exceptionally well.

The trip by speedboat, helicopter, and private jet was a blur. She occasionally saw Quan, who introduced her to Ming Tai, who became her constant companion and, realistically, her jailer. Quan, while reticent, did reveal that he and Ming Tai had known Stephen years before in Ireland. Beyond that, they would not go, no matter how many times she asked. They confirmed that a debt of honour was involved, which was being resolved. Nobody needed to get hurt as long as her ransom was paid.

She had long ago conceded that her life, Stephen's life, and the life of her family were worth the awful price of losing Barabbas. She also realized that behind their courtesies and politeness, these people would transform from threats to action in an instant. Following the sudden death of her parents, she fervently believed the only thing worth living for in life was life itself.

At the conclusion of the race, she rushed to Ming Tai, and the two laughed, cheered, and hugged for joy. She scanned the crowd inside and outside the ring to catch a glimpse of her aunt and uncle but to no avail. She wept as she saw Stephen leading the beautiful prancing horse to the winner's enclosure and the pride on the face of Dickey Beckett as the lieutenant governor presented the Royal Australian Cup to a beaming

Bill Burroughs. Untypically, Bill Burroughs refused to be interviewed by any of the clamouring radio and TV reporters.

Later that night, as she prepared for bed, Julie was surprised at a knock on her door. Ming Tai stuck her head in and, with a finger on her lips, whispered, 'Not long now, Miss Julie,' and was gone.

Chapter 36

Back in the owners and directors' suite, Bill Burroughs accepted the congratulations and good wishes of colleagues and contemporaries. A uniformed flunkey handed him a sealed package, which had gone through their scanning machine. He knew from the weight, size, and feel that it was a mobile phone. Summoning Stephen to the outside terrace, he inserted the accompanying SIM card.

Immediately the phone rang, and a familiar voice hissed across the ether, 'Congratulations, gentlemen, on a truly magnificent victory. All is prepared for the handover. I'm sure both sides require a neutral venue where we can avoid unwelcome surprises. Consequently, we will conduct our business on the top-floor restaurant of the Sky Terrace on Victoria Peak on Hong Kong Island. We are expecting you in Sha Tin quarantine centre no later than the day after tomorrow, the 12th. A three-bedroom suite has been reserved for your party at the Peninsula Hotel. I understand all the paperwork is in order?'

Bill Burroughs and Stephen exchanged worried glances. 'Extra formalities on the Australian side will cost us a day. The Equestrian Olympics are causing slight problems. We'll arrive on the 14th. Presumably, you'll check we're in situ. We don't want any chance of anything going wrong. We are anxious to conclude our business on the 15th.'

There was a momentary pause.

'Agreed. We hold all the cards. Don't dare try to cross me, Stephen. You are now in my backyard. We have made a great effort to be civilized about this matter. I will not be able to help you or Julie if the velvet glove has to come off. Mr Burroughs, I know you have discreetly mobilized some ex-SAS types. Stand them down, Mr Burroughs. They are totally unsuited to the task at hand.'

As instructed by Heffernan, Stephen and Burroughs stayed at the Marriott airport hotel for the following two nights. They spent their time making preparations for the transport flight to Hong Kong. Barabbas and Poyak were in fine fettle, helped by the constant presence of Stephen and Dickey Beckett. The black rage simmering in Stephen was barely held in check. The physical, mental, and financial suffering being felt by the others was a constant torment. Even now, he couldn't contemplate telling Dickey of his uncle's murder. Everything was on hold pending the safe return of Julie. He knew with certainty he would have gone off the rails without the steadying hand of the ever practical and pragmatic Bill Burroughs.

The night before their departure, they received a visit from Commander Wakefield accompanied by Superintendent Deegan. The commander confessed he had been rebuffed by the Federal Department of Justice in his attempt to prevent their trip to Hong Kong. He was incensed when he learned that Stephen Doyle was to be allowed to leave the jurisdiction on the undertaking of Bill Burroughs to guarantee his return. However, he insisted on a thorough search of their rooms, belongings, and horse transporter. He was looking for the ransom, usually demanded these days in the form of diamonds and/or bearer bonds. Cash was old hat for many reasons, principally being too bulky and traceable.

'Think you're too smart for the dumb police, Burroughs? Your itinerary and story that this trip to Hong Kong is to run Barabbas in Happy Valley is a load of crock. You are going to the home turf of the very triads who kidnapped Miss Dundon. I am also forbidden to alert the Chinese authorities by those geezers in Canberra. The whole thing stinks, Burroughs, though I have to say you carry a very big stick. Now Superintendent Deegan here will fill you in on another side to this sorry mess.'

Stephen was intrigued to hear the pronounced Dublin accent. He went paler, if that were possible, as he heard the Interpol policeman's opinions.

'I'll lay it out for you, Doyle. Some very undesirable people from your home county have disappeared, and we suspect they are somehow involved in what's going on here. Your old schoolmaster, Hughie Heffernan, and his shadow, Chris Murphy, for example, and friends of theirs by the name of Moran and Brody are most probably involved as well—all members or former members of the Provisional IRA and all capable of murder and mayhem at the drop of a hat. We don't know the link except we now believe there is a link. Whatever you know will be used with the utmost discretion. I'd like to feel we can rely on your sense of decency and help us put these scum out of action and secure the release of Miss Dundon. What do you say, gentlemen?'

Stephen and Burroughs had endlessly discussed all the permutations and possibilities. They were compromised whichever way they turned. The reputation of Julie's captors and their first-hand experience of Heffernan's capabilities were deciding factors. The involvements of two different police forces, however professional, and now Interpol, were risks they were not prepared to take. A further complication was the Chinese Communist Party. They enjoyed playing cat and mouse with Westerners since regaining control of Hong Kong from Great Britain. The eyes of the world were on China during their hosting of the Olympic Games. Their heavy-handed management of their own civil rights protesters in China and Tibet were an indication of their preference to use a sledgehammer to crack a nut.

'Both Mr Doyle and I are fully cooperating with the authorities. We are going about our lawful business and not interfering with your enquiries. Our only concern is for the safe return of Miss Dundon. Now if you both will excuse us, we really must be on our way.'

Chapter 37

Back at Ballymore Estate, a maid sent to the cold room uncovered the frozen corpse of Davy Beckett. Her piercing screams alerted the head housekeeper. She in turn raced outside to inform the new 'security' people. They, of course, had slipped away days before. Unable to contact her employer, who was in the air en route to Hong Kong, she telephoned the police.

Chapter 38

Landing at the commercial terminal at the new Hong Kong International Airport, the Burroughs party was efficiently processed and on their way within an hour. Sha Tin was a revelation. A huge complex, once miles outside the city, had been transformed. Hundreds of horses and their support teams of farriers, harness makers, handlers, grooms, riders, Olympic officials, the international press, and hangers-on jostled for space. Including the famous race track, Sha Tin was also home to the Hong Kong quarantine centre.

China spared no expense or resources in their determination to make their Olympics the best organized and most memorable in history. The opening ceremony at the Bird's Nest stadium in Beijing was testament to that. All Olympic equestrian events were taking place in Hong Kong, in part to minimize the spread of equine disease to China. The facilities and security were truly amazing. Horses and their transports were coming and going in what appeared to be organized chaos. So as not to leave everybody and everything to the final day, horses eliminated or injured were constantly on their sometimes-long journey home. At the same time replacements in still-eligible teams were simultaneously arriving.

Having stabled Barabbas and Poyek and completed the paperwork, Stephen and Burroughs prepared to return to their hotel.

'This way, if you please, gentlemen.'

Stephen turned at the sound of the familiar voice.

'Quan Song Li, out from under your rock, you piece of shit. What did Julie Dundon ever do to you? Only a lowlife would threaten a woman. If you've harmed one hair on her head, you'll pay. I'll get you no matter what it takes. If you have, you better kill me right now.'

Despite knowing the stakes and rehearsing with Burroughs the absolute need for calm and a cool head, Stephen felt the floodgates of all the emotions burst open. Quan heard him out in silence, secretly glad of the outburst. It was completely natural and in keeping with Stephen's temperament. Also it confirmed their plan to keep their opponents unnerved and on the wrong foot.

Quan was enjoying this immensely, though not a flicker of emotion could be seen on his face. 'Mr Burroughs, I hope you can teach my old friend the value of a civil tongue—all being equal. Miss Dundon will be restored safe and well to her family at the conclusion of our business tomorrow. Now if you would be so kind, I have arranged alternate accommodation for you tonight. Your reservation at the Peninsula will still stand. You may wish to sample its delights before your return to Australia.'

Chapter 39

In Bridgetown, frenzy erupted at the discovery of the body in the freezer. Martha Burroughs collapsed with the strain. She refused to say one word even when heavily armed police safely brought Miriam and little Benjamin to her. Superintendent Deegan, recognizing the cause of death as the signature of one Joe Moran, asked Commander Wakefield when he had last seen or heard from the Monahans.

'Speak to them at least twice a day. Can't get a word except sailor's abuse from him. She's very quiet—understandable in the circumstances. Must be a nightmare for them'

Deegan, who had the files on each of this IRA gang sent by courier from Belfast, Dublin, and Interpol, explained to Wakefield as they raced the 30 miles to the Monahan farm, 'Forget the gadgets and women. Joe Moran and Ray Brody are as close as you will ever get to a real-life 007 and 008. They are on a mission sanctioned by the chief of staff of the IRA. To them, that's the same as M giving Bond the go ahead. I sense your disbelief. Let me elaborate. They only acknowledge the authority of the first Dail (Irish parliament) in 1922. After the split in Sinn Fein and civil war over the Anglo-Irish Treaty, the remnants of the IRA were hounded by both the British and Irish governments. They were ground down but never out. Then the unionists and their British masters caused the dying embers to reignite by their disgraceful treatment of the civil rights marches in the late 1960s and early 1970s. The IRA and their successor the Provisional IRA were reborn with a mission to reunite the stolen six counties of Ulster into an all-Ireland republic. They're organized all over the world. They have support everywhere. Whatever their mission, Brody and Moran will move heaven and hell to carry it out. Commander, they have the skills and the means to attempt almost anything. I don't mind admitting they scare the hell out of me.'

Chapter 40

Burroughs and Stephen were ushered to a black Mercedes people carrier with darkened windows. Quan explained the obvious, that his father and uncles were prominent members of the Hong Kong Jockey Club and so had carte blanche in and around Sha Tin. They were brought to a luxury apartment in a secluded block overlooking Hong Kong Island. There they were instructed to prepare a meal for themselves from the well-stocked kitchen. Four sinister-looking triad members remained—two inside and two outside the complex.

'You will see Miss Dundon tomorrow at the handover. At precisely 12 noon, she will sign the papers you have with you, making you the sole owner of the horse. She will leave with Mr Burroughs. At 1 p.m. my father and his associates will join us for lunch. After lunch, you, Stephen, will sign the papers transferring ownership to my father for the amount owing to us. By this time, Mr Burroughs will have communicated to you that Miss Dundon is safe. No need for your SAS hooligans after all, Mr Burroughs. In the meantime, try to relax and know that this trying time is almost at an end. Do not attempt any foolishness. It will be fatal and final for you and the fragrant Miss Dundon. Every eventuality has been anticipated. I will be here at 11.15 in the morning. Please be ready to leave immediately. Now hand me your mobile phones for safekeeping, if you please.'

Chapter 41

Superintendent Deegan and Commander Wakefield were having a difficult time at Bramble Cottage. The strain was evident in the drawn features of the Monahans, who had aged ten years in as many weeks. The policemen outlined what they had found at Ballymore. Again they faced point-blank refusal to cooperate.

Superintendent Deegan summed up, 'Your niece is kidnapped by the triads. One of the gang is killed by, we suspect, Joe Moran, a very dangerous member of the IRA. The same Joe Moran left a sample of his handiwork at Mr Burroughs house. Davey Beckett's body was found in the freezer a few hours ago. I see they've left you with one of their souvenirs, Mr Monahan. Get that seen to quickly, or you'll have a permanent reminder. What's the common denominator? Stephen Doyle and Bill Burroughs are in Hong Kong at this moment. What's the connection between the IRA and the triads? It has to be something to do with Doyle, but what's the ransom?'

The Nag's mouth opened and shut without emitting a sound, his prominent Adam's apple bobbing up and down.

'You can't or won't talk. You're too terrified for your niece. Why are they all converging in Hong Kong? The triads have made a fortune from blackmail, kidnapping, and extortion. We can't just sit on our hands and hope everything will turn out okay. Commander Wakefield and I intend to alert the Hong Kong authorities and travel there to assist later today.'

The bluff had the desired effect. Shrugging off Susie's clinging arms, the Nag reached under the table and produced a double-barrelled shotgun. Both policemen sat frozen as the weapon weaved between them in shaking hands.

'You're going nowhere, shipmates. We sit tight here 'till we get word Julie is safe. You can do what you like with me after that.'

Deegan, the first to recover, leaned across and gripped the barrel of the shotgun. 'You're not going to shoot police officers, Mr Monahan. It's not in your nature—particularly because you're a decorated former naval commander and also because the safety catch is still on. Now level with us please. We have many resources available to us, which are useless unless we get a pointer.'

The very air seemed to leave the distraught aunt and uncle as their resolve wavered. Susie, gripped with uncontrollable sobbing, collapsed in her husband's arms. They confirmed the recent happenings at Ballymore and the fact that the IRA had both residences bugged for months. They also confirmed Quan's method of communication by using one-trip mobile phones. A whistle of admiration escaped from the lips of the Interpol officer. Beyond that, the Monahans would not go. Their love and fear for their niece defied all pleadings from the two policemen.

Leaving two armed officers to keep an eye on the couple, Deegan and Wakefield sped back to the command headquarters at Bridgetown. On arrival, they were dismayed to see a veritable horde from every branch of the media assembled in the courtyard of the station. The news of the body in the freezer couldn't be contained, and the fig leaf, the D notice concerning the whereabouts of Julie Dundon, was now discarded. Their only hope was that a connection with Hong Kong would not be made before the authorities formulated a plan.

Superintendent Deegan concluded a series of phone calls and made his decision. He called Commander Wakefield out on the rear veranda, where pipe and cigarette were produced and fired up.

'Commander, I've spoken with Interpol HQ. We've agreed events have moved from here to Hong Kong. They have informal relations with the Chinese authorities. China and Interpol have agreed I meet with a high-ranking military official in Hong Kong strictly on a 'need-to-know basis'. I'm leaving straight away. Somebody is being thrown off the last flight from Perth tonight. I'll be in Hong Kong in the early morning. I know your hands are tied here in your own backyard. Thanks for your help and courtesy. I'll keep you posted.'

Chapter 42

After a restless night, Burroughs and Stephen awoke to a crisp, clear morning as yet untainted by Hong Kong's usual smog of pollution. Not knowing if the apartment was bugged, their conversation was necessarily compromised. They had to appear natural for the benefit of definitely one and probably two sets of listeners. Mindful of Heffernan's dire warning, they hid the transmitter/receivers out of sight of their two internal minders in the bag of a vacuum cleaner. Hopefully, the listeners would pick up what was said.

At 11.15 a.m. precisely, Quan arrived accompanied by the two outside minders. A short conversation in rapid Cantonese with the inside minders produced grunts of satisfaction. Quan then ordered Stephen and Burroughs to strip and watched as one of his henchmen ran a hooped scanning device over their naked bodies.

'This is not prurience, gentlemen, but a necessary precaution. After all, we do not wish the world to know our business. Also we are using the 'double bluff' scenario. When I informed you the meeting would take place on Victoria Peak, that notion would have been dismissed by other interested parties—too public, too obvious, too Hollywood, a giant red herring, as you might say—which is why the meeting will take place precisely there. Now that you are presentable once more, we really must be on our way.'

In high good humour and under the unflinching eyes of the triads, Quan conducted them to the black Mercedes. They swiftly navigated the short distance to the harbour through streets teeming with vehicles and humanity. Aboard one of the fabled Star Line ferries, they set off across one of the busiest stretches of water in the world. A momentary distraction was the magnificent sight of the sun shining and reflecting on the glass, chrome, and copper of the tall buildings and skyscrapers as they approached Hong Kong Island. Four more triads met them at the dock and ushered them to a pair of Porsche Cayennes with darkened windows.

Moments later, they drew up at the Peak Tram Terminus. Other triad members waited inside, and leaving three at the bottom, they entered a reserved carriage. This journey is one of any tourist's most memorable experiences. As they waited for their slot, Stephen studied the information poster. They were travelling to the highest peak in Hong Kong, standing at 554 metres.

The Peak Tram, first installed in 1888, travels 373 metres up a lush mountainside. The steepest point is 27 degrees, and the remarkable trip takes a mere seven minutes. The Sky Terrace at 396 metres is a short distance from the upper terminus and is an architectural dream or nightmare depending on the individual point of view.

Soaring over the peak plateau like a giant glass-and-chrome Lego creation, the Sky Terrace could not be ignored. Various levels contain bars, restaurants, and viewing areas. Amongst other offerings, the terrace includes Hong Kong's very own Madame Tussauds, containing exhibits of particular interest to the Chinese population. Ripley's Believe It or Not! museum is another popular attraction. Throngs of people of every nationality eating and drinking and coming and going with cameras at the ready complete the picture.

Quan conducted them to the top terrace to admire the panoramic vista. It was truly breath-taking. The picture-perfect view looked out over the skyscrapers and across the Harbour to Kowloon and the New Territories. Stephen noticed houses, obviously a roadway at a slightly higher altitude, and a double helipad to the rear.

'All this is once more ours since we got rid of the British in 1997. They grabbed it in 1842 after they forced the emperor to sign the accursed Treaty of Nanking. Do you know what they fought over? I remember you telling me in Wexford about the Irish experience at the hands of the British, particularly the Penal Laws. Well, here, imperial China lost what became known as the Opium Wars. The British produced Opium in India and insisted they be allowed trade it in China in exchange for goods and services. Can you imagine it? The emperor and his court hated the influence opium was having on millions of his subjects. They became zombies and slaves, all for the wealth and glory of Britain at the barrel of a gun. Those of us who understand these things take some satisfaction every time a consignment of our heroin hits the streets of England. Now I hear through my earpiece that its time. Shall we go inside gentlemen?'

As they approached the glass door to the private dining room, Quan held up his hand. 'One final instruction, if you please. You are not permitted personal contact or to speak. Miss Dundon has the same instructions and has agreed to abide by them.'

Inside, a dining room table was set with glittering cutlery and sparkling glasses on a linen tablecloth of brilliant white. The top floor they occupied was designed like spokes on a wheel. Seven separate opulent suites radiated from a central hub containing massive kitchen areas and rest rooms. Off to one side stood a plain oak table with matching chairs. Four triads with bulging jackets stood guard, one of them facing the terrace door.

An inside door from an adjoining room opened. Stephen's heart pounded in his chest, his mouth dry as he caught his first glimpse of Julie Dundon since that fateful day in Port Douglas. Mixed emotions coursed through him. He had brought this on them all, but maybe now he could bring it to an end.

Julie looked fabulous, wearing an emerald-green gown from neck to ankle, with a high collar and a knee-length slit. What looked like a string of pearls adorned her throat, with a mini version in her piled-high hair. The effect was startling; she stood in matching stiletto heels with her head high, emphasizing the graceful curve of her beautiful neck. Her eyes and teeth were sparkling as she kept herself in check by clenching her hands tightly together.

Holding out a chair, Quan invited Julie to sit at the wooden table. When she was seated, never once taking her eyes from Stephen, Quan beckoned Burroughs forward.

'Please present the bill of sale for Miss Dundon's signature, Mr Burroughs. I have much experience in these matters. I am certain everything is in order. Now would not be the time for silliness.'

Bill Burroughs stepped forward, his face set in stone, as he handed the document case to the smiling Quan. After several moments of close scrutiny, he laid the transfer document in front of Julie and handed her a gold Parker pen.

Another glance at Stephen, a smile, and her signature rapidly written concluded the traumatic ceremony.

Chapter 43

Earlier that morning, Julie had awoken to the sound of humming. Ming Tai skipped through the apartment, pulling the drapes. Her humming gave way to laughter as she pulled back Julie's bedclothes.

'Up, up, little princess. A bath with special oils and perfumes awaits. This is the day. In two hours, we fly to Hong Kong. Forgive an old romantic fool. My heart sings for your happiness. Now look what we have chosen for you to wear when you meet your love.'

Julie gazed in wonder at the vision in Chinese silk laid out across the bottom of her bed. In a daze, she allowed herself to be led to a huge sunken bath where aromatic vapours steamed and clouded the room. Ming Tai talked incessantly in rapid English, switching to Mandarin when excited words failed her. Wrapping her charge in a towelling robe, she began the elaborate ritual of combing and coiling Julie's lustrous brown hair. Then with make-up artistically applied, the silken dress was slipped over her head. Placing pearls on Julie's throat and on her hair, Ming Tai led her by the hand to a floor to ceiling mirror

'Gosh, Ming Tai, what an artist you are. You've made me look and feel beautiful and really special. I can't wait to see Stephen's face when he sees me in this. Thank you for all your kindness. I know you have little choice that you are bound to your masters, but I couldn't have coped these past months without you. Who knows? Perhaps we may meet again someday under different circumstances.'

Waiting for one of the Audi A6s beloved of the Macau triads, Julie faintly heard the sound of raised voices. As this was so unusual, she strained to hear what she could of the argument. A loud male voice was shouting down the plaintive cries of an obviously upset Ming Tai. Moments later, a subdued Ming Tai joined her for the short drive to the airport, where they boarded one of the triad's corporate jets. Thirty minutes later, they were in the air on their way to Hong Kong.

Chapter 44

Now standing mere yards from the man she loved, Julie was on the point of rushing into his arms. She could see and sense the same trembling urge in him. Bill Burroughs gripped Stephen's arm as Ming Tai simultaneously gripped Julie's.

Quan, inwardly smiling, pretended not to notice. 'Thank you, Mr Burroughs and, of course, Miss Dundon. My female associate will conduct you to your suite at the Peninsula Hotel, where she has a final message vital to our mutual business. You may wish to stay on at the Peninsula and await Mr Doyle or move elsewhere. Either way, Mr Doyle will not be asked to conclude the transaction until he receives your confirmation that you are both safe and secure. I'm sure you have worked out a suitable method of establishing this.'

Bill Burroughs turned, looked Stephen straight in the eye, and untypically embraced the younger man in a monstrous bear hug. Then he stood back, gripped Stephen's shoulders, nodded briefly, and were gone.

Quan and Stephen faced each other, hatred arcing between them like electricity going to earth.

Quan broke the silence and, with it, his composure, 'You had one small chance to benefit from the restoration of my good name and good fortune. A gesture of generosity from the victor to the vanquished perhaps? But no, you had to interfere with my private wager in Perth. Don't bother denying it. It's been traced to Burroughs's syndicate. Who else could have known my little ways so accurately? A sizable fortune lost and my image tarnished. I curse the day we ever met'

'The feeling is mutual, Quan. We had our differences. I won't deny I let you down, but to grab an innocent girl and terrorize her and her family to get at me is the act of a lowlife. Why don't we go out on that terrace and sort this out man to man?'

Quan burst out laughing, and he laughed hysterically, with tears running from his eyes. Dabbing his face, he regained his equanimity.

'You don't get it, Stephen, do you? You are mine to do with as I please. We presented Miss Dundon in such a glamorous manner to show you what you will never again enjoy. Her good opinion and, dare I say, love for you is about to be altered. Did you not perhaps recognize anything about Miss Dundon's female companion? You should have, as you surely know every inch of her from our days back in Wexford. Yes, Stephen, none other than Ming Tai, your romantic mentor from the Red Dragon on Crescent Quay, and something else from those far-off times, that master tape of your sexual acrobatics with my female employees was, of course, copied. And Ming Tai's final instruction at the Peninsula Hotel will be to show Miss Dundon the tape in its entirety. Those two women have become close over the past months and Miss Dundon will appreciate that Ming Tai has no choice in the matter. Ming Tai will return here because she has no choice. You will sign over the horse and come back to Macau with us because you have no choice. You know I can reach out anywhere in the world and eliminate Miss Dundon any time I wish. Better for you and her and everybody concerned that you accept the inevitable. It may not be too bad, Stephen. My Father and uncles still retain a high opinion of your abilities.'

Reeling from Quan's venom, Stephen hadn't noticed the arrival of three older men. It was obvious from Quan's demeanour and the deep bowing of the four triads in the room that his father and uncles had arrived. Conversation was suspended until the noise of a helicopter landing outside had stopped.

The taller and leaner of the three, wearing a dark beautifully cut single-breasted suit, approached Stephen and held out his hand. 'I am Tan Song Li, father of Quan and father of the organization you know as Red Dragon. Please take my hand. It is offered in its original spirit to show I am not armed and come in peace. I understand you already met my companions, Chou and Ling, many years ago in your own country.'

Mesmerized by the directness so unusual in orientals and the aura of authority and power, Stephen involuntarily shook the offered hand.

'Now let us sit and enjoy our simple meal before we conclude our business. I am delighted that Quan was able to persuade you to join our enterprise in Macau.'

The five of them sat down to a succession of mouth-watering courses served by a continuous relay of white-gloved waiters. Innocuous conversation flowed with copious glasses of fine wines. Stephen and Tan Song Li ate sparingly and merely sipped the wines. Each awaited a call that would transform their world. Stephen, sick to his heart, could not expect Julie or any girl to accept and forgive the evidence contained in that vile video. Also Quan's threat to have Julie executed could not be discounted. Professional assassins were readily available for hire in every country to those with the money to pay for their services.

As for Tan Song Li, he would be able to retain control of their worldwide organization, whose income exceeded the GDP of most medium-sized countries. His hold had been weakened by Quan's misadventures. He had demonstrated that honour and face could be restored by guile rather than the crude recourse of murder so beloved of his occasional partners, the Italian mafia. The consideration on the bill of sale was the sum stolen from them by Stephen Doyle in exchange for legal ownership of the world's most valuable racehorse. His heart had swollen with pride while watching the manner of Barabbas's last victory. The congratulations of his rivals and peers were particularly gratifying.

The meal consumed at a leisurely pace was at last concluded. Tang Song Li signalled for the waiters to clear the dining table. The document case lay on the adjoining table, awaiting their signature. At the door to the serving area, the final waiter bowed to the room.

Suddenly, the piercing shriek of a fire alarm shattered the room.

Smoke poured from the central kitchen area. A triad rushed in from the terrace, shouting that Madame Tussauds waxworks on the floor below were ablaze. A balding low-sized middle-aged man wearing a loud Hawaiian shirt was frantically banging on the terrace door. The last triad in drew his weapon and, holding it down by his side, opened the door. The American-looking man pushed past. The triad tried to restrain him. The interloper turned inside the triad's arms and, dropping a stiletto down his sleeve, plunged the blade into the triad's throat.

Everything happened in seconds. Simultaneously, two figures wearing breathing masks and orange jumpsuits emerged from the smoke billowing from the kitchen. Both carried 9-millimetre Glock handguns and, without hesitation, shot the four triad bodyguards. Falling to the floor only one triad had time to draw his weapon, now dropping from lifeless hands. One of the gunmen covered Tang Song Li and the uncles, while the other expertly frisked them. Both uncles were carrying automatics in shoulder holsters. The 'American' tore off the vulcanized mask he was wearing.

Stephen's head was pounding from the noise and confusion. The 'American', none other than Hugh Heffernan, grabbed one of the automatics and stuffed the other in his belt. One of the uncles tried to reach the document case. Heffernan smacked him over the head with the automatic. As he fell, he kicked over the oak table. The other uncle dived under it, grabbed the AK-47 concealed there, and came up firing on full automatic. Sheets of shattered glass cascaded around the room.

One of the raiders crouched and, in one fluid movement, shot the uncle in the left eye. Heffernan shot the other as he lay on the floor and, in an exhilarated fit of bloodlust, turned his weapon on Quan and his father.

Stephen grabbed the spare automatic from Heffernan's belt and kicked him in the crotch. He backed towards the white-faced Tang and Quan, waving the automatic at the room.

'Enough, for the love of God. Enough killing, Heffernan, you murdering bastard.'

Heffernan, rage and hatred out of control, flecks of foam in the corner of his mouth, raised his weapon. Moran, six feet away, shot him in the shoulder. Heffernan squealed in pain, the automatic dropping from his hand. Thick, oily smoke poured from the kitchen and out the shattered windows, the five sprawled bodies and shards of glass making the scene surreal. Barely two minutes had passed to produce this carnage. Grabbing the sobbing Heffernan from behind, Moran used him as a shield and snapped off two warning shots, one of them nicking Stephen's left ear.

'Doyle, I have my orders. Pick up the document case and throw me the gun. You're coming with us or staying here dead with those other two. No time, no choice. You come, they live. You stay, they die.'

Stephen, looking into Moran's emotionless black eyes, believed him. He slid the automatic across the floor. Moran scooped it up. Stephen turned for one final look at his tormentor. Quan lay slumped, cradled in his father's arms. Tang Song Li held Stephen's gaze for a moment and slowly inclined his head in acknowledgement of the unspoken debt of honour. Moran beckoned them out the terrace door, ordered Stephen and the other shooter—revealed as Chris Murphy—to support Heffernan, and made for the waiting helicopter.

Brody at the controls had the machine with both doors wide open, hovering 4 feet off the pad. Murphy and Stephen heaved Heffernan aboard and piled in after him. Moran, who had confiscated the AK-47, was spraying the terrace on full automatic. Brody, with a referee's whistle clamped between his teeth, blew a piercing blast. Moran promptly dropped the assault rifle and dived aboard.

No time to admire the fantastic view as Brody, with feet dancing on the rudder and pedals, lifted the helicopter over the peak. They struggled to fasten seat belts and close the sliding doors as Brody flew over northern Hong Kong Island and swooped down the other side and across Hong Kong Harbour. Moran leaned over Heffernan, now delirious with pain, and whispered in his ear.

Heffernan mouthed, *No, no, no.* Moran shot him through the heart, slid back the door, and kicked him out. Stephen, with open mouth and eyes like saucers, waited for his own final dispatch. Moran reholstered the Glock and closed the door. Taking out a satnav phone, Moran sent an encrypted code in a two-second burst. Immediately, five bleeps replied, and Brody swung the helicopter towards the Kowloon shore.

Three minutes later, they settled down on the roof of a multi-storey car park. Leaving the orange jumpsuits and gas masks behind, they ran crouching from the downdraught of the slowing propeller. At a brisk walk they entered the car park, found an empty lift, and descended to the ground floor. Taking a key fob from his holdall, Brody swung his arm 360 degrees, continuously pressing the button. He was rewarded by the nearby sound of unlocking doors and flashing orange lights.

A Ford Transit with the logo 'Irish Olympic Equestrian Team' was revealed. Inside were changes of clothes for each in the Irish Olympic colours. Stephen, in a daze, marvelled at how well the four sets of clothes fit each of them. On the dashboard was a canvas bag containing false passports, accreditation documents, and badges identifying them as bona fide Irish Olympic personnel. With Brody at the wheel, they drove up a ramp and turned left on to a main road. Not a word had been exchanged since Moran's ultimatum back on the Sky Terrace.

'Okay, Doyle, here's how it goes. We're on our way to the airport. We've exchanged your horse at the quarantine centre for another due to travel home. We had time to insert a small team, including a vet. We have friends in the Olympic movement and the Department of Agriculture, so it was easier than it might have been. Also there was a major doping scandal involving one of the Irish Olympic horses and an unfortunate fire as soon as your horse left—enough confusion, but not enough to shut down the city or airport. This may or may not work, but I'm hopeful. I really don't fancy our backup plan. When we get to the airport, you go straight to the horse and keep him calm. We want as little fuss as possible.'

The commercial side of the enormous Norman Foster–designed airport is well away from glaring lights. They drove to the equestrian terminal, where officious and efficient Chinese authorities awaited. Leaving the vehicle with their clothing and weapons in a reserved short-term car park, they presented themselves at the registration desk. Interminable minutes dragged by as their documents were checked and verified. Forged credentials in this modern age of embedded microchips had to be impeccable.

Professionalism and the IRA are two sides of the same coin, forever striving for perfection in an imperfect world. At last they were ushered through to the departure concourse. There a pale, freckled, red-headed Irishman, who introduced himself as Declan Roche, met them. This nervous, jumpy individual, chewing already well-bitten fingernails, brought them directly to the waiting air transport. The sight and rumbling sound of arriving and departing aircraft fogged the air with the unmistakable smell of burnt and unburnt aviation fuel.

Chapter 45

Superintendent Deegan waited and fretted at the Peninsula Hotel. A foul-tempered police colonel assigned by the security authorities closely attended him. He shared his one meagre lead that the Australian contingent they were interested in was registered there, including one Julie Dundon. Their enquiries revealed only that the booking was in the name of an offshore company based in Macau.

Suddenly, the oasis of calm was filled with squawking police radios. The colonel in perfect English informed him that mayhem and worse had broken out on Victoria Peak. Before dashing away, the less-than-inscrutable oriental conveyed by look and manner that the event probably involved Deegan's suspects.

Deegan, acting on every policeman's basic gut instinct, elected to stay. An hour later, he sprang from one of the lobby's deep-cream leather sofas as two familiar people came through the revolving doors. Bill Burroughs, supporting a sobbing and shivering Julie Dundon, approached reception.

Chapter 46

Knowing the hierarchy under which Ming Tai operated, Julie reluctantly agreed to accompany her to the back room of a glitzy music store. Ming Tai was obviously distressed. She was agitated and effusive in her promise that as soon as the video she was ordered to show was viewed, Julie was then free to go.

The store, located a mere 100 yards from the Peak Tram terminus, was obviously a triad enterprise. The manager expecting them, showed them through the bustling store. Bill Burroughs, feeling control slipping from his grasp, demanded Julie remained in sight. Ming Tai demurred, insisting this was a private matter. To everyone's amusement, including two burly triad minders, Bill Burroughs solved their dilemma by simply lifting the manager's office door from its hinges. Now he could see her plainly, sitting facing him with Ming Tai, both looking at a VCR screen.

'You must view it all, Miss Julie. These Triads have strict orders from Quan. As you will see, I am a woman without honour, but I begged them to spare you this. My life is now in your hands.'

Bill Burroughs, looking directly at Julie, saw a complete transformation. Gone was the excited, slightly giddy, beautiful young woman. Instead, a broken person was being dismantled before his eyes. Tears flowed freely down a ravaged face, while occasional sobs racked the hunched young body.

Eventually, the torment clicked to a close. One of the triads ejected the tape, and both of them escorted Ming Tai, who was crying uncontrollably out the door.

Chapter 47

The Lufthansa air transporter left the People's Republic air space four hours later. Moran listened intently to a brief telephone call on his satnav mobile phone. They had adequate, if spartan, accommodation on the wide-bodied Boeing jet specially modified for transporting horses. A full complement was forty animals, whereas they were currently carrying twelve. Moran summoned Stephen back from the stalls, where he had been petting and soothing a very agitated Barabbas. The highly-strung animal sensed things in his world were amiss, and he was also without Poyak, his stable companion.

'I've just heard from Brother Superior. We're on our way to the Quarantine facility at Frankfurt Airport. You will travel on to Ireland with the horse after quarantine, go back to Wexford, race the horse in group one events in Ireland and the UK. In two years, he goes to stud. He is legally and officially signed over to you. This so called Good Friday Peace Agreement has starved us of funds, and your stunt before you left Wexford didn't help. Adams and McGuinness sold us out. Blair, Ahearne, and Clinton might have won this round, but we're here for the long haul. Our cause is simple and just—the return of the occupied six counties of Ulster and the departure of the Brits from Ireland.'

Stephen sat with his head in his hands, bewildered by the pace of events and the intensity of the tall lean dark-haired man sitting before him.

'Look at their record around the globe, and the fucking mess they leave behind. Partition, divide, and rule have always been their trademark—one pinprick of a country run for centuries by pompous bullies who really think they are the master race. Look at the fuck-up of India and Pakistan, millions killed and still going on to this day; Afghanistan and the northwest frontier, for God's sake; and the South African Boer War even *before* the First World War; then the artificial

116

creation of Iraq from Mesopotamia; and the fuck-up in Palestine *after* the First World War; then Aden, Cyprus, Kenya, Malaysia, and Rhodesia *after* the Second World War; and Ireland, always Ireland. We've been asking them to leave politely and impolitely for over 600 years.'

Stephen sat there almost nodding his head in agreement and occasionally looking out the window at the panorama of deserts and snow-capped mountains.

'Now you, Doyle, will train and run this horse to the best of your ability for the financial benefit of the Irish Republican Army. That's not a request. It's a direct order from your superior officer. We won't rest until our mission is accomplished. You knew this when you took the oath. Naturally, you're curious about Heffernan. Heffernan was tried by a military court of the Army Council and sentenced to death for bringing disgrace to the movement. Apparently, he was a practicing paedophile for years as a teacher under Brother Superior's very nose. We received word of the sentence and our orders while we waited for you in Hong Kong. You belong to a large family, Doyle. Your father is not a well man. Every one of them is a potential hostage. Brother Superior has arranged for the prodigal son routine for your return—all a terrible mistake, everything okay now, etc. They will believe it because they want to, especially your mother. All other charges will be dropped. We expect to be arrested when we land, but certain matters are being negotiated. Never forget, Doyle, you chose to serve this cause for life the day you took the oath. I really hope Brody or myself or somebody like us won't be sent to sort you or your family. Want to hear something really funny, Doyle? We're good at what we do because we've been trained by the best. When we were a lot younger, Brother Superior arranged for dozens of us to join the British Army. We were to concentrate on getting as much practical experience as possible—no birds, booze, or time wasting. Eventually, eight of us were accepted into the SAS and SBS. We were the best of the very best. Of course, the Brits have copped on long ago. They know this is to the death and that we will never give up or give in.'

Brody, an amused listener, clapped his hands. 'Doyle, you should be honoured. That's the longest mouthful I've ever heard coming from Joe Moran.'

Stephen, at a loss for words, stared into the fathomless black eyes and knew the nightmare he began would never end.

Chapter 48

The Chinese authorities threw a security blanket around the events on Victoria Peak. The entire area was sealed off, and the Western press neutralized. The official version was that a crack Red Army Unit had carried out an unannounced antiterrorist exercise, which was all part of their ever-vigilant security concerns, especially now with the eyes of the world upon them.

Superintendent Deegan persuaded the ranking paramilitary officer at the bottom of the Peak Tram terminus that he had permission to travel to the Sky Terrace. After a swift cell phone call and another on an army-issue handheld radio, the officer assigned an NCO to accompany him to the top. The cars coming down as they went up were crammed with curious tourists with noses pressed to the glass windows.

Picking his way through the carnage of the restaurant, Deegan slowly paced inside and outside the shattered premises. Deegan had no doubt of the identity of the attackers. The enormity of it in the middle of the Olympics shook him to the core. The police colonel from the Peninsula Hotel was roughly interrogating Quan and Tang Song Li when Deegan approached.

The colonel, who was spitting fire, turned on Deegan, his voice at screeching pitch. The invective abruptly stopped at a single word from a tall, extremely thin middle-aged Chinese in civilian clothes, with a smouldering cigarette glued to his bottom lip.

'Please ask whatever questions you wish, Superintendent. I know we will have the same objective. This buffoon will not trouble you again.'

A rapid exchange between both Chinese resulted in the colonel slinking away.

Deegan squatted by Quan and Tang, showed them his credentials, and told them of his suspicions. Tang realized they had to cooperate, as the government who tolerated them to their mutual benefit could crush them at will. He confirmed the details of the 'business arrangement' in progress when they were interrupted by the fire alarm. Also the descriptions of the attackers and that Doyle knew at least one of them was the clincher. Tang's description of Doyle's intervention that saved their lives and then one gunman shooting the other were intriguing.

'One final thing, Superintendent. Doyle was not part of this. He was terrified and went with them unwillingly. I hope you bear that in mind if and when you catch up with him.'

Chapter 49

A furious Chinese government detained Julie, Bill Burroughs, and even Superintendent Deegan. Their outrage was complete when they learned how their stringent procedures had been breached, the living proof of which was the disappearance of Barabbas. Threats and counter-threats were exchanged. The presence of so many world leaders and their advisers in China for the Olympics was both a help and a hindrance. Containment was the only issue on which there was agreement. With the plane, passengers, and cargo now effectively under arrest in Frankfurt, wise council was desperately required.

Enter William Augustus Florentine Penrose, duke of Carlisle, former British foreign secretary, and confidant of the mighty. Gus, as his intimates called him, was a superb diplomat. He managed to persuade the Chinese that their demand for the extradition of the people and the horse from Frankfurt would be counterproductive. The problem the EU had with China's human rights record would make it politically impossible to extradite EU citizens to China. Also the ensuing publicity would expose the ineptitude of the Chinese authorities. The EU also implied that millions of loosely documented Chinese citizens scattered throughout the twenty-seven EU countries might have their status scrutinized.

Lord Carlisle eventually achieved consensus. Stephen Doyle would be allowed to return to Ireland as the legal owner of the horse. Eventual ownership would be a private and moral matter between Stephen Doyle and Bill Burroughs's syndicate. Brody, Moran, and their henchmen would be spirited away to Northern Ireland, where outstanding warrants for past activities awaited. They would be charged and jailed until the lawyers eventually secured their release.

This would inevitably happen as the warrants predated the Belfast Agreement and would therefore qualify them for parole. Both wings of the IRA would be mollified, a fact that the wily Gus had established in a telephone conversation with Brother Superior back in Ireland. Gus fervently believed in knowing your enemy and dealing with them if necessary. It was, of course, your 'friends' who usually were the problem in the diplomatic world.

Chapter 50

Julie, Bill Burroughs, Dickey Beckett, and Superintendent Deegan returned to Perth on a regular Qantas flight. All of them were changed and traumatized by their recent experiences. Susie and the Nag, delirious with excitement, were waving and shouting by the barrier at the arrivals area. They flung themselves into each other's arms, shocked at the changes they saw in each other. Sobbing and hugging, they were led to a twelve-seater turbo prop for the short hop to the airfield at Bridgetown. Before leaving Hong Kong, Deegan had given his opinion on what had occurred and, according to the triads, how Stephen had saved the lives of both Tan and Quan Song Lee. Deegan thanked and commiserated with them before being driven off to brief Commander Wakefield. As he shook hands, he reminded them that the federal police would demand their own interview. He promised he would try to square things at a local level.

Thoroughly confused and exhausted, Julie sank into despair as the others recounted their experiences while she was in captivity. Dickey Beckett was inconsolable when told of the murder of his uncle. He was angry with everybody and everything and found it hard to accept that he had to be kept in the dark until Julie was freed. Susie, trying to soften the blow, told Julie what Stephen had told them and how, at an impressionable age, he was inducted into the IRA. She also confided that Heffernan had molested Stephen at a very young age.

The Nag refused to be placated. 'He's a bloody Jonah. From the day he appeared, he's been nothing but trouble. Seems to me he must've been in on the scam with the Chinamen. Only for those bloody Irish terrorists, they woulda got clean away—no one injured, papers legit, and Julie safely home. Whatever grief he gets from those madmen won't be half enough as far as I'm concerned.'

With these untypically bitter words, the Nag picked up his crutch. They listened in silence to the sound of his limping footsteps fading down the hall.

Chapter 51

Sod's law now came into force in earnest, or as the Nag was fond of saying, 'God never closed one door, but He slammed another.'

Sarah Bright and Julie were always best friends. Now, with Susie's encouragement, Sarah came to stay for a few days. During the endless nightlong talks, barriers came down with confidences shared and exchanged. Young women know in these circumstances if the other is holding back. The degree of intimacy is at a level that no male could remotely understand. Neither of them suspected the consequences before they went into the 'total female honesty' routine.

Julie described her closeness to Ming Tai while she was held in Macau. Then with fresh tears pouring, she described the video she was forced to view by Ming Tai in Hong Kong. Like a child fascinated by fire, Sarah hesitated, then plunged her hand into the flames. In graphic detail, the secrets hoarded in her heart came pouring out. All that transpired in Sydney before Sarah went home was laid bare. In the telling, Sarah omitted to confess that it was in fact Stephen who threw her out and sent her packing. Such was the detail that Julie could not doubt its accuracy. The betrayal by the two most important people in her life was now complete.

Numbed in a mindless vacuum, Julie went along with Sarah's recipe for mending a broken heart. Even though Sarah wasn't the smartest, she realized Julie had experienced something unique and meaningful. She had found love—ah, love, that corny state romanticized by crooners and writers, longed for but seldom found. Sarah's cure was to party, party, party.

Chapter 52

The Nag and Susie looked on in despair as the two friends plunged into a hedonistic lifestyle. Many a dawn would greet the pair as they drunkenly weaved their way home, sometimes dragging whatever male flotsam and jetsam they picked up along the way. Cleaning up after them as they breakfasted in the afternoon was distressing to Susie. She was worried sick at their behaviour and the possible moral and physical consequences of their actions. The Nag refused to discuss the matter, refused his medication, and spent long hours doing hard physical work without resting his damaged leg.

Inevitably, antibiotic-resistant infection spread, necessitating hospitalization. Gangrene set in and could not be controlled. Despite the advances of medical science, amputation became the last resort. Julie, shocked out of self-pity, spent every waking hour with her beloved uncle. Nearly too late, she realized that Susie and the Nag were actually the two most important people in her life.

Her heart hardened, and a calculating coldness consumed her as she obsessed with the notion of revenge. Susie spent all her time at the hospital and soon realized the house, farm, horses, and the horticultural business were in need of firm management. She sought advice from Bill Burroughs, who in due course turned up with a highly rated husband-and-wife team of Japanese extraction.

Chapter 53

Tako Toida and his wife, Naoki Okado, were a revelation. They took control of Midship Industries and Bramble Cottage and, in a tsunami of activity, had everything humming again within a matter of weeks. Sometimes exceptional people who are both academically gifted and practically minded come along. Tako and Naoki were such people, and happily for all concerned, had found a niche where all their talents were required. They were fulfilled, and bit by bit, an aura of calm descended on fractured lives. They came to know and respect each other.

Julie, Susie, or the Nag often came across Tako and Naoki sitting back to back in absolute stillness and silence. They exuded harmony and tranquillity and, as Susie swore, a scent of roses. Sarah was politely and discreetly peeled away and discouraged. Dickey Beckett, being loved to death by Miriam and adored by little Benjamin, stepped up to the mark and accepted more responsibility in the yard. Discretely in the background, Bill Burroughs kept a watchful eye and began sending out feelers across the worlds of intrigue, commerce, and terror.

Tako and Naoki learned and absorbed the recent dramatic and traumatic events in their employers' lives. Their hearts went out to them, but their concern was disciplined as was their custom and training. Both belonged to a Buddhist Shinto warrior sect which practiced self-control and self-defence.

After some hesitation, Julie approached the Japanese couple. All work having been completed, the pair were seated back to back on a floor mat, legs tucked under, elbows tucked in, and palms upturned. Wearing loose white trousers and crossover white tops, they stood in one fluid motion as Julie entered their open door. The three bowed deeply in a display of respect.

'Please excuse my intrusion. I have a personal request I really hope you can help me with. My mind and my body are all over the place. I have no peace or contentment. The recent troubles in my family have left me unable to cope. I want to be strong and capable for my aunt and uncle and a task I have set for myself.'

'Miss Julie, we have hoped and longed for this day. We have felt your pain. Fate has brought us together. Your road back to the light will begin at five o'clock tomorrow morning. All is in readiness.'

And so began a regime of rehabilitation, gently at first and then growing in intensity. Gradually, the negative toxins were expunged from Julie's mind and body. The physical side was no less intense, initially causing her to collapse nightly on her bed with aching bones and joints. Tako and Naoki's regime made her fit, focused, and competent in armed and unarmed combat. Bit by bit the transformation took shape, and now months later, she was restored and prepared for what lay ahead.

Chapter 54

Christmas came and went in a haze of oppressive heat. Temperatures of 40 degrees was really too much even for native-born Australians. Decorative Christmas candles melted before being lit, and an air of lethargy hung over Bridgetown and Balingup. The federal police had been and gone several times. Again the hand of Bill Burroughs was evident in the way they were treated. The press were kept at arm's length with all enquiries handled through Ballymore Estate's PR office.

Superintendent Deegan called to say goodbye and promised to keep them informed of any future developments. He had a long heart-to-heart with Julie and told her how pleased he was at the change he saw in her. Her composure slipped as they hugged farewell. A stab of poignant memory pierced her as she caught his male scent of aftershave and tobacco. A bittersweet flashback conjured a picture of her father laughing and swinging her by the elbows in the back meadow of faraway Katoomba.

'Julie, I'm here for you at the end of a phone. Take this card with my private numbers. Keep well, and let time do the healing.'

Chapter 55

The Nag went from hospital to rehab, where he met his match. Sister Clare was a nun of immense proportions called Alli Baba on account of her forty chins. She had a big red happy face with wisps of hair hanging out of her nun's headgear. The Nag awoke fierce emotions of love, tenderness, and contrariness in the old battle-axe. She bullied, bested, shouted, and cajoled him as he began the long journey of recovery, wearing an artificial limb.

The entire process of fitting and shaping was frustrating and painful even before the device was strapped on for the first time. When the prescribed painkillers fell short, Sister Clare would, surprisingly for a big woman, slip noiselessly into his room in the dead of night and administer a morphine injection.

He teased her about her religion, particularly when she confided that all nuns were married. She showed him her wedding band.

'What's going on, Sister Clare? Or should that be Mrs Clare? Mr Clare must be one hell of a man to get on the lee side of such a mighty woman.'

'Hold your tongue, you filthy heathen. I'll have you know nuns are consecrated as brides of Christ, who is husband, lord, and master. Who would want a miserable specimen like you with your old turkey giblets swinging down to your knees?'

'Well, shiver me timbers, I've heard it all now—my pride and manhood destroyed by the very same stroke.'

On it went, giving and getting in equal measure. The Nag had forbidden visitors until he had mastered the artificial limb. However, Sister Clare had shown Susie and Julie an annex where a glass panel was in fact a two-way mirror. This was necessary for the consultants and doctors to privately study the progress or otherwise of their many patients. Susie and Julie would arrive together unannounced on odd occasions.

On one such occasion, they bit their lips and hankies to stop laughing at the scene on the other side of the glass. The Nag had woken from a deep sleep in obvious pain and distress. His shouts brought a vision of a galleon in full sail as Sister Clare burst into his ward. From her voluminous pockets, she produced a vial of laudanum. In a trice, she had him in a headlock, pinched his nose, tilted his head, and poured the contents down his throat. They watched as he almost disappeared into her ample bosom. Then she shushed, soothed, and rocked him until blessed sleep claimed him once more.

Sister Clare was always 'accidentally' leaving relics, holy medals, and rosaries under his pillow or in his locker. The two of them laughed uncontrollably the day she shook holy water from a blessed well. As she sprinkled, the unscrewed cap flew off, drenching both him and his bedclothes.

'Good grief, sheila. I've bin keelhauled. If'n I die of pneumonia, I'll be back an' drag you down, down forever, Sister, to Davy Jones's locker.'

The day at last arrived when Susie and Julie were summoned to fetch him home. It was a clear, bright, sunny day with a hint of autumn in the air. The nun and the Nag arranged a little tableau. When the ladies entered reception, they were greeted by the sight of the Nag standing, propped by a crutch, and wearing an eye patch, with the hospital's pet African grey parrot perched on his shoulder. This remarkable mimicking bird had been coached and, when prompted, repeated 'Pieces of eight' over and over.

Waves of infectious laughter washed over them, with the assembled staff members joining the fun. This simple effort had the effect of bursting another of the remaining black clouds hanging over their family. They held their breaths as the Nag, unaided, walked down five shallow steps to the waiting Land Rover.

Tako and Toida were at the door of Bramble Cottage to greet them. They were eminently qualified to undertake the ongoing fitness rehabilitation regime, which would restore some equilibrium to their lives.

Chapter 56

On the other side of the world, Stephen Doyle was trying to cope with a dramatic change in his circumstances. The Olympic air transport from Frankfurt quarantine was diverted at the last minute from Dublin Airport to Baldonnel. This was the airbase of the Irish Air Corps located in west County Dublin and was also where government aircraft were maintained.

Stephen was escorted to the commandant's office, where two grim officials awaited. They neglected to give their names, except to confirm they were from the Department of Foreign Affairs and Special Branch respectively. Without mentioning his name, they confirmed with distaste the deal arranged by Lord Carlisle.

Stephen smiled to himself at their discomfort, and he left with threats as to what lay in store if he as much as incurred a parking ticket. As he supervised Barabbas's unloading from the aircraft and loading into a horsebox, Stephen was approached by a nondescript individual in a cap and waxed jacket.

'I won't shake hands. I'm Nick Kelly with Special Branch. I've inherited you. Your file reads like a disaster movie. I've served with Superintendent Deegan for years before he went to Interpol. He's filled me in off the record. He says you're okay and to give you the benefit of the doubt. We'll see. Now I've arranged that horsebox and a Garda escort to Wexford. After that, you're on your own—except you won't be, what with me and Brother Superior keeping an eye on you.'

Driving down the Naas dual carriageway, Stephen wondered if Nicky Kelly was a servant of the state or the IRA or both. He was only back in Ireland an hour, and already that special ambience of nothing and everything and anything was at work. They went past the town of Naas, on to Carlow, Bunclody, Enniscorthy, and finally, over the bridge at Ferrycarrig, which dominated by its Norman castle. Taking the bypass

around Wexford Town, he arrived in Bridgetown, drove up the poplar-
and birch-lined drive, into the yard, and back to his past.

The Garda car peeled away at the gate and left him struggling with
a thousand emotions. A recent rain shower had washed the cobbles, and
they glistened in the weak spring afternoon sunshine. The front door of
the Georgian farmhouse opened, and a tall gaunt figure leaning on a
walking stick emerged. Stephen stepped down from the Range Rover,
walked over, and stood before his father.

'Hi, Dad.'

'Hello, son.'

'From the bottom of my heart, I'm sorry for all the hurt I've caused
you, Mam, and the family. I've no words for it, Dad. I hope you can find
it in your heart to forgive me. If you want to, I'll move on as soon as the
horse is rested and leave you in peace.'

Both men gravely regarded each other. The tears in Stephen's eyes
were not of self-pity but for the reckless manner he had abused the love
and affection of his family.

Leaving his stick aside, Black Jack Doyle placed his hands on Stephen's
shoulders. 'Welcome home, son.'

A stooped figure appeared in the doorway, shading her eyes from
the setting sun. Stephen handed his father's stick to him and turned to
greet his mother.

'Hi, Mam.'

'O God, is that you, Stephen? Praise be to the Almighty. My prayers
have been answered. Oh, my son, my son, my son . . .'

As she broke down, shedding copious mother's tears, Stephen held
her in his arms, stroking her hair, murmuring his sorrow, repentance,
and regrets.

Next, one by one his brothers and sisters emerged from the house
until the entire family surrounded mother, father, and prodigal son.

'Before we go in for the bit of grub, let's have a look at this horse of
yours. He'll be in the first stall nearest the house. Everything's prepared—
fresh straw, hay, oats, water, infrared heater, and the latest CCTV. Who
called him Barabbas and why? Okay, okay, tell us later.'

As a family born and reared with horses, they knew not to crowd a
new arrival.

However, Stephen felt he had to put down a marker. 'He's not your
typical highly strung young thoroughbred. He's calm, mean, and deadly.

He'll stalk you and crush you in a confined place if he can. Funny thing is, that all disappears when a saddle goes on his back. Seems all he wants to do is run.'

Stephen dropped the tailgate and, taking a halter, went around to the small door at the front of the box. Talking continuously in a low voice, he backed Barabbas down the ramp. The Doyles looked in awe at 16 hands of exquisite horseflesh as Stephen ran him around in a circle on a loose rein. After ten minutes of this loosening-up exercise, Stephen led Barabbas past his family standing in line on the path to the stables. They were all intrigued, particularly Stephen, when Barabbas suddenly stopped in front of his father. The horse eyed the old man leaning on his stick and slowly dipped his head. They stood nose to nose for an interminable moment, communicating without words. Each nodded to the other, and the spell was broken.

With Barabbas comfortably stabled, the Doyle family sat down to one of Liz Doyle's fabled meals. Assisted by her daughters, the table looked a delight of culinary perfection. Boyhood memories of other times flooded back as his mother led the family in the traditional grace before meals. The married sons and daughters brought their respective spouses. Liz was in seventh heaven as she watched her healthy brood devour the delicious food. She had banned any quizzing of Stephen until the table was cleared, the dishwasher filled, and the cups of tea poured.

Stephen was shocked at how old his parents had become, particularly his father, who was now quite frail. The black head of hair was gone, replaced by a few tufts of silver. The once-ramrod back and strong voice were bent and faltering.

Now as patriarch, he addressed his family, 'Brother Superior from your old school came to see us. He explained how he discovered that Chinese so-called friend of yours implicated you in his massive gambling debts, how you foolishly tried to cover up by stealing from the order and from us. He can't understand and we can't understand why you didn't come to him or us with your problems. As Brother Superior says, Oscar Wilde knew a thing or two when he said, 'Youth is wasted on the young.' And to cap it all, he said they were so well insured against their loss he was able to convince their insurers to cover our loss as well. Don't ask me how he did it. He's a remarkable man. When he told us you were on your way home, your mother and me and Brother Superior knelt down right there in the parlour and thanked Almighty God, who does indeed move in mysterious ways.'

Though seething at the deceit and manipulation by his former master, Stephen was obliged to go along with the charade. To protect them all, he spun them the agreed yarn dictated by Moran and Brody, 'Your welcome, your forgiveness, and understanding are more than I dared hope. As I've come to learn, unfortunately the hard way, there's no substitute for family. I've learned some bitter lessons since I left Ireland and, to be fair, some valuable ones as well. Now the horse is owned by a syndicate of which I have a small share. The syndicate got bigger since Barabbas's success. Some of the major players in the racing game are involved. The original owners and investors have sold on for huge money. My job is to prepare Barabbas for the British and Irish Classics before we have a crack at the States. The feeling is that an Irish base would be more strategic for this phase of the horse's career before we go back for the Melbourne Cup. Then, all going well, the horse will retire to stud. That's the plan anyway, folks. My only stipulation was that we build our own team here in Bridgetown instead of bringing an out-of-town circus from Australia.'

Chapter 57

And *circus* probably accurately described what came next. The media, first local, then national, and finally, international—descended on this rural backwater in south-east Ireland. Stephen adamantly refused interviews and forbade his extended family to entertain any contact with the press. Initially, the roads and lanes around the little village were choked with media vans of various members of the Fourth Estate. Inevitably, the public joined in, driven by the purple prose of the feature writers and the notion that this wonder horse was actually in their own backyard. In desperation, Stephen called Nick Kelly and asked for help when strangers were seen photographing his mother and sisters during Mass in their local church. A no-nonsense cordon was thrown up around the Doyle property. Interest gradually waned as days became weeks with nothing to see or report.

Stephen contacted Bill Burroughs through a secure line arranged by Nick Kelly. The Australian had been thoroughly briefed by Superintendent Deegan and said he understood Stephen's predicament. Stephen raised the possibility of contacting Julie. His heart broke and then sank when told Ming Tai had shown Julie the tape of his sexual exploits and had gone off the rails with Sarah Bright. Quan Song Li's revenge was now complete.

Stephen's training regime began to take shape. The gallops were extended and modelled on the successful Australian 3-mile version. Barabbas found a new comforter in the form of a young filly called the Diddler. She was a great-great-granddaughter of Stephen's original mare of the same name. The Diddler might become a problem when she first came into season, but that would be down the road. Select guests were invited to watch Stephen work Barabbas on the gallops. With his weight pared to the bone, supplemented by a professional jockey's diet, Stephen thrilled the onlookers with Barabbas's turn of speed. In the absence of Dickey Beckett, Stephen intended riding Barabbas at the next competitive outing. He knew he was being paranoid, but in the present circumstances, he couldn't trust anyone else.

At night, sitting by the big open fire, the priorities of Stephen's parent became obvious. They both cared for him absolutely, but his father's questions and interests centred on everything about the horse. He was immensely proud of his son, his rehabilitation, and the presence of the racing world's most famous animal here in his own yard. His mother wanted to know about the people he met, if there was a girl in his life (particularly, the girl they had seen on TV with Stephen and the horse). And hadn't she been kidnapped and released, and what did this have to do with her son, and whether he was sure he was not in trouble, etc. He explained again that he had worked for Bill Burroughs, who had put him in charge of the young, unmanageable Barabbas, that his success with the horse had earned him a minor share, and that the new owners, who wished to remain anonymous, decided to put his name up as owner.

He explained this was perfectly legal, done every day in business; that Julie Dundon and her uncle, James Monahan, were former shareholders; that, yes, Julie was very attractive but he had been doing a line with her friend Sarah Bright; and that Julie Dundon's ordeal was terrible for a young woman to endure but presumably a ransom was paid because she was released unharmed. Knowing his mother, he knew she would forensically probe until all the pieces in the jigsaw of her son's missing years fell into place.

Chapter 58

The 2000 Guineas is the first group 1 classic of the year in the British Isles and was always held at Newmarket in England. This would be Barabbas's first tilt at the best of the best in this part of the world. Promoters, sponsors, bookmakers, and every arm of the media were already hyping the fact that Barabbas was entered. The news also figured prominently in the tabloids and upmarket broadsheets. Everything about this horse was dramatic news, some vaguely true but mostly exaggerated.

As preparation, Stephen decided to enter Barabbas in the season's first official non-classic event, which in fact kicked off the flat season. This event, called the Easter Dues, was a tongue-in-cheek Irish celebration of the 1916 Irish rebellion, which began at Easter of that year. It was held at the Curragh, and any owner or trainer who wished to test the waters before the start of the classics entered here. That was the original idea. Unsurprisingly, when racing people came together, the result inevitably would be competition fuelled by massive gambling. And so the Easter Dues—or Dues, as it was affectionately known—quickly became the end rather than the means.

As a racing venue, the Curragh of Kildare ranked alongside the top destinations in the equine world. Home to all Irish group 1 classics, the Curragh was mentioned in the same breath as Churchill Downs, Royal Ascot, and Melbourne. Situated an hour from Dublin, the Curragh and its environs were a natural amphitheatre with a history as old as Ireland itself. This was where annual feiseanna (celebrations) were held to honour the high kings of Ireland. Swordplay, eating, drinking, and wenching were indulged under the benevolent Brehon laws in vogue at that time. Horseracing was the centrepiece, where provincial kings and princes matched their mounts and purse in age-old rivalry. And so it was to this day. The Curragh of Kildare was an emerald oasis, surrounded by thousands of ancient sheep-grazing commonage.

Chapter 59

During her wipe-out with Sarah, Julie became reacquainted with Georgina Naismith. Sarah fell in love with Georgina's older brother, Trevor. A match made in heaven was the regular comment. This was because both were utterly vain and self-centred, but with bubbly personalities endearing them to most. Julie's plans were taking shape, and she was alert to any means of furthering them. In Australia, amongst a certain class, there was a ridiculous attachment to England as the mother country. Trevor, who came from an immensely wealthy brewing family, decided to bring Sarah to Bond Street in London to select an engagement ring.

Georgina wished to buy at least two more mounts at Tattersalls to compete at the World Equestrian Games in Badminton near Bristol in May. Julie did not want to be next or near Balingup for the fast-approaching Bridgetown spring show. The memories of last year's events, which began with the Bridgetown Cup, were barely healed scars. Susie and the Nag understood Julie's desire to escape those memories and were reassured when she announced she would accompany the others to England. Tako and Naoki were delighted with Julie's physical and mental recovery and her natural ability with martial arts.

One evening after a week in London, Julie slipped away from their suite at the Clarence. She spun them a yarn that she was testing the romantic waters once more. They were delighted for her and deliciously thrilled with the presumption that the object of her affections was in fact a married man. Discretion naturally was the order of the day, and they readily promised secrecy until she rejoined them before returning to Australia. Later that night, she caught the last Aer Lingus flight from London Heathrow to Dublin.

Chapter 60

Out for a stroll and on her way back to Dublin's Westbury Hotel, Julie ducked into Clarendon Street Church to escape a sudden downpour. She emerged in shock, having heard the congregation recite the crowd's response to Pontius Pilate, 'Release unto us Barabbas!'

Her head reeled from Christ's message of love and forgiveness and the contrasting rage of murder and revenge in her heart. Across the street, skulking in a doorway, twenty-four-year-old Lorcan Ryan shook and twitched, waiting for a soft target. In Dublin parlance, he was a scumbag and a gurrier, two of the lowest descriptions applied to any young man in Ireland. Wearing a black hooded tracksuit, he shivered in the cool, wet evening air, desperate for his next heroin injection. He had to get money somehow, anyhow, to pay for the fix. He noticed a young woman leave the church before the rest of the congregation. Obviously confused, she started walking towards Wicklow Street. Ryan, like a hyena, ran on tiptoe after the young woman, closing the gap in seconds, and struck her a vicious blow to the side of the head.

Julie went down on one knee and felt her handbag being ripped from her shoulder. Shaking and clearing her head, she was up in a flash and flying in pursuit. Ryan's lifestyle was no match for the training and dedication gaining on him with every stride. At full velocity, arms and legs pumping like pistons, Julie launched herself feet first like a human javelin. Ryan never knew what slammed into his back as he hit the ground full force, breaking every bone in his face. Kneeling on Ryan's back, Julie retrieved her handbag. The streetlight glinted on a metal object fallen from Ryan's hand. She picked it up, studied it, and pressed a recessed button. A long thin blade shot out. She pressed again and watched the blade disappear. Rising slowly from the unconscious Ryan, she slipped the flick knife into her pocket and walked back to her hotel.

Chapter 61

Earlier that week, Laurence Power was in an impossible position. With the match on a knife-edge, he had to pitch on to this deceptively fast green, let the ball trickle down 20 feet, and make the putt. The eighteenth hole at Royal Kingstown Golf Club in South Dublin was a severe test of nerve and skill. Laurence and his chief executive, Martin Carroll, had never beaten their opposition during their regular Wednesday four-ball competition. Their opponents, Declan and Cormac Coppinger, were irrepressible property developers and speculators. The property game was their natural environment, and since 1992, they had been spectacularly successful. But now in 2009, their empire had crumpled and collapsed. Once so certain, they were now bewildered. They owed tens of millions secured by worthless property assets. Their world had gone mad; the property bubble that was supposed this time not to fail had burst.

Laurence was their banker of choice, who had never refused them. He held their mortgages and personal guarantees. They all belonged to a wider privileged golden circle who socialized and holidayed together. During the round, they had discussed the possibility of saving their distressed loans being taken over by NAMA (National Asset Management Agency). If that happened, their loans backed by their property would be subject to a savage 'haircut'. NAMA would eventually, at a huge discount, sell their entire property portfolio lovingly built up over the years, and they would still be liable for the balance. The Coppingers hoped Laurence and his bank could shield them for a little while longer until they could come up with a viable business plan. Like Charles Dickens's optimistic Mr Micawber, they were certain 'something would turn up'.

Laurence knew differently. He knew the weight of thousands of Coppinger-type property deals had brought the bank to its knees. He did not expect they could survive the central bank's stress test next week.

But now in this rare oasis of tranquillity, he contemplated what he hoped would be his second last stroke. Oblivious to the beautifully manicured surroundings, he looked down at his ball. Just 4 feet off the green, the ball was lying in the second cut. Unfortunately, the thick, heavy grass was lying against it. This was one of the toughest golf shots in the book. Too much, and it would fly out; too little, and it would stay there. Using a pitching wedge, he managed to delicately flip the ball on to the edge of the green. Mesmerized, they watched as the ball seemed to settle but then, with one extra half turn, began to roll, gathering pace, heading beautifully towards the flag.

'Excuse me, Mr Power.'

Laurence turned to see two men in white boiler suits bearing the club's logo, with white baseball caps pulled low over their foreheads. Exasperated and annoyed, Laurence watched his ball roll 5 feet past the flag.

'It's urgent, Mr Power.'

'Look, you two, you should know better than to interrupt a member before he finishes out.'

One of them walked briskly up to Laurence, grabbed him by the shoulders, and broke his nose with a vicious head butt.

'What the fuck is going on?' Martin Carroll and both Coppingers came running up the green.

The other intruder sprinted towards them, drawing a matt black 9-millimetre Glock handgun. Martin Carroll raised his putter and was promptly shot through the left kneecap. The Coppingers echoed his screams of pain; the attacker reversed his grip on the automatic and, in seconds, beat them unconscious. A Ford Transit reversed across the green with open rear doors. The two grabbed Laurence and threw him head first into the back of the van. With added weight and wheels spinning, the van gouged and tore deep tracks across the pristine surface. The van roared past the clubhouse and the stunned open mouths on the members' balcony.

Chapter 62

The next morning, Julie boarded a train at Connolly Station. Leaving Dublin with the glittering sea to her left and houses, apartments, golf courses, and mountains on her right, Julie Dundon was at last on her way to Wexford.

Dun Laoghaire, Bray, Greystones, Wicklow, Arklow, Gorey, and Enniscorthy passed, each a contrasting visual delight. Finally, through the tunnel at Ferrycarrig and a glimpse of the Norman castle guarding the river. Then the conductor's voice announced their arrival in Wexford as the train eased to a halt in the time-worn station. Julie took a taxi and was driven along Wexford Quays to the Talbot Hotel. As they drove around Crescent Quay, her eyes were inexorably drawn to the scarlet logo of the Red Dragon Chinese restaurant, which was visible behind the imposing statue of Commodore John Barry, founder of the United States Navy.

After booking into the Talbot Hotel, Julie had a shower and a meal and, on impulse, joined a walking tour conducted by the Wexford Historical Society. The Americans, Japanese, French, English, and German tourists she joined were intrigued by the knowledge and enthusiasm of the guides. For the moment, she was lost in these simple pleasures, putting off in her mind the task she had set for herself.

She saw the old well-preserved town walls with their tower gates built by the Norman invaders after 1169 and Selskar Abbey, where the Norman king Henry II did penance for the murder of Thomas, a Becket. They stopped at the Bullring with its imposing statue of a pikeman, which was dedicated to the rebellion of the United Irishmen in 1798. This was also where Oliver Cromwell, the lord protector of England, butchered hundreds of men, women, and children in 1649 for refusing to surrender to his Confederate army. They went to Redmond Square, where John F. Kennedy, descended from Wexfordmen, addressed the people of

Wexford as president of the United States of America. The soaring spires of the Pugin-inspired twin churches built so shortly after the Great Famine, which lost Ireland four million people in 1847, were testament to the resilience of Wexford people. The narrow, winding streets of the medieval town were reminders of ghostly times past but at odds with the friendly greetings from townspeople encountered every step of the way.

Pleasantly tired after two entertaining hours, they strolled back along the boardwalk on the quay front to their hotel. Later as she lay on her bed, Julie pondered all she had seen and compared the visual reality to the images described by Stephen all those months ago and half a world away. She also dispassionately reviewed the reasons she was here. She was going to kill Stephen Doyle for all the hurt and harm he brought to her family; for the betrayal of her love and trust; for the murder of poor, harmless Davey Beckett; for the loss of her dear uncle's leg; for the muffled sobs from her aunt's bedroom and her swollen red eyes in the morning; and for the theft of Barabbas, who was theirs, a part of them, a part of an Australian dream.

The following day, Julie made preparations for her visit to Bridgetown.

Chapter 63

The road from Wexford to Bridgetown meandered for about 7 miles through a rustic, rural landscape past Kerlogue Nursing Home, with death clamouring to get in; up pretentious Coolballow Road; on to Murrintown; and past Johnstown Castle, now home to the Agricultural Institute. Wild daffodils, primroses, and bluebells decorated the sides of the haphazard road. The hired Ford Focus hummed along on a bright spring morning, the sun coming and going behind fleecy clouds. One could blink and easily miss Bridgetown if not for the gates of a railway crossing. A few clustered houses, a shop with petrol pumps, a pub, and a cooperative store completed the picture. The church was out on the road in the half parish of Mulrankin.

Before leaving Wexford, Julie bought an Ordnance Survey map and also studied the surrounding area online on Google Earth. The ribbon road network formed a natural boundary around the Doyles' Kiltealy Estate. Time was short, and Julie discarded crackpot James Bond solutions to gain access to Stephen Doyle. Instead she would use her natural attributes in the time-honoured fashion. From experienced observation and common sense, she knew that grooms, stablehands, and foremen from a particular yard usually socialized at the same place. A few discreet enquiries brought her to John Sinnott's pub in the tiny village of Duncormick. This rough and ready establishment, smoke-cured from generations of cigarettes, pipes, and the occasional cigar, was a last-ditch bastion of male preserve.

As this could be a long day and longer night, Julie sensibly decided to fortify herself with a solid meal. On a recommendation, she drove a further 5 miles to the seaside village of Kilmore Quay. A picturesque whitewashed seaside village sloping down to the water and distinguished by the thatched roofs of many houses. She walked the beach and the busy fishing harbour, taking in the mysterious Saltee Islands on the near horizon. Standing on Forlorn Point, Julie felt a calmness settle over her. With nerves soothed and resolve strengthened, she walked back the sea wall to the Silver Fox. Following a nourishing meal of local fresh seafood, she slowly drove back to Duncormick.

Richie Cleary couldn't believe his luck. Richie held court, propping up the bar, surrounded by back-slapping men of all ages. A broadly built, curly-haired thirty-year-old stock foreman, he was obviously popular and full of self-confidence. A gorgeous Australian brunette calling herself Susan Black singled him out and gave him her undivided attention. She was dressed in dark denim jacket and jeans, and her mustard silk scarf emphasized the glint in her hair and the warmth of her lovely brown eyes. His mates urged him on and for once resisted the temptation of spoiling the chances of one of their own.

Darkness had fallen, and Julie made a decision. After two hours of moderate drinking—she on a vile white wine and he on pints of Guinness—she made her pitch, 'Richie, you're a man of the world. As I've told you, I'm a photo journalist. What I want comes with a price. I want a photo of Barabbas in his stall tonight. I need to get it to my editor before he runs in the Easter Dues. This will be a world exclusive and naturally good for my career. Everybody knows he hasn't been seen, let alone photographed, since he left Australia. There's phenomenal interest in him there. What you get is me for a whole night—adult to consenting adult. Anything goes except kinky violence. I'm a woman of the world who knows what a man likes and wants. You get me in, we have our bit of fun, I get the photo, and you get me out. What do you say, sport?'

Richie licked his lips. His brain whirled as he computed the consequences. Maybe he could get her in and out without being discovered. Security at the staff gate had never been too tight, and he did have a bit of authority as a foreman. There was just too much activity going on day and night, plus the fact nothing had shown up during the thorough random searches they had carried out. On the other hand, if he was caught, he was finished and probably blackballed from every farm and yard in the country.

Richie appraised this gift from the gods, his eyes devouring her from head to toe. She coolly gazed back at him, chin up, shoulders back, breasts out.

'I've always looked at life as a hand of cards, Susan. You've got to do the best you can with the hand you're dealt. You could be bluffing—maybe you are. I could be bluffing—maybe I am. I'm calling your bluff. Okay, you're on. Let's go.'

Ten minutes later, his car was waved through the gates at the staff entrance. Julie was mightily relieved it wasn't any further as she bounced inside the boot of his Toyota. She had established Richie had his own room plus a tiny kitchen and a small separate bathroom. These were in the main staff quarters in an old converted stone barn. As she emerged from the boot, she inhaled the heady mix of horse, straw, dung, oats, and leather. It was like a tonic to be once more in her natural element.

Richie had his own side entrance, and with most of the staff off duty, they had little fear of discovery. With the big race coming in two days' time, now was the last opportunity for time off before every hand was needed. Time off for most, but not for all. Julie was certain Stephen would be close at hand, barely resting in that intense concentration she knew so well.

They slipped unnoticed into Richie's room. After some preliminary kissing and groping, Julie persuaded Richie to show her how she would access Barabbas's stall. Once she had the lie of the land, they would return to his room for what he quaintly called 'the bit of auld divilment'. She put her hair up, jammed a woollen hat of his on her head, and slipped into one of his old wax jackets.

Skirting the rear of the stable block, Richie showed how a new gravity chute had been fitted behind each stall. This allowed the stable to be swept out and then hosed down the chute and on to a conveyor belt. This belt then discharged on to the flat bed of a waiting trailer, eliminating a lot of tedious labour. The chute was snugly fitted with a slippery surface to prevent access by vermin. However, by pressing the chute upwards, it could be unhooked from the catches, keeping it in place. Richie demonstrated this to a delighted Julie, who rewarded him with a tongue-tingling kiss of Hollywood proportions. They quickly hurried back to his room, each with a different agenda.

Julie winked at the gagged, trussed figure secured to a stout wooden chair, which was in turn secured to the iron frame of his bed. With her training, it was not difficult to overpower an unprepared person. Even though Richie was burly and powerful, pressure points and nerve endings were vulnerable to paralysis when properly applied. She laughed at the woebegone expression on his round face.

She kissed him on the forehead. 'Don't fret, mate. I'll be back before dawn to cut you free. You can take me back to my car, and no one will know I was ever here.'

A few minutes later, Julie silently unclipped the chute behind Barabbas's stall and crept into his stable. A black shape materialized out of the darkness, white vapour streaming from flared nostrils.

'Barabbas, it's Julie, Barabbas. Do you remember me, Barabbas? Good boy, there's a good, good boy. I've missed you so much, Barabbas.'

She repeated his name over and over as she continuously stroked his familiar muzzle. They stood nose to nose, breathing each other until they were sure. Julie was fairly certain the CCTV cameras were not pointing in her direction at the back of the stable. With her eyes adjusted to the near darkness, she climbed the short rough ladder to the hayloft above.

Barabbas was completely unsettled after his encounter with Julie. She was counting on his agitation registering on the CCTV. Her gamble paid off as minutes later a tall dark-haired figure unlatched the half door of the stable. Julie tensed as the person below turned on a dim-shaded light set high on the wall. The shade had the effect of making the loft darker and the stable brighter. Her heart beat like a trip hammer as she looked down on Stephen Doyle. Love and hate swirled unchecked as her hand unconsciously closed on the flick knife in her pocket. Adrenalin now pumping through her body, Julie prepared to launch herself on the man below.

Just then, a figure appeared at the half door with another slightly behind.

'Well, well, well, if it ain't Mr High and Mighty himself. Hope you're lookin' after our investment, Doyle. We wouldn't want anything to happen to any of your precious family then now, would we? Not like what happened to poor Hughie Heffernan then.'

'Chris Murphy and Oliver Meaney, Laurel and Hardy in the flesh. The Brits barely stamped your cards, and here you are. How did you get in here? Now will you kindly fuck off? Can't you see the horse is upset? Which is the last thing I need right now. Or do you want to be reported to Brother Superior?'

With that, the door crashed open. Murphy and Meaney, both strong and fit, bounced Stephen between them. Blows rained down as Stephen raised his arms, trying in vain to protect himself.

'Hughie was our friend, our special friend. After he showed you how much he liked you, you were to be our special friend too, but then you squealed on him after robbing the movement. You little fucker, you got him killed.'

'You dirty pair of perverts call yourselves Irishmen? I never squealed, though to my shame I should have. Brother Superior found out himself, which means Moran and Brody are on your case right now, and you know what that means.'

Murphy and Meaney exchanged looks and stopped for a split second. In that unspoken moment, they made a decision. Their renewed assault was now a vicious frenzy, kicks and blows pounding without pity. Stephen sagged to the floor, cut and bleeding, unable to protect himself. Murphy grabbed a two-pronged hayfork clipped to a bracket. Shouting obscenities, he raised the fork to plunge it into his helpless victim.

Julie dropped, lithe as a cat, ducked and spun as Murphy, sensing danger, reversed his grip and swung the fork in her direction. She stood so still with the stiletto blade extended. In one movement, Murphy dropped the fork and reached for the flat automatic at the small of his back. Bringing the neat deadly weapon to bear, he never felt the long thin blade slide under his ribcage and into his heart.

In the melee, Barabbas, initially frantic, was now strangely quiet and seemed to be leaning against the wall. Julie checked the pulse of the unconscious Stephen, grabbed a halter, and threw it over the horse's head. With a soothing voice, Julie led Barabbas to a hitching ring and made it fast. It was then she noticed the slumped form by the wall. In two strides, she was checking for another pulse. The protruding dead eyes of Oliver Meaney were an obvious clue. Crushed to death, he confirmed the warning of poor old Davey Beckett in another Bridgetown many months ago.

In passing, Julie noticed an ankle holster strapped to the exposed leg of the dead man. What were they doing here? It sounded like they were gloating and that Stephen was acting under duress for the sake of his family, just like how the Chinese had him jumping through hoops for her safety. How did he cope with all that stress? He obviously staggered from her crisis to this one. Julie sank to her knees in the straw and cradled Stephen's head in her lap. Her tears landing on his face brought him back from unconsciousness.

He opened his eyes, looked up, blinked, closed his eyes, shook his head, and opened his eyes again. 'Julie . . . is that you, Julie? It is, it is . . . I must be dead. I don't care. Stay with me awhile, my love. Say you will, Julie, say you will.'

Julie continued rocking and crying and stroking his hair as the sound of shouting and running feet reached them. Stephen's older brothers Eamon and Brendan were first on the scene, shortly joined by two of his sisters and their husbands. Their questions dried in their throats as they surveyed the surreal tableaux—a young woman kneeling and holding their bloodied brother and two obviously dead bodies, one with a knife stuck in the chest. Their semicircle parted to admit their parents. Black Jack was wheezing and leaning on his stick.

'Jesus, Mary, and Joseph! Oh my god, what's happened? Stephen, speak to me. Are you okay? Who's that with you? Oh my god, you're that girl from Australia. What's wrong with those other two? Sweet Jesus, are they dead? C'mon, Jack, our Christian duty, we might only have minutes to spare.'

Elizabeth and Jack Doyle first checked that Stephen was not in imminent danger, then went to each body. Jack painfully but determinedly knelt at the remains of Chris Murphy, while Liz attended to Oliver Meaney. They each whispered an act of contrition into the ear of both dead men. Their firm belief was that the soul does not depart a still-warm body and that if the spirit of the dead person acknowledges the contrition, then God will accept that soul into heaven. Such simple belief was the bedrock of their faith, which sustained generations of Irishmen and -women.

Eamon Doyle, taking the lead, reminded them to touch nothing until the police (An Garda Síochána) arrived. They would attend to Stephen's wounds while they placed the call. The CCTV would have captured most of everything, which should be of great assistance. Back at the house, they gathered around the huge dining room table, an open fire of logs and turf throwing welcoming warmth into the family room. Stephen and Julie sat there, fiercely holding hands like survivors of a shipwreck.

Julie, voice shaking with delayed shock, cleared her throat. 'I know you have a million questions, which we will answer as best we can. We also have millions of questions, but first, may I suggest I call Superintendent Deegan? He's with Interpol, and he's ex-Irish Special Branch. He knows nearly everything about our problems. I trust him. He's got all the contacts, and he'll be able to fill in some of the gaps. Do you think that will be okay?'

Julie had reached into her jacket and removed a card from her wallet. Looking around the room, she accepted the succession of nods as permission to proceed.

As she dialled the international number on her Blackberry, Stephen broke his silence, 'As Julie said, we'll fill you in as soon as we compare our own notes. A lot has happened since we were last together. In the meantime and more importantly, the people we are dealing with are really, really dangerous. My reason for being here was to try and protect you from them, at which I've spectacularly failed. So please be patient with us a little while longer.'

Julie held up her hand as she made contact. She turned the phone to speaker, heard her identify herself and launch into a description of their predicament.

'Touch nothing, Miss Dundon. We'll take care of everything. Believe it or not, I'm in Wexford at your hotel. We momentarily lost your trail. We've been tracking you since you arrived in London. Mr Burroughs is with me. We'll see you in a short while.'

An hour later, Superintendent Deegan and Bill Burroughs joined them at the dining room table. By this time, Liz Doyle and her daughters had worked their culinary magic. The table fairly groaned with food and other refreshments. Superintendent Deegan, having surveyed the scene in Barabbas's stall, instructed the forensic team and viewed the CCTV tapes. Bill Burroughs swept Stephen and Julie into his massive bear hug as the rest of the Doyle family looked on in amazement.

'Okay, folks, settle down while I fill you in. We've been keeping an eye on Miss Dundon in case of a fit of revenge by the triads. We really got nervous when she took off for Europe and then Dublin. We figured Wexford had to be her next stop when the trail went cold. She simply got the train instead of hiring a car in Dublin, and we lost her. The problem here and now is that events have interfered with our plans. We've been trying to roll up Brother Superior's dissident IRA outfit for a very long time. Ninety eight per cent of the people on the island of Ireland support the peace process and the Belfast Agreement, but not these jokers. We thought we would have our best chance with Brody and Moran tucked up in Castlerea Prison. The bad news is that despite a red flag against their release, the Northern Ireland Office released them—said they had to strictly adhere to the Belfast Agreement. And we're fairly positive they're behind the recent kidnap and murder of a leading Dublin banker. The death of these two IRA volunteers changes everything. Any arrangement made with Stephen will be history. That's the way their minds work. The IRA eyes and ears are everywhere. They probably already know what's happened here.'

A uniformed Garda sergeant called Superintendent Deegan outside. He returned five minutes later and called Stephen and Julie aside.

'One of my team discovered an irate farm foreman gagged and tied to a chair in his flat. He swears he was jumped by an unknown assailant. I know he's lying. Before we waste valuable time, I wonder if you, Miss Dundon, could shed any light on the matter?'

Julie blushed to the roots of her hair. 'How did you know, Superintendent? In the excitement, I had quite forgotten about Mr Cleary. Is he okay?'

'The big clue was when I removed the gag before the blindfold. His first words were choice, with lots of reference to *you fucking bitch.*'

'I'm afraid I took advantage of Mr Cleary's good nature to get into the estate. I'll explain the full story when you both have time. In the meantime, please don't punish poor Richie, it really was all my fault.'

Just then, Bill Burroughs approached, having been out in the yard for the past half hour.

'The forensic people are finished, Superintendent. Will it be okay to move Barabbas back to his box? We've put in fresh hay, straw, and water. The CCTV set-up is really quite good. Don't worry, Stephen. Everything is in hand. You look exhausted. Here, have a look at the monitor. See who's looking after Barabbas for the moment.'

Stephen looked and looked and still couldn't believe his eyes. Dickey Beckett, large as life, was fussing and petting and soothing the now tranquil Barabbas.

Burroughs said, 'Dickey and Miriam became very worried about Julie and her aunt and uncle. He knew I wasn't the sort to let matters lie. When I told him I suspected the gang who murdered his uncle had some hold over Stephen, he pleaded to be let come along. Supt Deegan's people spotted my people shadowing Julie in London. He had to create a showdown in case we were the other side. We agreed to join forces, and here we are. Can you contain matters here for a couple of days, Superintendent? I think we should race the horse—a sort of Trojan Horse—flush the bastards out.'

'I'll have to report up the line. Various departments in various jurisdictions are involved. Now don't worry. At this level, decisions are made very, very quickly. But first, we have to present them with a viable plan. Let's get a night's sleep and meet here at 8 a.m. after breakfast. I've arranged for extra security—the best. I've got to get back to Wexford Garda station to grease the local wheels.'

Chapter 64

Liz and Black Jack Doyle finished their night prayers and, sitting up in bed, reviewed the day's dramatic happenings. The waxed heavy oak bedroom furniture glowed in the reflected light from their bedside lamps. This was their nest, their cocoon, and their sanctuary, where daily events were discussed and tomorrow's plans were laid. Their vast queen-sized bed was where their six children were conceived and subsequently delivered by Bridie Stone, the local pint-sized midwife.

They were horrified at the killings and the treachery of Brother Superior. What was more terrifying was his fanaticism, his absolute conviction that his cause was right and justified by any means. And their poor Stephen was caught up in it like a leaf in a storm. The fact that he brought a lot of grief on his own head was not something readily conceded by most parents, and they were no exception. Another lifelong unwritten rule was shattered when Stephen and Julie hand in hand went up the stairs to Stephen's bedroom. Liz smiled to herself at her intuition now confirmed that they were in fact made for each other. Up the landing, the objects of her thoughts were fast asleep, fully clothed, wrapped in each other's arms.

Early the next morning, Superintendent Deegan arrived for breakfast with two other men. One was the nondescript Sgt Nick Kelly and the other a stern-faced broad-shouldered man whose bearing fairly screamed *military*.

There's nothing quite like the smell of a full Irish breakfast. Rashers, eggs, puddings, and sausages—all popping and sizzling, making the early juices flow. Liz, the girls, and indeed, some of the men soon had a supply line in full production. When they were fully fed and clutching their umpteenth cup of strong tea, Superintendent Deegan brought the gathering to order.

'On a need to know basis, only the following will sit in on the meeting. Don't take it personally. It's for your own safety. All I ask is that you carry out our instructions without question. The people we are dealing with have proven what they are capable of over and over. They have sympathizers everywhere, maybe even here. Sergeant Kelly will take details of all your mobile phones and leave an emergency number on each of them. Don't talk to anybody outside the family. Lives will depend on your ability to keep a closed mouth.'

Superintendent Deegan, Bill Burroughs, Stephen, Julie, Dickey Beckett, Jack Doyle, and the unidentified other breakfast guest repaired to the vast conservatory at the back of the house. The garden outside, neatly clipped and trimmed, was a riot of flowering spring plants and shrubs.

Superintendent Deegan rapped the table. 'This is Colonel McGarrick, CO of the Irish Rangers battalion. A company of his rangers has been seconded to this operation. It's proof to me how serious the govt. are about these dissidents. You hear very little about the Irish Rangers, and that's the way they like it. The description *elite* is much abused but deserved in this case. They are trained with the SAS, American Special Forces, and the Israeli Army. We are going to agree a plan this morning which involves the horse running in the Easter Dues at the Curragh in two days' time. Sgt Nick Kelly outside there will be involved but at arm's length. His contacts with the dissidents are both a curse and a blessing. The rangers are deployed in and around the Doyle estate. Nothing, but nothing, will get in or out or past them. Now let's get down to business.'

Chapter 65

In deference to the sincerely held beliefs of Elizabeth and Black Jack, Julie was assigned her own room at the other side of the house. The morning after their traumatic reunion, Julie noticed the relief in Elizabeth's eyes when they emerged from Stephen's room, wearing the clothes of the day before. She appreciated that to flout the conventions of generations, which had reared so many children and grandchildren, would be insensitive and insulting. They would naturally make other more-discreet arrangements.

Chapter 66

Tuesday morning of Easter week dawned with preparations well under way. An early start was essential for a two-and-a-half-hour journey on the day of the actual race. They had considered and dismissed the option of travelling the day before, although at Colonel McGarrick's suggestion, a horsebox with a Garda escort had already travelled as a diversion.

Tensions were ratcheted up a notch when a blushing Richie Cleary knocked on the kitchen door.

'Got a call on my mobile, said to tell the gaffer straight away, said he was to remember what happened to Shergar. Don't know who it was. Lots of people have that number. Didn't sound pleasant at all.'

A sombre silence followed. Every person in the world remotely connected with racing and every man, woman, or child in Ireland knew the story of Shergar. The 1981 Derby winner owned by the Aga Khan was kidnapped in 1983 from Ballymany Stud near the Curragh. Such was Shergar's racing form that his kidnapping became worldwide news for weeks on end. The Provisional IRA never admitted it but was known to have carried out the kidnapping. Blame and counterclaims still existed to this day. Some ransom negotiations were carried out, but nothing transpired. The upshot was that the most famous racehorse of his day had never been seen alive or dead again. Rumour had it that they couldn't handle the volatile animal, shot him after he broke a leg, and allegedly buried him in a vast, remote bog in County Leitrim.

'No surprise there. Thank you, Richie. We're depending on you and the others to carry on your normal duties and anything the superintendent requires of you. Now I believe Miss Dundon would like a word in private.'

Even though unfolding events were grim, there was something quite amusing at the sight of the burly foreman and young Australian beauty closing the door behind them.

'Don't say a word, Richie. There's too much going on at the moment. I'll make sure you're not blamed for smuggling a girl past security. I know the staff look up to you. You can really help by keeping them onside. There was nothing personal in the way I treated you. I would have used any means to get inside the estate. When this is over, I promise I'll tell you as much as I can over a pint down at Sinnott's. Do we have a deal?'

As per her request, Richie didn't say a word, nodded, shook her hand, and walked back up the yard.

Three hours later, after an uneventful journey, their procession of dark-tinted SUVs, horsebox, official Garda cars, and four Garda motorcycle outriders, arrived at the Curragh.

Chapter 67

An air of unmitigated excitement sang in the air. There is no joy more fervent than an Irishman's appreciation of a good horse. A full card promised a feast of racing from the finest collection of horseflesh invited or entitled to race.

A nearby nursing home, Lilac Hall, catering mostly for elderly retired country folk, added an extra twist to the day. Such was the clamour from these walking wounded of life that ambulances, coaches, and cars were used to ferry them, their wheelchairs, and rugs to the track. Their spokesman, Jake Purcell, declared there was no way they were going to miss the chance to see the Australian wonder horse racing against the cream of the crop in their own backyard. Red Cross and St John Ambulance Brigade were on hand to attend to their well-being.

This news and other snippets, including the expected attendance of the sheiks, sultans, and the millionaire and billionaire owners of nearby studs and estates, were broadcast through the radios of thousands of cars and coaches inching their way through traffic jams and tailbacks to the Curragh of Kildare.

The weather, as was often the case this time of year in Ireland, stuttered fitfully with heavy clouds and a wild wind from the west. Then at approximately 11 a.m., the sun popped out, the clouds dispersed, and the day settled down. Up the road in Fairyhouse, the week-long Steeplechase Festival of racing was in full swing. These five- to twelve-year-olds were the selective-breeding by-products of previous competitors of the Easter Dues and other great thoroughbred events around the world. To facilitate the avid racing fraternity, Fairyhouse featured only four races, all in the morning.

Between both tracks, helicopters ferried the high and mighty, who were then whisked from one VIP area to the next. The ordinary punter found this hilarious. Most of the glitterati were jumped-up builders, developers, estate agents, spivs, and other scavengers, who were just dying to look down on somebody else. Lots of them were still in denial of their financial reality. And head and shoulder beneath them all were their lapdog politician cronies, fit to burst from swilling at the trough.

The happy throng of everyday Irish citizenry, with their trilby hats, peaked caps, headscarves, crombies, blazers, sports jackets, jeans, suits, sensible shoes, and high heels, were oblivious to their 'betters'. All were joined in one purpose. This was going to be a race to be remembered, to be able to say they were there when the cream of five continents kicked off the flat season. Though it didn't rank as a classic, it was more important in that peculiarly Irish way that turns logic on its head.

The colourful on-course bookmakers, hoarse with excitement and shouting the odds, were doing a roaring trade. Nobody knew how much cash was gambled on this day except for the certainty that it was vast. Equally busy were the tipsters, three-card-trick merchants, pickpockets, and fortune tellers. 'A day at the races', long a school day composition subject, was truly a sight to behold.

Away from the bedlam amid tight security, Barabbas was being prepared. Everybody was nervous and trying not to communicate this to the horse. They weren't very successful as was evident by the antics of the high-strung animal. In the end, it took the combined attention and presence of Julie, Stephen, and Dickey Beckett (who had just been cleared for the ride) to restore order.

Separately, each knew without a word what their role should be— no over-fussing or sudden movements and only low voices until a calm descended. Up and down the competitors' yard, the normal sounds of a race day could be heard. Gradually, their own anxiety was replaced and reassured by the familiar homely sounds and smells of stamping hooves, whinnying, clinking tackle, fresh straw, fresh dung, and eye-watering urine.

Upstairs, the panoramic balcony of the thronged members' pavilion was being used by Superintendent Deegan and Colonel McGarrick as a lookout post and HQ.

Downstairs, Julie was summoned by Bill Burroughs and escorted to meet and greet a 'surprise' guest. They met at the elevators, where Julie was overwhelmed to see a grinning Georgina Naismith with outstretched arms.

'Bill and I have been in touch, Julie. I just had to come over for the big occasion. This place is amazing. In its own way, it reminds me of the

Bridgetown Derby. Sarah and Trevor are upstairs. Can you join us for a bite or a drink?'

Bill Burroughs, who was holding the lift, persuaded Julie to take a short break. Julie relented and stepped into the lift. A short ferret-looking man spoke briefly into his mobile phone and darted up the stairs.

Before the doors slid closed, Julie pressed the Open button. 'I'm truly sorry, but I just can't. I couldn't relax away from Stephen, Dickey, and Barabbas at the moment. I hope you understand. I'll see you back here before the race, Georgina.'

Bill Burroughs also made his apologies as he insisted on escorting Julie back to the stables.

Upstairs, Georgina's shrieks brought security running from every direction. When she calmed down, she told of being confronted by a low-sized man in a cloth cap when the doors opened. He had a knife and was shouting something like 'Where's the other fucking bitch?'

Deegan and McGarrick conferred and agreed that whoever he was, he had the correct badges and credentials to get this far. They prided themselves on establishing a tight, secure operation with several overlapping layers. Sarah, Trevor, and various officials comforted Georgina. They reasoned the perpetrator was probably a bit of a head case and would be found in the massive security sweep now taking place.

Three o'clock and the horses enter the parade ring. Eight runners—three Irish, three English, one French, and one Australian. The press went on overdrive when Julie and Stephen arrived.

'It's them, it's them, I tell you. She's the previous registered owner, then she was kidnapped. Now she's here with Stephen Doyle, the current registered owner. There's a mighty story here, lads, when it gets out—and it will get out. It always does.'

One on each side, holding Barabbas by the bridle, Stephen and Julie—a picture of youth and beauty—led the colt around the parade ring. The wall of noise and flashing cameras had the young horse skittering sideways. TV images flashing worldwide were watched with conflicting emotions in Macau, Beijing, Hong Kong, and Western Australia.

Eight superb equine specimens, with Barabbas joined as the odds-on favourite with Raptor, last year's Epsom Derby winner. This unbeaten three-year-old won all his five previous group 1 races, the last one being the Derby. Ridden by Danny Winters, Britain's champion jockey, the beautifully proportioned gray flicked his flowing near-white tail like the aristocrat he was.

This was the perfect preseason trial for such horses. The form for thoroughbreds for the racing year is always uncertain until tested under ideal racing conditions. If they were pulled up, as sometimes happened, no shame or blame was attached. It was back to the drawing board like Formula One on practice day. Mostly, however, they were there to win. The confidential prize fund and associated gambling opportunities were too massive to miss.

An observant punter might have noticed the unusual sight of several fit-looking young men with binoculars, scanning the crowds from various vantage points with no obvious interest in the runners or riders.

Last-minute instructions over, the eight jockeys, resplendent in multihued silks, mount up and trot the half-mile to the starting gates. Dickey, ignoring everybody else, talked non-stop to Barabbas. Drawn number 4, he burned with a righteous fever to show those bastards what he and Barabbas were put on God's earth to do. The handlers were finding it nigh impossible to persuade Raptor to enter the starting gate, causing a further delay. This manoeuvre requires the touch and skill of master craftsmen. Everyone is aware of the risks involved when handling highly bred and highly valuable animals.

Chapter 68

With nothing else to be done, Bill Burroughs, Julie, and Stephen made their way up the three flights to the members and owners' pavilion. They were just in time to hear the booming voice of the Racing Board Secretary.

'So good of you to come, Brother Superior. Yourself and the Palladines have been such great supporters of the Irish horse industry at home and abroad. Here, let me introduce you to the chairman and board and the minister, who you probably know already.'

Superintendent Deegan and Colonel McGarrick turned in amazement to see a tall, gaunt figure with swept-back silver hair in clerical garb accept the handshakes of the assembled luminaries. Power and authority seemed to radiate from this austere-looking man so removed and oblivious to the trappings of wealth and privilege.

Julie and Bill Burroughs arrived, with Julie wearing a stunning hat donated by one of Stephen's sisters. Sarah, Trevor, and Georgina descended on her in a cloud and swirl of high spirits and excitement.

Sarah's vivid blue eyes snapping with excitement-'Georgina, tell Julie what happened to you in the lift. Most peculiar. Security are buzzing like blue-arsed flies.'

Julie is aghast. 'Georgina are you sure you're ok? I'm bursting for the ladies. According to those monitors, I'll just have time. Anybody coming? In this country, a girl never goes on her own for some reason.'

Sarah immediately jumped up, handing her drink to Georgina. 'I'll come with you. So much to tell, so much adventure, Julie Dundon. What a hat!'

Talking non-stop, they dashed for the loo, where Julie nipped into a stall, leaving the enormous hat by the sink. Instinctively, Sarah tried it on as girlfriends invariably did. Julie flushed the toilet, opened the door on the run, and froze in her tracks.

A low-sized man with his hand over Sarah's mouth from behind had plunged a broad-bladed knife into her back. He whirled around, and his jaw dropped at the sight of Julie. He brought the bloodied blade to bear, slashing the air in a frenzied attack. Julie shimmied left and right on the balls of her feet, caught the jabbing wrist, held his arm rigid, kicked his feet away, rolled him on her hip, and broke his arm with the sound of a snapping branch. In the same motion, she slammed him to the floor and jumped with both feet on his lower back, breaking his spine.

At that moment, Stephen entered the lounge. His first impression was of Superintendent Doyle and Colonel McGarrick staring fixatedly past him. He turned to his left to see what they were looking at. Both seismic shocks occurred together. Brother Superior and Stephen Doyle stared at each other as if hypnotized. Stephen's mouth had yet to close and engage his brain.

'Well, Master Doyle, I can see from your presence you are not after all riding Barabbas today. Such a pity. Good afternoon, gentlemen.'

With that, he turned on his heel, closely attended by an entourage of four fit-looking men. As they reached the door, one of them turned and Stephen's heart lurched as he looked into the cold, dead eyes of Joe Moran.

Something clicked in Stephen's brain.

Stephen turned to Superintendent Deegan, 'He thought I was still down for the ride. He never copped the stewards, had okayed Dickey at short notice. They're going to try something on the track. Quick, for the love of God, give Dickey the heads-up on his earpiece.'

They were thanking their lucky stars that Superintendent Deegan had arranged to fit first Stephen and then Dickey with a miniature state-of-the-art transmitter/receiver. Superintendent Deegan was about to press the transmit button when the public-address system blared into life with the immortal 'And they're off!'

Chapter 69

As the gates sprang open, Danny Winters in stall 3 slashed Dickey across the face with his riding crop. Dickey barely managed to right himself as his broken goggles flew over his head along with his transmitter/receiver. Valuable ground lost, he used reins and knees to help him stay on board. Barabbas, already skittish, pulled around in a complete circle. Dickey, using all his skill, gathered them both and set off in pursuit.

The PA system blared the news that the jockey was having trouble controlling Barabbas, and the roars of the crowd swelling in the afternoon air, already being heard at this distance.

Screams erupting from the foyer galvanized the dumbstruck group watching Superintendent Deegan failing to contact Barabbas's jockey. They rushed en masse through the swing doors and pushed aside the gagging crowd of women at the door to the ladies. Julie was on her knees on the tiled floor, pressing towels to the open wound gushing red in Sarah's back. Pinching Sarah's nose and forcing breath past whitening lips, Julie saw and heard her mother's fervent prayer in a flashback.

'Jesus, Mercy. Mary, help.'

An ignored moaning and withering heap on the floor, his face in torment, was in turn calling in agony for his own long-dead mother.

The Curragh emergency response unit now swung into action. Long practiced, they were prepared for any eventuality, particularly accidents involving the many helicopters constantly flying in and out on race days. The trauma team was staffed in rotation by the brightest and best.

Today, as luck would have it, Gerry O'Sullivan and Austin Breen, the number one and two at Beaumont Hospital, had just arrived on one of their rare days off. Summoned by the chief steward, who spotted them in the foyer, Mutt and Jeff—as they were fondly called for obvious reasons—went straight to work. They stabilized Sarah as best they could with bloods and fluids and, along with Julie and Trevor, were on their way to hospital by air ambulance within fifteen minutes.

Chapter 70

Clods of turf from flying hooves blinded Dickey as he urged Barabbas into a ground-eating stride. As he made up distance, he didn't notice the late arrival of the accompanying ambulance. This vehicle travels slightly behind the horses on a parallel track outside the rails at race meetings everywhere. Everybody takes it for granted because it's always there.

Colonel McGarrick, now back at his command centre on the terrace, used his secure military comm network to alert his rangers.

'Full profile. Attack imminent. Possible target, horse and or rider. Execute initiative.'

Dickey, moving Barabbas up the gears to a flying gallop, glanced to his left. His blood ran cold as the electric window in the ambulance slid down, revealing an arm, shoulder, and hand aiming a double-barrelled shotgun. With his left hand on the steering wheel, Brody's curly head appeared, wearing his usual toothy grin.

Lying prone in the TV tower 600 metres ahead, Cpl Tommy Roche swept the course below through Kahles ZF69 telescopic sights mounted on a Steyr SSG 69 sniper's rifle. With Colonel McGarrick's orders acknowledged, he knew he would probably have only seconds to act. The window of the ambulance became a shadow as it descended, disturbing the light patterns bouncing off the vehicle. His brain registered the protruding barrel of a weapon. He took one breath, exhaled gently, caressed the trigger, and unleashed a .50-calibre high-trajectory round at 1,450 metres per second.

The result was instantaneous. The ambulance seemed to leap in the air as the round tore through Brody and down into the transmission. The somersaulting vehicle then smashed through the rail and slid across the track. In seconds, with sirens blaring, a fleet of emergency vehicles sped to the scene. Up the track, stewards flagged the galloping horses until their jockeys gradually wound them down. Instructions were then sent to walk their mounts back to the start along the parallel track.

Back in the pavilion, Superintendent Deegan, Colonel McGarrick, and Bill Burroughs went into action. Superintendent Deegan immediately confiscated the TV tapes of the event. Colonel McGarrick conferred with the serving minister for defence, who was also the acting prime minister in the absence of the taoiseach. Wise heads prevailed as they agreed containment was the correct course. Other proposals from senior civil servants to declare a state of emergency were ignored as mere panic measures that would indeed give aid and comfort to the enemy. Bill Burroughs huddled with the stewards and owners and other interested parties.

The decision, which had to be unanimous, was conveyed to the police and military. After due consideration, an announcement was broadcast over the PA system. The decision to rerun the race at 4.30 p.m. was greeted with rapturous applause by the racing public. Mobile phone traffic overwhelmed the system as punters of every stripe sought to reschedule their arrangements for the rest of the day. The media and public had a fair idea that, contrary to soothing noises from the PR people, something momentous had happened. But then they said, as rumours swept the Curragh, that something equally momentous *was* happening. Raptor was installed as even-money favourite with Barabbas now at 2 to 1 on.

Down at the stables, Dickey Beckett approached Danny Winters. Both jockeys eyed each other with mutual loathing.

'Danny, you're riding one of the greatest Derby winners ever. Raptor is a super horse, so why demean the fucking animal by acting the bollix? We can have a proper race head to head, man to man, horse to horse, or if you pull that stunt again, I'll pull your head off. My gaffer has put extra cameras in so the world will see the real Danny Winters. What do you say, mate?'

Without saying a single word, Danny Winters nodded, stuck out his hand, shook Dickey's hand, and walked up the yard.

All form were now being reassessed by the world's most knowledgeable punters. The Irish racegoer seems to have an extra equine gnome in their DNA. Rumour and counter-rumours swept the track. Racing correspondents from around the world were lined up, talking to cameras, their take bounced off communication satellites and flashed in seconds around the globe.

One American was literally on his knees, begging his sports editor to let him continue broadcasting past their allotted time. 'It's not just a race, Walt. It's news, Walt. It's huge. Everything you need is here— glamour, sex, a kidnapping story, Australians, French, Brits, scary Irish, and rumours of a very iffy carry-on in China. Yes, Walt, China. And no, I'm not bullshitting. Forget the fucking golf just for once, Walt.'

The Lilac Hall residents were having the time of their lives. Some had led full lives; others, for various reasons, had not. Now all were united on this one occasion to live life to the full. Every institution threw up natural leaders, and Jake Purcell filled that role at Lilac Hall with distinction. A successful retired cattle dealer or tangler from County Galway, Jake literally knew everybody from his time attending cattle and horse fairs all over Ireland.

Still fairly mobile on frail legs, he manoeuvred his way with the aid of a sturdy stick down to the betting ring. At seventy-six, he was still a handsome figure who always looked well in his sometimes-extravagant outfits. Today, he sported a green hacking jacket, mustard waistcoat, check shirt, cravat, cavalry twill trousers, and brown trilby hat. He apologized as he bumped into an even taller man of similar age.

'Well, well, well, if it isn't the bould Jake Purcell done up like the usual dog's dinner. Have you no shame at all, man?'

'Well, bless my tired old eyes, is it yourself Black Jack Doyle from the County Wexford, the bastard who whipped the grandest girl in Ireland right from under me nose? How is the darlin' Elizabeth these days, Jack?'

The two old codgers, who had admired, respected, fought, and dealt with each other for over fifty years, went into a huddle. Reminiscences were exchanged as their backs were continuously slapped by dozens of passing acquaintances.

After the niceties were completed, Black Jack answered the unasked question, 'Barabbas's jockey was interfered with in the stalls. The horse is sweating up a bit, not enough to worry about, but he's sound and fit and gone very calm. Very definitely worth the price, but who knows for sure at this level? See ya, Jake. Best of luck.'

Jake hurried as best he could back to his cronies. 'Right, girls and boys, just got the word. Pa Ryan here will draw up a list of each payment. Give me all your money—yes, you heard me—all your money. IOUs will be accepted. The available cash will cover the IOUs. Barabbas has drifted to 2's. He'll surely go out to 3's. I'm going back to the ring and wait to pounce. Our previous bets stand, so it's going to be a roller-coaster ride. Are you with me, folks?'

Those who could stood, while those who couldn't waved their sticks, crutches, hats, and scarves.

'Go for it, JP. Go on, ya good thing. Rock on, Purcell. Here's to the greatest cute hoor of them all. Purcell's pensioners ride again.'

Jake looked fondly at his decrepit collection, some with (or without) hair, the odd toupee, teeth moving independently, make-up caked, and lipstick obviously applied with trembling hands. Waving his trilby, bowing and blowing kisses, he made his way back to the betting enclosure.

Chapter 71

The security ring around the stables was so intense that it was just short of a platoon with fixed bayonets. Inside, conditions could only be described as controlled bedlam. Thoroughbred horses were notoriously fickle and temperamental. Some react quite badly to an upset in their routine. The professional skill, which was there in abundance, was the ability to manage the unmanageable in difficult circumstances. Looking around them, some owners and jockeys began to fancy their chances a bit more as they saw the effect the rescheduling was having on their rivals. Nobody unauthorized could get in, but word most assuredly got out. Such was the swing and the weight of money that Richelieu, the French horse, and Raparee, one of the Irish horses, emerged as joint favourites as the eight competitors trotted once more to the starting gates.

Julie, though given the opportunity of returning to the Curragh in the air ambulance, elected to stay at Sarah's bedside at the hospital. A traumatized Trevor Naismith sat beside her with his head in his hands, still in a state of shock. Julie was devastated at what had happened and also at what was supposed to happen. A fraught transcontinental telephone conversation with Sarah's parents had left her shaken. A similar conversation with the Nag and Susie brought her to tears.

She had already agreed with Stephen and Bill Burroughs that to withdraw Barabbas now would be to hand a pyrrhic victory to their enemies. Now she stared numbly at a flat-screen TV in a waiting room as the RTÉ's racing gurus hysterically prepared the waiting world for the imminent restart of the Easter Dues.

At 4.30 p.m. on a brilliant, bright spring afternoon, the sun highlighting the coloured silks and gleaming coats of immaculately prepared horses and riders. All eyes were on the giant screens or glued to binoculars, watching eight, three- to four-year-olds trot to the starting gates. This time, all were loaded on the first attempt.

The gates spring open to the public-address racing announcer's 'And they're off!'

Dickey kept Barabbas on a tight rein. His suspicions are immediately confirmed as known front runners Rolando and Abbeville set off at a blistering pace. Their tactic, which often worked, was to put as much distance as they could between themselves and their pursuers as quickly as possible. At 10 furlongs, this could put a lot of pressure on the pack, which simply has to make up the ground. With hooves drumming the trembling ground, air snorting through extended nostrils, these magnificent thoroughbreds sweep round the first bend. Six horses knotted together, closing on the two five lengths ahead. Dickey knew Barabbas had the stamina and speed. But stamina and speed on their own are not enough.

As the half-mile marker flashed by, Dickey knew the others were waiting for his move. Pace, momentum, and nerve are everything now. The first to crack are Turkland and Figleaf, as they stream away to catch the front runners. Richelieu, Raptor, Raparee, and Barabbas are closely bunched on the rail stride for stride. The PA commentator is screaming the names in the order of their running. Dickey knows the winner would come from these four. The other three have only seconds to stop watching him and make their own play for glory.

Practically in unison, Richelieu followed by Raparee are let off the bridle and accelerate with the help of a few sharp backhanded smacks of the whip.

Barabbas, on the rail, is straining, straining, straining. People outside the profession have no idea of the fitness level of professional jockeys. Dickey, crouched in the stirrups, is holding ¾ tons at 35 miles per hour by the strength of his arms. All the while, they have kept in touch with the pack, but with ¼ mile remaining, Raptor began his beautifully smooth acceleration with gorgeous tail flowing in the slipstream.

The PA is screeching, and the roar from the crowd rising, now soaring like a living entity. Eight names being urged to do as their ancestors did across the plains, steppes, and pampas of the ancient world.

On the rail and without breaking stride, Dickey switched Barabbas to the outside. Only now would he know if the confusing events of recent times have taken their toll. All the great combinations of horse and jockey have it—this fusion of heart and soul, bone and sinew melded together as one.

He leaned along the neck of the horse, whose ears are pricked to hear the command. 'Go, Barabbas. Go, go, go!'

With ears now flattened, his great engine of heart and lungs slipped into fifth gear. Gradually, gradually his immense stride lengthened. First Rolando, then Abbeyville, their tactics undone, were passed. Then Raparee, Turkland, and Figleaf were reeled in.

Richelieu, who was really flying up ahead, was being overhauled by Raptor. Danny Winters flung a glance over his right shoulder to check on Barabbas. In that instant, he knew he had been outfoxed. Before he could turn his head to the left, the black shadow with purple and gold colours swept by.

Richelieu, running the race of his life, was passed. Danny asked for more from an empty tank, and Raptor drew level stride for stride, but one was faltering. Dickey looked over. One glance was enough. With his experienced eye, he saw a great horse with nothing left to give. Danny raised his whip once more and looked over at Dickey. Their eyes locked even through dirt-covered goggles. Dickey shook his head from side to side. In response, Danny lowered his whip and eased pressure on his mount. Barabbas, by now hurtling like a missile into a scene from *Babel*, flashed past the post three lengths clear.

As the jockeys allowed their mounts to run down, Danny Winters drew alongside Barabbas, with Raptor blowing like a bellows. He stuck out his hand, his Yorkshire accent rough and gruff, as he said 'That were champion, Oz, pure champion.'

Up in the stands, the citizens of Lilac Hall were in hysterics of excitement. They were not alone or unique. Everyone around the Curragh racecourse and anywhere within the beam of a radio or TV transmission were infected by the wonder and splendour of it all. On the way to the winner's enclosure, Dickey and Barabbas were escorted by mounted members of the army equestrian team. This courtesy was usually reserved for the winner of the official Irish classics, such as the Derby and the Oaks. However, Colonel McGarrick's influence and authority were unquestioned during the course of this operation. Dickey was glad of the extra cover as they faced a solid wall of noise from exultant racegoers. None of them, high or low, had ever experienced anything like the events just witnessed.

Chapter 72

The happy throngs were making their way from the racecourse when news swirled that a very well-known character had taken ill in the stands. Black Jack Doyle had a premonition. He and his wife, Elizabeth, and their Garda minder made their way back inside. Jake Purcell lay in the aisles, being attended by medical staff and surrounded by bewildered, distraught pensioners.

Pa Ryan stood there, wringing his hands. 'He had just handed me the betting slips and said I was to go down and collect the winnings. He said he was a bit tired after all the excitement. He said we were rich. I never saw him so happy as he was today. He pointed you out to me earlier on, said you were the best of friends. What'll I do, Mr Doyle? What'll I do?'

When the medics shook their heads, Jack and Elizabeth knelt by Jake and whispered an act of contrition in his ear. They moved away as a heavy, red-faced priest puffed his way up the steps.

'My poor old buddy, look at him, Liz. Told me today the reason he never married was he couldn't have you. At least he died happy doing what he loved to do.'

'Jack, he was always a gentleman even when we'd all meet up after the harvest below in Ballybunion during the Listowel Races.'

'Are you telling me, Elizabeth Doyle, that when I stayed with the horses in Listowel, you were gallivanting with the likes of Jake Purcell in Ballybunion?'

'I wasn't Elizabeth Doyle then, Jack. Mind you, he was a lovely dancer, though he always seemed to have a bottle in his trouser pocket. He didn't stand a chance and knew it, but a girl likes to have her head turned every now and then.'

Jack then offered to take the list and betting slips from Pa Ryan, explaining he would have everything sorted by the time he came back up for the funeral. The commanding presence of Jack, accompanied as he was by a uniformed Garda, was enough for Pa as he gratefully handed over the responsibility.

Chapter 73

Later that day at the hospital, Julie and Trevor were at last allowed in to see Sarah. Her pert little face was pale on the white starched pillow, and her blond hair was enveloped in a hospital bandana. Gerry O'Sullivan and Austin Breen—aka Mutt and Jeff—were in beaming attendance.

'Gerry served his internship at the Bronx Memorial, New York. They hold the world record of gun and knife attacks. He knew exactly what was best practice before, during, and after. Sarah was very fortunate. We think she will make a complete recovery.'

'In an emergency, our Austin is the best organized person ever. He makes all the difference when seconds are vital. Now say your goodbyes. This little lady is going to need a lot of rest for a week or so.'

Julie took Sarah's hand, which was so weak and fragile, and kissed her on the forehead. As she did so, they both uttered 'Sorry' in the same breath. Tears brimming, they both nodded, closing a strained chapter in their long friendship. Julie then left Trevor to say his goodbyes. Outside, Stephen and Georgina had arrived and were waiting with Sgt Nick Kelly in an unmarked black Special Branch BMW. In minutes, they were on the road to Wexford, with Julie instantly asleep, her head on Stephen's shoulder.

Keeping in touch by secure satellite phone, the various strands of the convoy met at the Seven Oaks Hotel in Carlow Town. Trevor and Georgina elected to return to Dublin to be near Sarah. All others, including the horsebox, were to return to the Doyles' Kiltealy Estate in Bridgetown.

After a light meal, Superintendent Deegan spoke before their departure, 'Stephen and Julie are not coming with us. They've already left. They need some time alone, and I agreed. They think I won't know where they are, but Sergeant Kelly's BMW is fitted with a tracking device. Wherever they stop, we'll have the watchers in place. I have this manpower and authority for a little while longer. I take full responsibility. I hope you understand.'

He was surprised and pleased at the silent nods of agreement, particularly the smile tugging at the lips of one Elizabeth Doyle.

Chapter 74

Out the Kilkenny Road, the BMW blazed along like the proverbial bat out of hell. Four miles out, an abrupt turn left brought them to Bagenalstown, then on to Borris on the River Barrow before wheeling right and left for Goresbridge. They barrelled along the narrow, winding country roads to the Gaelic hurling town of Gowran, then swept left past the racecourse and on to Thomastown. Twisting and turning through the riverside town, they slipped through the back gates of Mount Juliet Estate.

Stephen was well used to Mount Juliet. It was the massive country estate of the late Major Victor McCalmont, and Stephen had often taken mares to the world-famous stud standing there. Nowadays, it was the epitome of grandeur, grace, and beauty, with the main house converted to a stupendously luxurious hotel. The endless grounds were given over to hunting, shooting, and fishing, including one of the greatest golf courses in the world created by Jack Nicklaus himself. The River Nore, one of the principal rivers in the south and east of Ireland, flowed through the heart of the estate.

Stephen parked in the gravelled courtyard at the hotel entrance and, with Julie by the hand, skipped up the shallow steps and into reception.

Nothing fazes the receptionist or concierge of an international first-class hotel. A young couple arriving without luggage or a reservation is rare, but not completely unusual. A discreet check on Stephen's American Express card confirmed their status. Stephen would have been quite happy to take one of the chalets clustered in villages throughout the estate. However, a shared look between the receptionist and concierge meant being offered the suite reserved for a VIP who was delayed for two days. Their obvious joy, youth, bearing, and vitality struck a chord with the two hotel professionals; happy people made people happy.

In no time, housekeepers fussed and swept them to their quarters. As they opted to dine in their suite, their outer clothes and footwear would be taken away and returned in an hour, expertly buffed, ironed, and dry-cleaned. Towelling robes, nightwear, slippers, and choices of sealed packs of new underwear were laid out for their consideration. A silver ice bucket with a chilled bottle of Krug Champagne appeared.

Stephen shared one of his rare drinks of alcohol with Julie, while the staff primped and prepared their dining table. Finally, after Julie and Stephen selected their choices from the extensive menu, the staff withdrew, saying the first course would be served in exactly one hour and fifteen minutes.

Julie stood with one foot forward, expression serious, chin up, hands folded across her chest. Her hair, shaken out, cascaded down her shoulders.

'Now, Master Doyle, sharing separate rooms at Kiltealy House has been a strain, at least for me. We will not shower beforehand. I want to inhale every bit of you. You won't have to hold back the first time 'cos I know you're bursting and anyway I'm drenched.'

With that, she grinned an outrageously cheeky grin and furiously fluttered her lashes.

Just like the day in the dunes at Port Douglas, Stephen marvelled at Julie's directness. 'Okay, Miss Dundon, you help me with this buckle, and I'll help you with your bits and bobs.'

'Bits and bobs indeed, Master Doyle, how deliciously quaint. And *wow*, how he's grown. I think he remembers me. Just let me give him one little kiss . . . There, I really think he liked that.'

She shrieked as Stephen stooped, picked her up, and flung her on the bed. She shrieked again as Stephen dived on her, spun her over, whipped off her panties, and left a distinctive bite mark on her delicious behind. Then face to face, each reflected in the other's eyes; they gravely touched foreheads and lightly rubbed noses.

With one sweet kiss, he gently laid her down, raised her long legs over his shoulders, and drove his full length in and up as far as he could go. She rose to meet him in perfect rhythm, and in a short while, the exquisite intensity burst like a molten dam. Deep inside, she felt the torrent and knew as women sometimes did that nature's cycle had been fulfilled.

The meal that followed was truly a gourmand's delight. Quail eggs, lightly poached salmon, beef Wellington, roast venison, and delicious desserts—all washed down by separate wines chosen by Mount Juliet's world-famous sommelier. It was as much alcohol as Stephen had ever consumed, and yet the artist's hand was evident as each wine complimented each dish completely. Afterwards, they strolled the grounds for an hour, crossing and recrossing the river in the dusky twilight. The intoxicating smell of new spring growth was everywhere. The rising sap and nature girding her loins for yet another season was in perfect harmony with the mood of the two young lovers.

The morning sun filtering past the edge of the heavy drapes announced another new day. A booked wake-up call gave them half an hour before breakfast arrived.

'Good morning, cobber. My, what dark rings you have around your eyes. You must have been up all night. Now your sheila is wondering whether we have time for a shag and a shower—or a shower, a shag, and a shower? Are you shocked by this brazen hussy? I must confess I'm a bit shocked myself. Aha, and who do we have here? Seems like he's already made up our minds.'

They paused at the BMW in the courtyard, looking at the front of the magnificent manor house distinct with red-leafed ivy climbing its walls. Golfers and guests were coming and going, and in each silent interval, the plaintive cry and show of strutting peacocks could be seen and heard. Stephen and Julie silently captured this moment and stored it forever in their hearts.

Chapter 75

Stephen started the engine, and both jumped at the familiar voice of Superintendent Deegan coming from hidden speakers, 'Sorry for the shock, folks. I can actually see and hear you. There's a tiny camera monitoring you through the glass in the rear-view mirror. Get back to Kiltealy House as quick as you can. The brotherhood discovered you're not here. They've mobilized all their resources. A squad of rangers is close but not close enough. Anyhow, constitutionally, they can't act without a Garda presence—a lot of legal bullshit we cannot ignore in broad daylight. Do not come back through New Ross. Do not discuss your plans with me now in case the car is compromised. Good luck.'

Stephen and Julie exchanged glances. He watched her go pale and bite her lower lip. On impulse, he cut the engine and ran back into the hotel. The urbane concierge, who had been handsomely tipped, raised an eyebrow as Stephen declared an emergency. He explained that the electronic management system in the BMW was acting up again. As they had to be in Wexford for a vital meeting in two hours' time, he wondered if he could borrow the hotel's courtesy car. He promised to return that evening with their car, plus a pickup tow truck for the BMW. The hotel had several such cars, each covered by the most comprehensive insurance available. The clincher was the 500-euro-note deposit, plus the BMW car keys.

Fifteen minutes later, they drove out the Jerpoint gate in a sedate 220 Mercedes Benz. As luck would have it, this particular model sported tinted windows. As ill luck would have it, Corporal McDaid and his rangers, having just arrived, momentarily missed this development. As he gathered his squad, he only had an oblique view of part of the BMW, and so missed the departure of the Mercedes. Steven considered his options and made his decision. He decided to head into the lion's den in the hope that the brotherhood would never think him so stupid.

He made one call in a seven-second burst to Superintendent Deegan on his mobile. 'Rendezvous where the black-faced workers live.'

A sudden thought flashed in Stephen's brain as he struggled to hold back his impulse to drive like a madman. Why was he in Sergeant Kelly's car in the first place? They could have borrowed a vehicle from any of the others. When Superintendent Deegan handed him the keys, was he testing Kelly or using them as a stalking horse? Was it one or the other or both or neither?

They joined the main Kilkenny–Waterford road at Ballyhale, then on through rolling pastureland to Lukeswell to Mullinavat and Waterford City, over Edmund Rice Bridge, along the historic quays, past Reginald's Tower, and out the Dunmore East Road. Outside of the main urban areas, this was the heartland of the IRA. This was also the area where, as a impressionable young volunteer, Stephen was trained in terrorism and corrupted by his former schoolmaster, the late unlamented Hugh Heffernan.

All the while, Stephen pointed out places he had been and things he had done. It was an untypical outburst, much like a catharsis of the soul as they drove deeper and deeper into the stronghold of their implacable enemy. Julie listened in silence as the places fitted the names Stephen had described in his confessions after their reunion. She occasionally stroked his bare arm in reassurance and kept her silence.

They went down the hill to the riverside at Passage East to catch the ferry to Ballyhack on the Wexford shore. Both villages were plainly visible to each other. Ballyhack, pretty as a picture and dominated by its Norman castle, faced west and caught most of the day's sunshine, while in contrast, Passage East crouched under a cliff facing east, seemingly in perpetual shadow. As they waited in that shadow in a line to board the ferry, Stephen described the story of the betrayal of the romantic rebel known as the Croppy Boy and how he was hanged by the British in the infamous Geneva Barracks high above the village.

The car ferry only holds thirty vehicles and makes the crossing in less than ten minutes. Shortly after casting off from Passage East, the ticket and fare collector moved down the first line of cars. With a sinking heart, Stephen realized the collector had a companion he immediately recognized.

Liam Mackey was a hulking brute with a red scalded face and a talent for cruelty. Mackey and his kind were typical of the many foot soldiers needed and drawn to violent nationalist, religious, and racist organizations everywhere. Liam Mackey would not be operating alone.

'Julie, when I say go, open the door and roll under that SUV alongside us. No debate, okay?'

Stephen turned sideways and, with knees bent, held his feet against the driver's door. He watched as the ticket collector rapped on the tinted window. With repeated knocks unanswered, Mackey pushed the collector aside, slipped a weapon from behind his back, and held it down by his side. Stephen shouted 'Go!' and slammed his feet against the unlatched door, knocking Mackey off his feet. He sensed the passenger door opening and Julie sliding out.

Carried by his own momentum, Stephen jumped from the car, elbowed the hapless ticket Collector in the face, and turned to deal with Mackey. Like a lot of large men, Liam Mackey was surprisingly fast on his feet. Rising from the deck to a crouch, he let out a roar and raised his gun. Just as Mackey reached chin height, Stephen again swung the heavy Mercedes door, slicing Mackey's forehead to the bone.

Stephen felt the passage of bullets from overhead before he heard the chatter of the machine pistol. Running, he scooped Mackey's handgun and instinctively snapped two quick bursts at the gantry above leading to the bridge. Uncomprehending stares and screaming came from some of the other passengers as Stephen raced to the ladder leading to the upper deck. He spotted a figure climbing another short ladder and disappearing into the wheelhouse.

On a car ferry, the superstructure is all to the side of the vessel, leaving as much space as possible for the maximum number of vehicles. Julie now joined him, and after a brief huddle, she picked up a fire axe and climbed the next ladder. Stephen rapidly climbed over the top of the superstructure and, counting to 100, reached the ladder on the opposite sheer side of the vessel. He heard Julie smash the glass of the door on her side, which was immediately followed by a semi-automatic's burst. Thankfully, the glass in the door at his side was lowered on a strap so the skipper could look out and down while docking and undocking. Stephen dived through the open window, came up the other side on a half roll, and in the same motion, got off a shot slicing the back of the gunman's head.

The ferry was by now turning hard to starboard and heading downriver on a flood tide. Ballyhack and its jetty swung away as the vessel continued to turn.

Stephen jammed the pistol in the back of the captain's neck. 'Where you taking us, Skipper? One smart-arse move or wrong answer, and there's no tomorrow.'

The skipper, hands and voice shaking blurted, 'For God's sake, don't shoot me. They radioed just now, said to make for Dunmore East. The radio's open. Don't make me shut it down, or they'll kill me. Please, mister, I've a wife and family.'

Stephen promptly fired a shot into the radio receiver. Julie tended the badly wounded terrorist, using the ample supplies in the first-aid cupboard.

'Okay, Skipper, we're coming abreast of King's Bay. Hard a 'port, Skipper. Drive her in as far as you can, then drop the ramp.'

'O my god, mister, we'll never get her out. That bottom's all mud and silt. There's not near enough water.'

Stephen, from his gunrunning days, was well aware of the neglected state of the tidal harbour at King's Bay, Arthurstown.

A quick look at three trawlers coming at them from three different directions decided him. 'You've a flat bottom, Skipper, a full tide and no choice. You or these fuckers are not now or ever gonna take or ruin our lives. I'm sick, sick, sick of that fucking madman acting like God. Now get on with it. I don't give a shit about you, them, or this boat. Only me or mine matter from now on.'

Julie looked up from bandaging the gunman, worried at the murderous outburst and the wild-eyed look of a man pushed to the edge.

As they came into the small harbour, the skipper gave the engines a sharp burst, then quickly shut them down. The ferry smashed through a line of anchored small craft, its momentum carrying it almost to the sea wall. They felt the keel plough into the soft, clinging, muddy bottom and come to a shuddering stop. When the skipper lowered the ramp on to the sea wall, the main deck was slightly elevated. Unfortunately, the abrupt halt had the effect of tossing some vehicles forward. The ramp approach was now jammed with dislodged cars, vans, and SUVs.

Stephen handed Julie the revolver, picked up the machine pistol, and left the bridge with a warning that had the skipper bobbing his head like a metronome. They ran along the top of the wheelhouse and down a ladder to the well deck. They clambered over and around stalled vehicles, across the ramp, and down on to the road. Here they were exposed if the enemy were waiting. They ran crouched along the sea wall for about 200 yards, crossed the road, and ran through the doors of the King's Bay Inn.

The startled drinkers, frozen with glasses half-raised, gaped silently at the gun-toting couple. The first to speak spluttered the immortal words, 'If it ain't Bonnie and fucking Clyde.'

The pub dominated both roads entering and leaving the village. Stephen decided to commandeer the upper floor, which had windows on the front, back, and side and had walls four feet thick. Before he could implement his plan, they heard the unmistakable sound of a low-flying helicopter. Stephen slid his head around the open door, glanced up, and was rewarded with the sight of the GARDA logo on the side of the hovering craft. Just then, a convoy of cars and jeeps roared into the village, with flashing lights and shrieking sirens. Superintendent Deegan jumped from the lead vehicle, waving a semi-automatic rifle.

Rather than risk being accidentally shot, Stephen called Superintendent Deegan on his cell phone. 'Julie and I are okay. We're in the pub, which is clear. We can't come out 'cos we have a couple of weapons we picked up. Can you come in and collect us and them?'

An army officer handed Superintendent Deegan a megaphone he used to direct the armed Gardai and military personnel. With a perimeter formed, he walked across the road, shielding his eyes against the sun, and entered the gloom of the pub.

Their joyful reunion was interrupted by a small, wizened, unshaven, toothless man in a cap, who demanded, 'Is nonna youse gonna order a drink for the house after frightnin' the livin' shite outta decent country folk?'

With a relieved laugh, Stephen slapped two fifty-euro notes on the counter and followed Julie and Superintendent Deegan out to the waiting cars.

All place names and signposts in Ireland were in both English and Irish. Superintendent Deegan acknowledged he had made the connection to 'where the black-faced workers live'. Arthurstown, on the village signpost they were passing, was translated and shown as 'Coleman' in the Irish language.

Chapter 76

As the powerful Volvo roared up the hill, Superintendent Deegan brought them up to date, 'No chance now of keeping this under wraps. Everyone in the pub and on the stranded ferry will have a tale and a claim. You two are now on countless camera phones. You'll be all over the tabloids tomorrow morning and possibly the late TV news tonight. We're heading back to Kiltealy House for another strategy meeting. We've simply got to take the initiative. Our latest intelligence is that the brothers claim to be the direct unblemished descendants of an organization called the Irish Republican Brotherhood. This is very dangerous, and I'll tell you why. They were set up in 1858 to stir up rebellion before another failed Fenian Rising and have been behind every rebellion since. They united every strand of republicanism, particularly in the USA, down to today's IRA. Only the elite of Irish republicans were inducted into the IRB—very powerful and ultra-secretive. All the IRB were in the IRA, but very few of the IRA were in the IRB. They'd put the Masons to the pin of their collar.'

As they drove down the road home, Stephen pointed out places of interest to Julie, who was shivering from delayed shock and wrapped in a travel blanket in the back seat.

'That place we just left, the King's Bay in Arthurstown, was where King James supposedly set sail for France after his defeat by King William of Orange at the Battle of the Boyne. Now, here before Wellingtonbridge, you can see the monastic settlement and the ruins of the seven castles of Clonmines—more of Cromwell's handiwork—and Wellingtonbridge, called after the Iron Duke himself, the hero of Waterloo. Did you know he was born in Ireland but detested the Irish? I'm serious, folks. When challenged about his birthplace and that it automatically made him an Irishman, he famously replied, "If I were born in a stable, would that make me a horse? —Bloody Bastard."'

And so wearily and eventually, their convoy arrived in Bridgetown and turned up the long drive to the sanctuary of the Kiltealy Estate. Black Jack, Liz, the rest of the family, Dickey Beckett, Bill Burroughs, and the curly head of Richie Cleary were all there to greet them. Elizabeth Doyle and her daughters ushered them to the dining room replete with refreshments of every description.

A log fire blazed in the hearth, warding off the evening chill. Elizabeth, in her no-nonsense mode, forbade any talk of recent events until, as she put it, all plates were licked clean. The one exception was Black Jack's description of the life and times and untimely death of Jake Purcell. He had them choking with laughter at the antics of both of them as young men starting out in life all those years ago.

Superintendent Deegan and Colonel McGarrick came back into the house from the military communication vehicle parked outside. Both had given their report to their immediate superiors. Their demeanour could only be described as grim.

'Okay, people, before we get down to business, let's look at the RTÉ evening news. Our information is that the lid has blown, and the media is on the warpath.'

That turned out to be the understatement of the year. The news was almost entirely devoted to the lives and times of Stephen Doyle and Julie Dundon. The station cobbled together footage from Australia, a speculative piece from Hong Kong quoting informed reliable sources, more nods and winks and live film from the Curragh, and a host of uploaded camera phone pictures taken on the Ballyhack ferry. RTÉ's southern editor was also doing a piece to camera from outside the very gates of the house they were sitting in.

The one glaring omission was any reference to the Irish Republican Brotherhood, the dissident IRA, the Palladine Brothers, and Brother Superior. The supposition was some form of criminal conspiracy, involving cross and double-cross. The minister for justice was wheeled out to give the government's response. A complete professional, he spoke angrily from both sides of his mouth for five minutes without saying anything. He did leave a hostage to fortune by saying the Gardai were following a definite line of enquiry. He mollified the baying mob by promising a further statement within the next twenty-four hours.

Superintendent Deegan switched off the TV and addressed the gathering, 'Against the advice of both myself and Col McGarrick, I am instructed to arrest Brother Superior under the offences against the State Act and convey him forthwith to the Special Criminal Court in Dublin. As you may or may not know, the act allows a person before the Special Criminal Court be charged with membership of an illegal organization solely on the word of a Garda superintendent. As I am merely seconded to Interpol, my rank will be sufficient for the purposes of the act. We had hoped to roll up the entire brotherhood once and for all. However, events and politics have robbed us of the initiative. The government has persuaded the foreign media to run with RTÉ's storyline until their next press conference tomorrow evening. We are leaving now to be in place for a dawn raid on the Palladine Monastery and Novitiate. It's amazing how difficult it is to get at Rosbercon on the other side of the bridge at New Ross. We obviously can't cross that bridge. The car ferry, as we know, is out of action. We'll have to helicopter from here to Inistioge in Co. Kilkenny and take the back road from there to Rosbercon. All communication out of here by any means is forbidden. If any of us are killed or wounded, it'll be one of you who betrayed us. Oh, and by the way, the terrorist shot by the ranger in the ambulance at the Curragh didn't die. He was stabilized and miraculously expected to make some sort of recovery. Only now he seems to have disappeared. That's the kind of organization we're up against.'

With those ominous words, both officers left the room. Stephen caught Bill Burroughs's eye, and together they ran to catch up with the departing officers. After a quick conversation in the yard, Stephen and Bill made a convincing argument as to why they should be included in the raid. Colonel McGarrick informed them the rangers company plus relieves would remain at Kiltealy. A fresh company from the barracks in Kilkenny City would wait for them at Inistioge.

Stephen hurried back to the house to tell Julie and his parents that he was leaving. Three voices speaking at once were silenced by a hug each and a shake of the head. They knew their Stephen and responded with a return hug and a prayerful Godspeed. Grabbing a warm Burberry jacket, Stephen ran and caught up with the others.

Sitting in the waiting helicopter was the hunched figure of Sgt Nick Kelly of Special Branch. 'Still a walking disaster, Doyle. My BMW crashed or abandoned along with the Ballyhack ferry. A trail of wreckage and bodies follow you like a bad smell. The poor taxpayer and insurance companies will be cleaning up after you for years.'

Stephen eyed the policeman up and down. 'I've always been aware, Sergeant Kelly, that the IRA couldn't operate without the active or inactive support of what the *Irish Times* likes to call the 'sneaking regarders'. My life and my families lives are threatened, but I can promise you, if I survive, I will have my revenge.'

Superintendent Deegan looked from one to the other. 'Stephen, Sgt Kelly might not be exactly Mr Charm, but he is an excellent officer who enjoys my complete confidence. He is here to carry out an important role on our behalf. Now let's load up.'

Stephen was pretty sure Superintendent Deegan had included Sergeant Kelly precisely because he wanted him where he could keep an eye on him.

Chapter 77

Inistioge is often described as picturesque, which is like describing Tuscany as pretty. A beautifully quaint village with stone houses of perfect proportions and an ancient arched bridge spanning the River Nore. All lost to them as they arrived in darkness, flying wide of the village, guided by the assembled rangers and landing in a meadow on the back road to Rosbercon. The rangers had already reconnoitred the route and target. After a map-and-grid discussion, they set off, with Stephen and Bill firmly instructed to stay in the rear vehicle until told otherwise.

With lights doused, the small convoy crept along the dark narrow country road. Eventually, they slowed and stopped. Corporal McDaid directed them through a gate and into a half-empty hay barn. The day's events finally took their toll as they listened to the metallic sounds of their engine cooling down. Stephen and Bill Burroughs slept, propped against each other, until roused by someone shaking them awake.

A slight smear of light to the east extinguished the stars one by one. Corporal McDaid handed them a thermos of coffee and foil-wrapped corned-beef sandwiches. A tentative dawn chorus of birdsong swelled with each passing minute. Superintendent Deegan and Colonel McGarrick appeared with the look of men used to little sleep.

'Follow us to the stand of trees near the monastery. Stay concealed there until I call you on your mobile. Do not, under any circumstances, rush in if you hear gunfire. Wait for my call. We'll have enough on our plate without having to worry about you getting caught in the crossfire. Corporal McDaid will stay with you for your own safety.'

With that, they stole away into that strange half world, with the heavens getting brighter and the earth still wrapped in shadow.

Half an hour later, Stephen's mobile vibrated in his breast pocket. A terse Superintendent Deegan told them to drive through the main gates to the front door of the monastery. Stephen knew every inch of the way.

Childhood, boyhood, and manhood memories jumbled in his head as they drove through the massive gates, now open, under the stone arch and up the rhododendron drive to where one-half of the double front door was open. An armed uniformed ranger beckoned them inside and conducted them along familiar corridors to the main drawing room overlooking the quadrangle and playing fields.

Colonel McGarrick, his moustache fairly bristling, came into the room. 'We have the building secured. We've begun a thorough search for arms, ammunition, etc.—anything incriminating. Supt Deegan with two of my men is reading Brother Superior his rights while he gets dressed. They'll be with us shortly. We met no resistance whatsoever, which I find bloody peculiar.'

Just then, the door opened. Stephen felt Bill Burroughs's hand grip his elbow. Brother Superior stood there, tall and severe, surveying the room. He was dressed in the full-length black soutane of his order, complete with scarlet sash from waist to hem and a Roman collar visible at his throat. He moved aside to allow the person behind him to enter the room. Stephen's breath caught as he recognized Joe Moran, his dark eyes inscrutable, dressed in the same clerical uniform.

Brother Superior's eyes swept the room. 'Gentlemen, if you will permit me, I have something germane to our predicament in the order's safe. Please be seated. All will be revealed momentarily. May I also welcome the attendance of Master Doyle and Mr Burroughs. How kind of you to pay us such an early and unexpected visit.'

Brother Superior unlatched a portrait of the current Pope to reveal a substantial wall safe. He slowly dialled the combination, which was answered by a resolute click. Another click immediately followed, which was Colonel McGarrick chambering a round into his Colt automatic. Brother Superior pulled the heavy door open and stood back. He indicated a thick manila envelope, which the colonel withdrew and placed on the highly polished mahogany table. Brother Superior slit the envelope and tipped the contents on to the table.

He sat down and picked them up. 'Allow me to explain. As you can see, these are two Vatican diplomatic passports—one in my name, and the other in the name of Brother Moran. It seems the Holy Father needs my services in Rome as the new vicar general of our order. He has also requested Brother Moran be appointed Brother Superior in my absence and to accompany me from time to time visiting our monasteries and religious houses around the world. Such faith in our abilities is truly humbling. You will understand, gentlemen, why in the circumstances it will not be possible for us to—how do you put it?—ah, yes, to help you with your enquiries. Now if you could be so kind, I must ask you to leave and allow us to continue with God's work.'

A stunned silence followed this announcement, which was broken as Stephen shrugged off the restraining hand of Bill Burroughs. 'This is pure fantasy, farce, bollix, and bullshit. You know why I'm here. I know you and your operation. Who better? You probably have yourself covered by this charade. Bill Burroughs and I want a private conversation with yourself and Joe Moran. Don't dignify him with the title of brother. He's a killer, pure and simple, and you're his puppeteer. Now I suggest we go out to the pagoda in the walled garden, where we can have a conversation in private.'

Brother Superior, elbows on the table, chin supported by steepled fingers, silently contemplated his former protégé.

'I agree, but only for the sake of your mother and father. Not another word until we're seated outside.'

Superintendent Deegan re-joined them with the passports, having spoken with the secretary of the Department of Foreign Affairs. 'Your diplomatic status has been confirmed—one govt. dept. completely unaware of what's happening in the other. But of course, you are well aware of that, Brother Superior. My instructions are that you are free to go. One curious fact you may help me with—at least thirty fit young men are exercising in the quadrangle at a time of zero vocations generally. How come you can attract so many seminarians?'

Brother Superior gravely regarded the policeman, and without a trace of irony, 'The Lord is faithful to His servants who obey Him. The harvest is indeed great, and the labourers are few, but He will not allow the gates of hell to prevail against us. Now shall we go, Master Doyle and Mr Burroughs?'

In single file, with Joe Moran bringing up the rear, they walked across the pebbled courtyard under an arched opening in a thick yew hedge to a striking structure in the middle of the garden. The pagoda, open at all sides, had a marble cupola supported by slender Doric columns. Stephen, without being asked and with a nod to Bill Burroughs, lifted his arms to permit the expert hands of Joe Moran to pass over his body. Joe Moran in turn nodded to Brother Superior, who gestured to polished granite benches, where they sat facing each other.

Bill Burroughs took the initiative. 'Gentlemen, all practical men in the business world, which is my world, know the art of compromise, and negotiation will always find a solution to any problem. Only fanatics and the truly stupid try to impose their way as the only way and to hell with the consequences. Financially, I can make things happen even with the financial world in the mess it's in at the moment. We would, I'm sure, all like to get back to some sort of normality in our lives.'

'Mr Burroughs doesn't understand us or our world, does he, Master Doyle? We are simply on a mission to set our country free. Many have died for this cause in the past, and many more may die in the future. All that blood will not be in vain.'

'Bill Burroughs has a generous financial proposition—either accept it and move on or I go to the British tabloids, who are slavering to know the true story. You or the brotherhood could not survive the media storm. Your supporters and sympathizers in government will not be able to help you. You will be back to the old days—on the run and hiding wherever you get shelter or maybe granted asylum by those other great freedom fighters in Tripoli or Zimbabwe. Either way, I don't give a damn. One way or another, this has got to stop, and stop now.'

A terrible moment of mutual hatred shimmered between them; it was so tangible that the only outsider, the tough old Australian, shivered to his bones.

'Master Doyle, I will not be spoken to in that manner by a subordinate. Brother Moran advised you on the Olympic equestrian flight from Hong Kong that the oath you took as a volunteer still binds you to the brotherhood. However, I am mindful of the suffering inflicted on you by Heffernan and the Christian charity extended by your parents to volunteers Murphy and Meany as they lay dying. Also Miss Dundon's action saved the life of another volunteer on the car ferry. These are important matters in your favour. If the financial negotiations with Mr Burroughs are fruitful, then you personally have a grave responsibility in order to resolve this matter. Our preference, as you know, would be for you to run and eventually breed Barabbas for our future benefit. We are not totally unreasonable, Master Doyle. You will be rewarded for your efforts. Either way, the decision you make must contain the virtues of restitution and repentance. These and only these will be sufficient.

'Brother Moran and I must travel to Rome tomorrow. Our duties there will detain us for two months exactly. I suggest we meet here one day after our return. In the meantime, I can assure you of a tranquil period in which you can contemplate your decision. You will recognize the right decision when it occurs. Otherwise, the wrong decision will have the most frightful consequences. Regarding the British tabloid press, Lord Carlisle, who was so helpful in Hong Kong, has been advised to encourage the two major press barons that the torrent of misfortune that would visit them, their business, and families would not be worth the effort. Now I must leave. Brother Moran has some further information which may interest you.'

They turned and watched the departing Brother Superior in the ankle-length soutane seeming to float along the ground. They turned back to be met by the unblinking coal-black eyes of one of the most dangerous men on the planet.

Moran's lip curled in distaste, 'Doyle, I won't waste words. You swore to obey your rightfully appointed commanding officer as I did. You have broken your pledge, and I will break you and yours the minute I'm given the order. Brother Superior is throwing you a lifeline, but you're probably too proud and stupid to appreciate that. You have two months, don't waste it.

'Two things you should be aware of. Tan Song Li died last week in Macau, and has been succeeded by Quan. Mr Burroughs will be able to confirm this. Knowing Quan as you do, you can imagine revenge and recovery will be a priority for him. Also, any future race you enter Barabbas in will get a genuine bomb warning. He will not race again until we finish our business, as you put it, one way or the other.'

Stung, Stephen retorted -'*Brother* Moran, it occurs to me you never told Brother Superior that Meaney and Murphy were part of a paedophile ring with Heffernan. He'd be very disappointed if the eyes and ears of his chief enforcer forgot to mention that.'

'Fuck you, Doyle. You're a dead man if you try to drive a wedge between me and Brother Superior. I've served him all my life, but I'll break orders for the first time and personally gut you if you ever try that stunt.' Without another word, Moran left them, moving away in the opposite direction, an air of controlled aggression and menace in every stride.

Chapter 78

The trip back to Kiltealy House was a sombre affair. On the way, they each gave an account on their meetings with the Palladines. The colonel and superintendent in turn transmitted a report to their superiors. They were promised decisions by the time they arrived back in Bridgetown.

Following a welcome homecoming and another Doyle culinary production, both security officers informed them that they would be recalled to their units in a week's time. This presupposed the tranquillity promised by Brother Superior. In fact, both officers were seething and furious that this renegade cleric had such influence and access to the higher reaches of government.

'Both Colonel McGarrick and I have gathered that this Brother Superior has already been in touch with our superiors and that they have accepted his assurances of a truce for two months. Can you believe it? However, they say it has huge implications for the Belfast Peace Agreement and that they need this time to prop up the Unionists. Also, Adams and McGuinness will have trouble keeping their Provisionals in line if these dissidents are successful, particularly if this blasted cleric can peddle the line that they are the successors of the IRB and the legitimate predecessors of the IRA,'

Julie and the Doyle family sat silently, trying to absorb the implications for them and the country by this turn of events.

Julie asked-'Superintendent, you have been a great friend to us. Can you give us your honest assessment? Are we being thrown to the wolves?'

'Julie, the answer is yes and no. The government has to look at the larger picture, and individuals would be considered pawns in the wider scheme of things. On the other hand, politicians in my experience are mainly cowards, always currying favour with one interest group or another. Col. McGarrick and I have threatened to resign and go public if anything untoward happens to you or Stephen or your family. Luckily, both our ministers are strong characters. If any related harm comes to you or your family, they also have threatened to resign unless internment without trial as an emergency measure is subsequently introduced. This in turn has been passed to the reverend gentleman, but by then, it might be too late. You've already seen what kind of a fanatic we're dealing with. For all intents and purposes, we're dealing with our own version of al-Qaeda and Osama bin Laden.'

"Black" Jack Doyle spoke up, 'Thank you, Superintendent and Colonel, for your frankness. I don't intend to remain a prisoner in my own home one moment longer. I intend to go to my dear friend Jake Purcell's funeral in Kildare tomorrow. Plus, I also have his winnings to distribute.'

'Jack, as your wife and old friend Of Jake, I intend to go with you—and that's final!'

After a moment's silence at this outburst, someone started laughing, soon joined by all. Elizabeth Doyle, face flushed from passion and cooking, stood with hands on hips, a smudge of flour on her nose, blowing a damp curl from her defiant eyes.

Just then a knock on the door brought the burly Richie Cleary into the room, his curly dark hair and sallow skin hints of his gypsy blood. On cue, he blushed at the first sight of Julie.

'Beggin' your pardon, boss. I got a call on the mobile a minute ago. The same voice I told you about before, said to tell you the local Volunteer company was ordered to stand down until further notice. I'd love to get me hands on that bastard's neck—honest to God, I would—sorry, missus, sorry, Miss.'

'Nothing to be sorry about, Richie. By the way, any idea who he might be?'

'Sorry, Boss, but there's probably at least one sympathizer on the staff. You know how tight security has been this past while? Well, last week, I copped damp hay in Barabbas's feed box. If he'd eaten that, the colic coulda' killed him. Wouldn't be the first time that stroke's been pulled. I've been on double alert ever since. If he's here, I'll get him.'

Chapter 79

A week later, all overt signs of security were gone. The only remaining irritant was the constant presence of national and international paparazzi. They could and would pop up literally anywhere. Superintendent Deegan had arranged for a tough no-nonsense lady from a well-known PR firm to coach them. Anne Maloney, in her long career, had defended the indefensible and explained the inexplicable. A short, aggressive, bulldog-type person, she had a filthy tongue, which she used to cow the media and family alike. She had one iron rule—all statements would only come through her.

Superintendent Deegan left them with national and international phone numbers for himself and Colonel McGarrick. Bill Burroughs and his son-in-law, Dickey Beckett, left for Australia. Dickey was literally aching to be reunited with Miriam and little Benjamin. Both offered to stay but were graciously declined. They could do no more in Ireland, and in fact, Bill Burroughs needed his own time and space to work out and raise the money needed to satisfy the brotherhood. Grateful tears, kisses, and promises were liberally exchanged. And so began the two-month period (now less than one week) in which their future would be decided.

Julie and Stephen visited Sarah several times in the hospital in Dublin. She was making a steady but slow recovery. Trevor absolutely refused to leave until Sarah was fit enough to travel home to Australia. In fact, he and his sister, Georgina, leased a nearby modern apartment with stunning views of the Dublin Mountains. Stephen and Julie stayed there overnight on some occasions, strengthening and building bonds of friendship. Julie was delighted for Sarah to see how events had shown that Trevor had character. His reputation, upbringing, and family wealth could have been severe handicaps in a crisis.

Back in Bridgetown, Julie and Stephen delighted in each other's company, spreading their infectious happiness to the rest of the family.

Sometimes late at night, after tiptoeing to his room, Julie awoke to find him with hands behind his head, staring at the ceiling. After hard work and lovemaking, he should be sleeping the sleep of the just. However, the passing of each day without a decision or a solution was an ever-increasing burden. The one point of total agreement between himself and Julie—and with the rest of the family—was the determination that Barabbas would not belong to the brotherhood.

Stephen on Barabbas and Julie on Stephen's mare, the Diddler, were to be seen on the gallops early morning and late evening. Black Jack and Liz were usually on the viewing platform complete with binoculars and stopwatch. After one such morning workout, Julie left with Barbara, one of Stephen's sisters, for some shopping in Wexford.

On their return later that evening, Stephen and Julie were in the tack room, gathering bridles and saddles for their evening exercise. Barabbas and the Diddler were stamping in their boxes, eager for the gallops. Stephen wondered at Julie's behaviour, as she seemed to be checking inside and out.

Satisfied, she led him to a wooden bench. 'Stephen, I missed my period, which—if you had half a brain would know—is like clockwork. Barbara took me to see Dr Crosbie in Wexford today. He confirmed what I felt. Stephen, I'm pregnant. Now, Master Doyle, I want to know what you're going to do about it. Think carefully before you reply because the Nag will shoot you and Susie will load the shotgun.'

A slow grin spread across Stephen Doyle's face. One hundred and one conflicting emotions and calculations churned through his head. He shook that self-same head to clear the confusion, jumped to his feet with a roar, ran across the tack room, and hit the wall with both feet. In a second, the rebound propelled him back to where he scooped Julie up under her arms and held her aloft over his head.

'Oh, Julie, Julie, Julie, my darlin' girl, are you sure? Of course, you're sure. What am I thinking? Who should we tell? Should we tell everybody? Nobody? I'm so, so happy. Are you happy, Julie? Guess how Wexford folk would describe our news? They'd say Stephen Doyle has puddened that young Julie Dundon wan—y'know, that Australian wan with the horse!'

Julie laughed aloud at the effect her news was having. Inside, she hugged herself at the delight of it all. The happiness, the joy, the awareness of her body already subtly changing was simply overwhelming. Stephen, suddenly officious, immediately decided Julie would not sit on a horse until the baby arrived. Julie countermanded and told Stephen she was the arbiter of her own body and that she would decide when and where and what to do. And anyway, as he would soon find out from the *Dad's Beginner Book* she bought today, she could ride out until at least six months. So there!

At dinner that evening, they made their announcement. Most of the clan were present, and the remainder were swiftly phoned or texted. Black Jack and Liz went around the giant table, hugged, clasped, and kissed the young couple. The others followed and, with the same feeling since the dawn of time, gave thanks for the new life beginning amongst them.

Liz dried her tears on her apron. 'Julie and Stephen, God does indeed move in mysterious ways. Stephen, you've come back into our lives like a bolt of lightning. Julie, I've loved you before I ever knew you. You're all a mother could wish for her son. This news is a sign of God's blessing. He'll show you the right way to overcome your difficulties. I know you probably think we're old, cracked, religious nuts, but we've been around long enough to know that God loves us, each and every one, and wants us to be happy. Now, Julie, go and phone your uncle and aunt this very minute.'

Julie returned twenty minutes later, tears streaming down her cheeks. She said they were overjoyed in Australia; Susie would start knitting immediately, and the Nag promised to stop cursing straight away. They longed to see her either here or there and wanted word of the date she or they should travel. She had spoken with Bill Burroughs, who was making progress on the financial side. Alas, despite his best efforts, the deportation ban imposed on Stephen by the Australian authorities was proving very difficult to change. Julie then announced she had a date of long standing with Richie Cleary and that she would see them later. She arranged for Stephen to drop her off at Sinnott's in Duncormick and to pick her up when she phoned later on.

Julie had already found out Richie would be drinking in Sinnott's that evening. She quietly entered the pub, stood listening for a moment, and followed the sound of 'The Bonny Shoals of Herring' to the back bar. Head thrown back in full flight, Richie squawked to a halt in mid song at the sight of Julie leaning in the doorway. She beckoned him over to a vacant table, and when he joined her, she stood on tiptoe and kissed him gently on both cheeks. Richie clasped his face with both hands, his face crimson with embarrassment. A great shout went up from his buddies and singing cronies, further mortifying the gentle soul.

They ordered their drinks, and as promised, Julie told Richie as much as she could of their adventures to the present day. She thanked him for his steadfast loyalty to her and the Doyles. Julie nursed a glass of wine as Richie imbibed numerous pints of Guinness. After referring to the night she duped him, and apologizing again, she told him she wanted to share the news and joy that she was pregnant.

Richie's jaw dropped open in disbelief. 'But . . . but, Miss, you couldn't—I mean . . . I mean, we didn't . . . we didn't do anything, Miss!'

Julie hooted with laughter as the penny was dropping. Arthur Guinness had a lot to answer for. Eventually she phoned Stephen, who made the mistake of coming into the pub. Nothing would satisfy Richie or his mates but that Stephen had to have a drink, and that was final. An hour later, when they did leave, Julie held out her hand for the keys. They drove the narrow road home, singing 'They tried to tell us we're too young' at the top of their voices, unaware of the dark-panelled van with dimmed headlights keeping pace.

That night, Elizabeth Doyle smiled as she heard the besotted couple go straight to Stephen's room and gently close the door. They were engaged now, and that was the way of the modern world.

Stephen as a person was fearless and reckless. But now he was very fearful for the safety of Julie, their unborn child, his elderly parents, and his extended family. The days passed so swiftly as he struggled with his heart, conscience, and imagination. The years he had known and served Brother Superior gave him some insight into the mind-set of the cold and distant cleric. The acts of restitution and redemption so strongly emphasized were obviously of huge importance. There was a way if he could only think of it—something unique, something different that would pique the interest and remove the stain of dishonour obviously existing in Brother Superior's mind.

Barabbas continued to be exercised and trained. They should be looking forward to the British, Irish, and French classics. The road to equine immortality beckoned with other stops at Dubai, the Breeders Cup in the USA, and most of all, the Melbourne Cup back home in Australia.

Chapter 80

A week before his fateful appointment, Stephen sat on the top rail of the fence of the two-acre paddock. The lush green sward highlighted the coal-black coat of Barabbas as he dashed here and there, stopped, started, galloped, and walked. Looking at the young horse at the peak of perfection brought a lump to his throat. The sins of his youth had brought them to this. Barabbas might never race again.

Anne Maloney, their PR, was running out of excuses to the media as to what, when, or where Barabbas would run next. 'For shit's sake, Stephen, what the fuck is going on?'

'Anne, I've just now made a decision, and it's breaking my heart. I can't tell you this minute, but we'll need all your skills in the very near future. I want to check up on something and talk to the others. You'll know before the week is out, and that's a promise.'

That night with the dishwasher stacked and everything put away, Stephen put his proposed solution to them. Present were Julie; Black Jack; his mother, Elizabeth; and Richie Cleary. They were appalled and shocked at his proposal. Arguments raged back and forth, indignation and anger scorching the ceiling. Gradually, he wore them down with the logic of his argument. It was the worst possible way to win the argument, as the consequences were dreadful. And yet, finally, one by one he had their grudging assent.

Chapter 81

The day of his appointment dawned. The sun popped up to give radiance to a beautiful cloudless summer's day. Stephen was extremely quiet over breakfast; in fact, they were all untypically quiet. Julie and his mother had to coax some food into him. They only succeeded by pointing out that this could be a long day and not one for feeling weak and faint later on. He had contacted Rosbercon and was told he was expected at noon. He assured his family yet again that he had no fears for his personal safety on this particular day. They also knew that somehow and somewhere, Superintendent Deegan and Colonel McGarrick and/or their agents would be close by.

Stephen's mood shifted and changed along with the sunlight flickering through stands of trees as he drove the road from Bridgetown to New Ross. He scarcely noticed the forty-minute journey until he saw the glittering swell of the River Barrow as he descended the hill to the famous little town. Minutes later, he was over the bridge and driving up the long avenue to the Palladine Monastery. The Angelus bell in the tower overhead began ringing its eighteen peals as Stephen drew to a halt outside the main double doors.

Sitting in the car, he closed his eyes, and with his forehead touching the top of the steering wheel, he asked again for God's help for himself and his family. He managed a wry smile as he guessed the same god was being invoked by the people inside those doors to also bless their endeavours. As the last peal died away, one half of the massive door opened, revealing the tall dark figure of Joe Moran. Stephen opened the boot of his Land Rover, removing a small picnic-sized cool box. He walked up the familiar steps to the unmoving figure dressed in black clerical garb.

'Moran, I am here alone. I will not open this box until I am with Brother Superior. After that, you may search me and it for wiretaps or whatever. Either way, I don't think I'd stand a chance against you and the Beretta I know is in your left-hand pocket.'

'There's always a chance, Doyle.'

Stephen then noticed the tiny earpiece and aerial behind Moran's ear. He was also positive CCTV was monitoring them. Moran nodded and stood aside for Stephen to enter. As the door clicked closed, Stephen fought down a wave of nausea and terror. Without waiting for Moran, Stephen strode down the long, wide corridor to the main drawing room. With senses tingling, he absorbed the sound of their footsteps ringing on the black-and-white tiled floor, the sight of religious paintings, and the smell of beeswax polish.

Standing behind a bare table with his back to the window was the tall angular figure of Brother Superior. 'Good of you to be so prompt, Master Doyle. I see you have something for me. Do you wish to reveal its contents now, or would you prefer a chat first?'

'I presume Bill Burroughs has been in touch? Do you find his financial offer satisfactory?'

'Eminently satisfactory, Master Doyle. I presume you did know he's been in touch, but did you know it was through our old friend Lord Carlisle? I thought not. Lord Carlisle and his ilk are pragmatists. We met in Valetta in Malta—on neutral ground, so to speak. He's not keen that the brotherhood through the order has such a worldwide reach. He seems concerned that in frustration we might be of assistance to other bodies in rebellion in other parts of the world. Where do they get such fanciful notions? He did point out that Britain was happily divesting herself of colonies of the empire until the advent of Margaret Thatcher. Then those idiots in Argentina invaded the Falklands. She took a huge gamble to reinvade, and it paid off. Such a recent precedent was of such comfort to the unionists. They believe that now Britain cannot ever shed part of what they like to call the United Kingdom of Great Britain and Northern Ireland. However, Brother Moran and others will attempt to persuade them otherwise. And as you know, Mrs Thatcher personally had a narrow escape in Brighton.'

Stephen stared in fascination as Brother Superior spun his magic, the same magic that captivated and convinced him so many years before. He rubbed his face in his hands to clear his head and then placed the cool box in the centre of the table. From the corner of his eye, he saw Joe Moran slip the Beretta from his pocket and hold it down by his side.

'Brother Superior, I have here a VCR which explains repentance and restitution better than any words of mine. With your permission, I'll set up the TV to play the tape.'

Brother Superior nodded and, with the preparations complete, indicated that Stephen should sit on a dining room chair beside him. Joe Moran remained standing, having closed the heavy drapes. Stephen pressed the remote control and closed his eyes as the first images flickered on the screen.

The camera panned lovingly on the perfection that was Barabbas. The pricked ears, intelligent head, and unique stride were traits now recognized everywhere in the racing world. The film showed Stephen leading the magnificent animal down the ramp of a horsebox. The camera then shifted to a sign in the yard, which read 'John Devereux, Veterinarian Surgeon'.

A very large balding man in a white coat was seen talking to Black Jack, who then turned to the camera. 'Yes, yes, yes, I know what you're saying, but I'm saying this is the worst case of criminality ever in the whole wide world as far as I'm concerned. Have you any idea what you're doing? Is there no other way? Sorry, Jack. Sorry, Stephen. You wouldn't be here otherwise. Okay then, if that's the way of it. Let's do this professionally. This way please.'

Just then the camera swung wildly, and Julie's voice was heard. 'Oh God, Stephen, I can't hold the camera. Will you do it for me please?'

Stephen was seen taking the camera from Julie's shaking hands and turning it on Richie Cleary holding Barabbas tightly on a halter. Upset and sensing danger, Barabbas went berserk, rearing and bucking and lashing out. Richie fought to hang on. John Devereux grabbed the other side of the halter, while two assistants swiftly secured a padded rope behind the horse's back legs. Another plunged a syringe of sedative into the animal's rump. Minutes passed with the entire team straining and holding down the frenzied animal. Then gradually the muscles relaxed, and the fire died out in his eyes. The restraints were released, and Richie, followed by Stephen with the camera, led Barabbas into the veterinarian's equine clinic. The vet's team took over, gently securing the sedated animal, and when he became drowsy, they pushed him on to a very large operating table. John Devereux appeared in shot, swabbed the affected area, and deftly removed the horse's testicles. These were then placed in the cool box and packed with ice.

Finished, the tape stopped running on the VCR. Stephen switched off the machine, and Joe Moran pulled back the drapes. Stephen said nothing, just sat there with tears streaming down his face. The only sound was the ticking of a stately grandfather clock standing in the corner.

Brother Superior regarded the younger man for several long moments. He then reached into his robes and handed Stephen a crisp white linen handkerchief. 'Your actions indeed contain the virtues of restitution and repentance. Some might consider them extreme. However, as I told you at our last meeting, you would recognize the correct way when it presented itself. I have no reason to doubt you. I presume the box on the table contains the animal's gonads and that the blood and tissue samples are a perfect match? No need to speak for the moment. I must repair to the chapel to pray for guidance. In the meantime, Brother Moran will convey you to the brotherhood's battalion HQ.'

Chapter 82

Stephen never felt the needle until the tip pierced the skin on his neck. He couldn't tell what time had passed or where he was, only that he seemed to be swimming upwards towards the light. Gradually his senses cleared, and he found himself sitting, tied by the wrists and ankles to an upright chair. He looked down and saw he was dressed in a very dark, black- green uniform.

He looked up and saw Brother Superior opposite him at the centre of a long refectory table. He was wearing a similar but more ornate uniform, complete with cloak, embroidered in gold. Looking to the left, he saw ten young men and, to the right, ten more, all dressed in the same plain uniform. And behind Brother Superior the brooding dark figure of Joe Moran in a captain's uniform complete with Sam Browne belt.

On the wall behind them were emblems of previous historical insurrections and rebellions. In pride of place was the Fenian flag displaying a golden harp on a plain green background. Brother Superior began with the invocation and renewal of the oath of allegiance to the brotherhood and the Irish Republican Army. Two volunteers then cut the cords binding Stephen and hauled him to his feet.

Brother Superior intoned, 'Stephen Doyle, you were sentenced to death by a properly convened court martial of the Irish Republican Army for acts of betrayal and treachery. That sentence has been revoked following the satisfactory completion of the tasks we set for you. Also your parent's Christian actions towards two of our members and that of Miss Dundon, whom we believe is expecting your child, have mitigated your offence. Accordingly, you are hereby dishonourably discharged from the Irish Republican Army with a permanent stain on your character. You are dismissed with ignominy and the promise that any future interference by you with our organization will result in your summary execution.'

All through Brother Superior's address, Stephen stared into the dark, fathomless eyes of Joe Moran, certain he could never expect pity or mercy from that quarter. Caught unawares, Stephen again felt the prick of a needle. As he sank to oblivion, he managed a thought for the gelded Barabbas, who was also drugged so that others could have their way.

Stephen awoke fully dressed at the steering wheel of his car. The Range Rover was parked in a garage, formerly a stable, backing on to the main monastery building.

Sitting beside him was Joe Moran back in clerical garb. 'Drive home slowly, Doyle. We've perfected that sedative. It's completely worn off by now, maybe a slight headache. Brody is dead, Doyle, didn't make it. I wanted to leave him in hospital till he was strong enough, and I wanted you to pay for it. Overruled on both counts. You're as lucky as a cut cat Doyle.'

'Hang on, Moran, I presume that was Brody in the ambulance at the Curragh. He thought I was on Barabbas. He—in case you've forgotten— was going to shoot me out of the saddle. Surely to God you don't expect me to mourn for him.'

'Brody was a patriot, Doyle—on a mission, carrying out orders, killed in the line of duty. Now fuck off outta my sight forever, you fucking traitor.'

With that, he was gone. After a few moments, Stephen started the engine, drove out the garage door, across the yard, and down the long avenue to the quayside of New Ross. As he crossed the bridge to the Wexford side, an enormous weight seemed to lift from his soul.

At the edge of the town, a Garda in traffic police uniform waved him down. He pulled over and pressed the down button on the offside window. The Garda leaned in the open window and put his finger to his lips.

Superintendent Deegan in a mock thick rural accent said, 'I'll have to ask you to step out of the vehicle, sir. We have reason to believe you may be carrying an illegal substance. You will come with me, and my colleague will drive the vehicle to the nearest Garda station.'

Back in New Ross Garda Station, Stephen and his clothes were subjected to a forensic examination for embedded tracking or listening devices. Colonel McGarrick joined them while the Range Rover was being similarly examined. Stephen recounted as much as he could recollect, including the news that Brody was dead and that they were somehow aware of Julie's pregnancy.

Superintendent Deegan sighed, 'Go home, Stephen, and try to rebuild your lives. For us, the struggle will continue until one side or the other prevails. Obviously, Col. McGarrick and I must make sure this cancer is rooted out for all our sakes, not least for the future of our democracy.'

Chapter 83

Two hours later, with the sun heading towards the western horizon, Stephen drove up the avenue to Kiltealy House. Seldom, if ever, had Bridgetown sparkled so much to Stephen's eyes. He had phoned ahead to say he was okay and was on his way. The Range Rover had barely stopped on the gravelled driveway when Julie yanked the door open, pulled him from his seat, and planted a large moist kiss on his lips.

'Quick, quick, inside now to the others with your news. I know, I just know by you that the news is good.'

For the next hour, Stephen held them spellbound as he recounted all that happened since they shared breakfast that morning. After the questioning died away, a thoughtful silence descended on the family. Liz was later heard to remark that in all her long years, she had never prepared so many pots of tea.

Into the silence, Stephen tapped his cup with a teaspoon. 'God knows this is not rehearsed. On this special day, with my family as witness, I ask that you, Julie Dundon, consent to be my wife. The love I have for you is nearly unbearable. Every day when I wake up, I just touch your cheek to make sure you're real. I want us to become as one in the eyes of the Lord, the Doyles and the Monahans—What say you, my Antipodean sheila?'

The gathering looked at the normally undramatic Stephen, who was dramatically on his knees before the blushing Australian.

Julie in turn knelt before Stephen, 'Well now, cobber, first off, you need my aunt and uncle's permission. Secondly, as you so charmingly put it recently, I've been puddened. And thirdly, you were going to have to answer to Richie Cleary if you didn't do right by me. I'm going to take a chance on you, Stephen Doyle, with all my heart.'

Talk immediately began on the logistics of the wedding. It would be in Ireland, as Stephen was still barred from Australia. Late September after the harvest was discussed and agreed, particularly as Julie's baby was due at the end of November. Everybody and anybody would be invited. Going to bed that night, the various couples agreed that such a joyful occasion would be a welcome relief at the end of a terrible nightmare.

The long summer days began, and gradually their thoughts strayed from their preoccupation with the flat-racing season. Black Jack Doyle's Bridgetown operation specialized in producing animals for the hunting and steeplechasing business. However, that selfsame business, like lots of other businesses, was taking a hammering. The economic downturn was affecting everybody's pocket. In the boom, the seemingly casual cost of keeping a horse in training was now becoming an impossibility for some. The racing game was never easy or for the faint-hearted. Stephen, however, slipped effortlessly back into this world he'd left behind.

Their last moment of high drama was a press conference fronted by their PR, Anne Maloney. She wept at the news she would have to deliver. Stephen took her into his confidence and was rewarded by the most invective bout of foul and filthy language he ever heard. He hugged her and said he wouldn't be surprised to hear that a certain religious establishment in New Ross had been struck by lightning.

The press conference was held in the Slaney Room, the main ballroom of the Talbot Hotel in Wexford. Such was the national and international interest that the partition with the smaller ballroom next door was rolled back to accommodate the army of correspondents and their equipment. Anne Maloney then demonstrated why she was the best in the business. She deftly separated the issues surrounding the family and the horse. Rumours and counter-rumours had inflamed the coverage of events, fuelled by an unchecked tabloid press.

'Ladies and gentlemen of the Fourth Estate, I will answer some of your questions after I've read my statement to you. I will try to be fair. After all, this is my profession too, but I will not answer any question from that section of our profession accurately known as the gutter press. Now you know and I know precisely who they are and where they are in this room. I leave it to your common sense to shut them up. Otherwise, you'll get no information, and we'll be here all day.'

A chorus of outrage followed a stunned silence. Anne Maloney stood at the lectern with arms folded until the hubbub eventually died away.

'I am constrained from discussing any personal details involving the Doyle, Dundon, or Monahan families. You will be aware, better than most, of the onerous libel laws existing in Ireland. I can tell you that numerous members of the legal profession are preparing a multitude of litigation involving these three families. Your editors won't thank you for going down that road. Go there at your peril.

'The really sad news is that Barabbas has undergone cryptorchidectomy surgery. This procedure, as some of you may know, is necessary in some instances for the removal of a retained testicle. The procedure, which is difficult, was not a success. The subsequent risk of testicular cancer necessitated castration. This has since been carried out. Barabbas is recuperating physically. The family is recuperating emotionally.

'Amidst all this gloom and on a much happier note, I am pleased to announce the engagement of Miss Julie Dundon of Balingup, Bridgetown, Western Australia, to Stephen Doyle of Kiltealy, Bridgetown, County Wexford. They intend to marry later in the year. Now I will take your questions.'

Stephen and Julie sat in a bedroom upstairs, listening to Anne Maloney's press conference through an electronic feed. They marvelled at her commanding performance; she was like a Serena Williams sending and returning serves at lightning speed. Eventually she wore them down. The true professionals amongst them realized she was never going to drop her guard. When she brought the meeting to a close, some of the brightest and most cynical gave her a round of applause.

As the older hands filed out, heading for the bar, the tabloid pack, now off the leash, shouted and howled their inane questions. Anne held up her hand for silence and said her assistant would now hand them a further statement. The young lady then moved amongst the mob, handing each a white envelope, some of which were torn from her grasp. The only sound was the ripping of envelopes. Each envelope contained a single sheet of paper on which were written the immortal three words: 'Piss off, asshole.' When they looked up, Anne and her assistant had gone.

Upstairs, Julie stood at the window, looking across the harbour at the white sails tacking around the Ballast Bank. Beneath her, the Dublin–Rosslare train snaked along the edge of the water. Stephen came up behind her, his arms wrapped around her middle, and his hands cradled the new round of her belly. He savoured the intimacy of the moment, inhaling the female scent of his soul mate. Julie leaned her head back, resting it on his shoulder.

'I've a little secret to share with you, Miss Dundon. This morning I got word from Tom Lacey, one of my many cousins over in Galway. He does a bit of breeding like a lot of small farmers in the west of Ireland. We send him suitable mares to breed with their heavier animals—mostly for hunting, which is like a religion in Galway. To cut a long story short, I sent him the Diddler. I know I lied to you about her absence. Before he had her covered, he sent the word I was hoping for. The Diddler was already in foal—just started, but definite. Richie Cleary spotted she was coming into her first season. We moved her to the old breeding sheds my father used years ago. Then the two of us snuck Barabbas down to say hello. God, he nearly killed us. Richie is one of the very best stockmen I ever met—on a par with the Nag. It wasn't the most professional covering in the world, but we felt we had to take the chance.'

Julie slowly turned around, her face and eyes alive with excitement. 'Stephen Doyle, you never cease to amaze me. Isn't this the greatest news ever? Isn't it just delicious when you think of the way that old scoundrel Davey Beckett had Barabbas's dam covered? Now go and lie on that nice bed while I think of your reward, which you richly deserve. No, no, not another word. Let me loosen that trousers to give yer man a bit of air. He'll give you a hernia if he doesn't get out.'

Later, they lay together listening to their thumping hearts recede, daring to believe in their own fairy tale and perhaps yet to 'live happily ever after'.

Chapter 84

The summer drifted along, each day bringing them another step towards normality. Their lives settled into Black Jack's busy routine—breaking, training, and preparing their own and their client's horses. The jump season was in full swing, with horses being prepared for the hundreds of hurdle and chase meetings all over Ireland and the UK.

Most important of all was the progress being made by Barabbas. He made a rapid recovery following his surgery. John Devereux called nearly every day to make sure the wound was healing free of infection. Now a gelding, Barabbas and his nature changed bit by bit. Richie Cleary and Stephen spent every spare moment schooling the young horse. Next year, he would have finished racing as a four-year-old and retired to stud. Now in jump racing, he would be considered a young horse, starting off in novice handicap hurdles.

They always suspected Barabbas could jump. They often reviewed the tape of the Australian Royal Cup at Belmont Park in Perth. The way he soared over both stricken horses without hesitation showed a natural instinct. But that was then, and this was now, and an awful lot had happened in the young horse's life in between. Black Jack, Stephen, Julie, and Richie Cleary all agreed to go back to basics and school Barabbas properly from day one. They were glad they did, as the horse's true quality and innate talent quickly became obvious. After the wedding, they would introduce Barabbas to a new audience, beginning with the local Lingstown point-to-point meeting in October.

In the meantime, new dreams began to take root. Talk and thoughts of competing at Punchestown, Fairyhouse, and Leopardstown were discussed. And what about the 4-mile Grand National at Aintree or the holy grail itself, the Cheltenham Gold Cup, steeplechasing's ultimate prize?

Racing people themselves are a breed apart, eternal optimists living tough lives in difficult conditions. Non-racing people, who got a glimpse of the non-glamour side of this business, shudder at the thought of the relentless daily grind that must be endured.

In the meantime, their lives were full. They enjoyed family outings to some of County Wexford's fabulous sandy beaches and lots of shopping in Wexford and nearby Waterford City. However, their greatest family pleasure was in attending the many race meetings scattered all over Ireland. These trips, which were sometimes for business and sometimes for pleasure, reconnected them to the ordinary lives of ordinary people.

Stephen, keeping a promise made to Susie while in Australia, never gambled on the outcome of any race. Julie, on the other hand, developed a natural flair for a flutter. She had a good eye and, more importantly, a good ear. She gave them all a great laugh when she seriously told them Paddy Power, Ireland's most prominent bookie, would finance her baby's education.

Sarah Bright, now fully recovered, and Trevor came often to Kiltealy. They delayed their return to Australia when Julie asked Sarah to be her bridesmaid. The modern magic of Skype kept Julie, Susie, and the Nag in touch more intimately than a telephone call. Julie particularly loved keeping in touch with the estate manager, Tako Toida, and his wife, Naoki Okado. She thanked them often for helping to get her head and life back together. The Monahans planned to be in Ireland a full month before the wedding. The Burroughs family and Dickey Beckett would arrive a week before the event and stay for an extended three-week holiday afterwards.

Stephen was often in touch with Bill Burroughs, that stalwart friend with whom he had shared his troubles, and to whom he owed so much. He was able to lay Stephen's concerns to rest regarding outstanding monies owed to the syndicate. The last of the serious wagers with the big overseas-based punters had been paid in full. The Irish and UK heavy hitters had long since settled up on the result of that remarkable day at the Curragh. After paying the ransom, a significant amount remained to clear all remaining debts, including a very tidy share for Julie.

Chapter 85

The month of August arrived and, with it, the Etihad flight from Australia. The scenes at the arrivals hall at Dublin Airport were straight out of a Failte Ireland brochure. Susie and the Nag abandoned their grossly overloaded trolleys, which were rescued by an alert airport policeman. They walked and then half ran as if in a daze to the barrier. Black Jack and Liz were amazed to see Susie and then the Nag gently stroking Julie's face. Then they all burst into tears.

Then they were off in convoy to the Shelbourne, the doyen of all Irish hotels, fronting St Stephen's Green. They stayed for four days, each morning beginning with a post-breakfast stroll through some of the 22 acres of the gorgeous Victorian layout of the Green, then morning coffee at Bewley's, and shopping in nearby Grafton Street, Dublin's favourite pedestrian thoroughfare.

After lunch one day they took a taxi to the Dublin Horse Show, held annually at the Royal Dublin Society's showground in Ballsbridge. There they met up with lots of family, friends, and acquaintances, all with the love of horses as their common bond. Susie and the Nag were enchanted by the glamour and colour of this hallowed 150-year-old institution still located in the heart of Dublin City. The icing on the cake was to witness the 500/1 Italian equestrian team on the final day beat all comers to lift the fabled Aga Khan Trophy.

Numb from joy and non-stop talking, Susie and the Nag slept for most of the journey back to Bridgetown. On arrival, the entire Doyle extended clan were on hand. The weather over the past week had softened to a mellow late Irish summer. To honour their guests from the country of the great outdoors, the Doyles had set up a barbecue on the large patio, which led to the sunroom, which in turn led to the kitchen. Never people to sit and be waited on, Susie and the Nag rolled up their sleeves and cut and carved, ate and drank, talked and sang on this perfect afternoon.

Leaving the youngsters to clear up, Julie and Stephen, Black Jack and Liz, Susie and the Nag left the house and walked the short distance to the stables. Black Jack and the Nag had established an immediate rapport since they met and had talked into the night every night, sharing a bottle of Jameson. Now they lined the rails of the small paddock in the centre of the yard. Stephen led Barabbas from his box and walked him around the paddock. He then slipped the halter and joined the others.

Barabbas kicked up his heels, galloped in one direction, checked, and galloped back. Even though the Nag knew what had happened and agreed with what had to be done, he was still heartbroken at the awful waste. Trying to be pragmatic, he noticed the beautiful proportions of the young horse. Gelding has the side effect of filling out an animal, and Barabbas right now looked superbly fit and alert, with fire still in his eyes.

To ease the pain, Susie asked the Nag to tell the story of how they first saw Barabbas, the day Davey Beckett drove his battered old horsebox into their yard at Balingup. A natural storyteller, he had them in stitches as they strolled back to the house and the Irish hooley now in full swing.

Chapter 86

August slipped into September; the hay long saved, and the second cut of silage under way. The grain harvest was also in full swing, with great yields of wheat, oats, and barley, some as high as 3 tons to the acre. The first Sunday in September arrived with an epic All-Ireland hurling clash between ancient rivals Kilkenny and Tipperary. Black Jack used a lot of favours to secure tickets for the game. Prime seats in the Hogan Stand at the HQ of the Gaelic Athletic Association on Jones's Road in Dublin is heaven for most Irishmen.

The Nag and Susie were fascinated at the speed and skill of Ireland's national game. The colour, pageantry, and passion were infectious as they witnessed Kilkenny once more triumph over their old enemies. Sunday papers were bought but not read that day due to the early start and late return from Dublin.

Buried deep in one edition was a short report from *L'Osservatore Romano*, the Vatican newspaper.

> It is with profound sadness we report the sudden and untimely death of Rev. Brother Philip Larkin, putative vicar general of the Palladine Brothers. Brother Larkin and Brother Moran, his successor as Brother Superior of the order, were about to be confirmed in their new roles by the Holy See. A further announcement will follow in due course.

Superintendent Deegan and Colonel McGarrick were informed by various intelligence agencies. After conferring, they decided to alert their sources, as this was new, uncharted territory. They also agreed not to contact or alarm the Doyle family at the moment. They were both invited and had provisionally accepted an invitation to Julie and Stephen's wedding.

Chapter 87

Preparations for "The Wedding", as it was now being called (as if for royalty), were gathering pace. On 21 September, the autumnal equinox was the chosen date. Julie was in girlie seventh heaven. The fittings, the fun, and the finery were intoxicating for all the ladies. Sarah, Susie, Liz, her daughters, and daughters-in-law were all involved. The menfolk were dismissed with airy waves of dainty hands. This was women's work in the women's world, an infallible fact of life observed through the ages in every country and by every creed.

Originally, the marriage service and reception, in their particular circumstances, were to be held locally in Wexford. That was until, returning one day from the Galway Races, Black Jack decided to fulfil a promise made at the funeral of his old friend Jake Purcell. Jake's nephew Rory and his wife, Maeve, had extended an invitation to call and stay at Ardattin House outside Portumna in County Galway. Rory and Maeve had followed up the invitation with several phone calls, which Black Jack now decided to accept.

Jake Purcell's home place was not only a delight but also a hidden delight. A gentleman's residence, it was situated below rather than above the road. The half-mile tree-lined drive curved down, sweeping around two gentle bends. Then, the sudden sight of the Regency pile, complete with turreted tower and annex, were a surprise and a feast for the eyes. In front, a glistening lake fed from the hinterland discharged via a weir into the nearby River Shannon. Julie fell completely in love with the ambience and the setting. Ardattin House operated as a private hotel which never needed to advertise. Exclusive weddings were a specialty, with accommodation for the principal guests. The bride and groom had the use of a special suite at the end of the annex jutting into the lake and supported by massive pillars. Other guests would be accommodated in the nearby luxurious Shannon Oaks Hotel.

The first time Black Jack brought them to Ardattin House was the clincher. Rory and Maeve conducted them on a thorough inspection tour of the house and demesne. Julie clapped her hands together and then put them to her mouth, uttering a string of 'Oh my, oh my, oh my'. It was all they needed to hear.

After finishing some light refreshment, Black Jack steered Elizabeth out to the verdant lakeside lawn. 'This could have been yours, Becky. Jake was mad about you, as you well know. He had all this before I could even dare write my first cheque. I often thank God for letting you see whatever you saw in me. Sorry, love. Now, don't take on. I really didn't mean to upset you—honest, I didn't.'

'Ah, Jack, my love, Jake Purcell was fine and dandy, but Jack, you were and are my oak—tall and strong, decent and kind. We've weathered many a storm and reared a fine family. It was very easy to love you, Jack. And when God calls us, I'll be happy for us to be together for all eternity.'

Chapter 88

Another hysterical day dawned at Dublin Airport with the arrival of Bill and Martha Burroughs, Miriam Burroughs, little Benjamin, and her beaming husband, Dickey Beckett. They were absorbed into the Doyle clan, who all lived within a few miles of Bridgetown. Later at Kiltealy Estate, Stephen saw tears welling in Dickey's eyes. First one and then another began to roll down his cheeks. Bill Burroughs was biting his lower lip as they sat on the rail of the paddock, watching Barabbas being exercised over gentle jumps. Without a word and, as males sometimes did, the three men embraced and walked back to the house.

Two days before The Wedding, Stephen accompanied the Burroughs and Monahan families to Ardattin House. He would stay with the greater mob in the Shannon Oaks until the day of the wedding. The Shannon Oaks and its proprietor were, in Irish colloquial terms, 'as well known as a begging ass'. They were famous worldwide for their hospitality and as the best place on God's green earth to hold a stag party. In view of Julie's delicate condition, her hen night would be held at Ardattin House.

Early on the day before the wedding, Stephen collected Bill Burroughs and Dickey Beckett. As they drove the road from Portumna to Galway, he promised they would enjoy the beautiful scenery and maybe a little surprise. Eventually, on the outskirts of Recess, he turned into a neat yard under an arched sign, which read 'Tom Lacey and Sons'. Tom stood waiting under a second arch leading to a cobbled yard surrounded by loose boxes. Following introductions, Tom led them to a cosy stall with a familiar head looking out over the half door. Stephen slipped an apple from his pocket, cut it in halves, and watched it being nibbled from his palm and chomped on by big strong teeth.

'This is the other lady in my life. Meet the Diddler, the daughter of a succession of mares I've had since I was a boy. This lady is so well bred she should be in Burke's Peerage. I shipped her up to Tom, hoping she was in foal. She was, and she is. The sire, gentlemen, is Barabbas. We had a one and only opportunity to pass on his line. You can imagine how dangerous it could be if this news got out. Tom's kept me informed of her progress. She's in top condition, and with an eleven-month gestation period, she'll drop her foal late next month.'

Stephen stood back and watched in amusement as Bill and Dickey approached the mare with what could only be described as reverence. Four experienced eyes swept the Diddler from every angle. Then inside the stall, four expert hands ran up and over every inch of the young filly. Stephen leaned on the door, listening to the soothing murmurs of approval.

Tom eventually said, 'Right, lads, inside now and meet Sally, my good wife, and have a spot of refreshment. Fortunately—and unfortunately—our four rascals are at school, so we have a few hours to ourselves.'

Sally settled them in a lovely living room with stunning views of the Twelve Pins of the Maumturk Mountains of Connemara. Bill Burroughs remarked that of all the places he had been, he had never imagined any place could be so beautiful. Tom persuaded Bill and Dickey to sample a shot of poitin, the local moonshine, used in rural Ireland for every possible ailment in animals and humans. As a drink, when distilled by those with the 'knowledge', poitin is as smooth as a twelve-year-old whiskey.

Stephen declined, as he was driving, and as the second glasses were refilled, he produced some documents from inside his jacket. 'Julie and I, the Nag, and Susie have agreed that the foal will be registered three-fourths in the name of Bill Burroughs and one-fourth in the name of Dickey Beckett. Now not another word from you two. It's our gesture of appreciation for the endless help and friendship from both of you over the past two years. Tom will fill in his part on the papers when you come to collect the foal. Maybe you should re-register the foal to one of your offshore companies, Bill, just in case, okay?'

Bill Burroughs sat there wordlessly, shaking his great shaggy head, while Dickey jumped up, hugged, slapped backs, and shook hands over and over. A few more glasses of poitin followed and then a few more with toast after toast like a Soviet-era celebration. Eventually, Stephen and Tom, with help from Sally, loaded the highly inebriated Australians into the car for the return journey to Portumna. Song after song and verse after verse deafened Stephen as he enjoyed the feeling of having brought such happiness to people who richly deserved their reward.

In Dublin, Superintendent Deegan placed a call on a secure line to Colonel McGarrick. 'Colonel, some disturbing news. You'll remember my sergeant in Special Branch? Nick Kelly, the one with the perpetual bad attitude? Well, he's been found locked in his car in Limerick with his throat cut. Nick never made friends, only enemies. It may not be who we're thinking, but I'm pretty sure it is. Nick was my double agent in the IRA. Somehow, Moran figured it out. He'll be out of control now with Brother Superior gone. I don't think we should alarm the Doyles or Monahans right now. The wedding's tomorrow. They won't be back in Wexford for a while yet. Also, that murdered banker, Laurence Power? Seems all the clues and evidence point in the same direction. Looks like we'll have to send our regrets. Pity.'

Chapter 89

The 21 September dawned gloriously as the Indian summer continued to bathe Ireland in soft golden light. Stephen arrived at Ardattin House wrecked from the stag party. The wedding service would be a civil ceremony in the great hall at eleven o'clock. Julie and Stephen had successfully persuaded Black Jack and Liz that Julie couldn't be a hypocrite and have a religious ceremony. Liz felt in her heart that Julie would one day find her way back to the church. In the meantime, she had the couple agree to accept a blessing from a brother of hers, a Dominican friar from the priory in Tallaght. They had met Father Gerrard several times and had no objections to the jolly avuncular priest sprinkling them with holy water.

Stephen's eldest brother, Eamonn, was best man. The other brothers, all resplendent in morning suits, were ushers and groomsmen. Stephen stood with Eamonn before the registrar, sweating and waiting for the opening note of 'Here Comes the Bride'. Stephen turned as the organist's fingers crashed to the keyboard, releasing the gloriously familiar strains. Julie stood at the open double doors to the great hall. All brides are beautiful on their wedding day. They seem to radiate the happiness burning inside and bursting to get out. Julie was all that and more.

Julie Dundon was naturally beautiful. Her light sallow complexion, enhanced by her pregnancy, emphasized that beauty. Sunlight streaming from windows above the organ gallery illuminated her and made her positively glow. A simple ivory dress with flowing lines neutralized her pregnancy bump. Julie looked cool and dignified with her mother's pearls at her throat and seed pearls woven in her hair. The Nag, with Julie on his arm, slowly processed with barely a limp. They were followed by the bridesmaid, Sarah Bright, her blonde hair complimenting a startling blue dress, which perfectly matched her eyes. Susie then followed as matron of honour in a remarkable creation of flowing orange silks and was promptly nicknamed Jaffa by the legion of Stephen's nieces and nephews. Susie smiled to herself because she knew in years to come she would never be forgotten, and would always stand out in every wedding photograph.

The Nag reached Stephen and, before giving Julie away, stuck out his hand. Stephen looked into the stern grey eyes, feeling the power still in that calloused hand. It was an unspoken moment, each recognized by the other. Julie leaned over and kissed the Nag on the cheek. His eyes immediately misted over as he stepped back alongside Susie.

Julie turned to Stephen with a wicked glint in her eye and whispered, 'Our moment has arrived, Master Doyle. It's like a fairy-tale, only my poor bladder is being compressed by this ragamuffin of ours. Could we get to the kissing part pronto?'

Stephen and the registrar, who was listening, burst out laughing. The ceremony began, all tensions now gone. Vows were made in clear ringing tones, and the rings exchanged. When the concluding 'I now pronounce you man and wife' and 'You may now kiss the bride' arrived, the hall erupted in a spontaneous round of applause.

This set the seal on the rest of the day, which was a rip-roaring success. Ardattin House didn't do things by halves. A traditional jazz band set feet tapping in the ornate bar where they gathered for pre-dinner drinks and from where they were summoned as required by the wedding photographer. The decibel level increased as the drink level rose, and before long, the band had volunteer singers. Black Jack and the Nag brought the house down with their impromptu 'Won't you come home Bill Bailey', while Liz and Susie stole the show with their quivery version of 'Summertime'.

The exquisite dinner was accompanied by a string quartet, played by four ravishing young women in formal evening wear. The speeches were very witty and in the true spirit of the occasion. Most said a few words, and some said a lot. The Nag and Black Jack, with collars undone, had them in stitches with yarns and reminiscences. Susie and Liz had tales from Stephen's and Julie's childhoods.

Stephen said he instructed the hotel to do a head count, as he recalled the antics he and a friend employed to infiltrate weddings as young men in Wexford. Julie, who was a great mimic, spoke briefly in Australian, Dublin, Cork, and Wexford accents, poking fun at herself and lots of her new friends and acquaintances. There was one goodwill message she kept to herself. It was a note from Ming Tai in Macau, which was in an envelope with a scent she vividly remembered.

A twelve-piece orchestra played in the ballroom, where Stephen and Julie led the dancing beneath antique Waterford chandeliers. The ballroom opened on to one side of the bar, while the other side opened out to the breakfast room now set up and blaring as a disco. Julie and Stephen made several forays to both venues and were quietly pleased and gratified at the success of their wedding day. People of all ages were talking, laughing, singing, and dancing.

When Stephen saw Julie's energy level begin to drop, he quietly and discreetly led her around the back of the grand staircase to the private elevator, which brought them two floors to the annex. A member of the hotel security staff was posted there to ensure their privacy from well-meaning well-wishers.

Chapter 90

Julie and Stephen walked half a long corridor hand in hand, passing suites which would later be occupied by the Monahans and senior Doyles. The next corridor they met turned at right angles and ended at the presidential suite, which today doubled as the honeymoon suite. This corridor was built to resemble a glassed-in cloister and extended on pillars out over the lake. The low lighting afforded glimpses of water on either side as they walked and listened to their footsteps echo on the granite tiles.

The suite itself was stunning with every imaginable luxury. The bathroom—a designer's delight of backlit marble with a sunken bath, Jacuzzi, and enclosed sauna—was straight out of *Hello!* magazine. The bedroom was done in restful autumnal brocades, thankfully without a claustrophobic canopy bed. Folding double doors led from a separate living room to a dining area with a compact kitchenette. Glass doors in the bedroom opened on to a balcony wrapped around the building.

Julie and Stephen walked three sides of the building along the balcony suspended above the dark waters of the lake. Julie leaned as far as her belly would allow over the railing, asking Stephen to hold her while singing and laughing through the theme tune from *Titanic*.

Eventually, as their laughter subsided, Julie turned to kiss Stephen. 'Husband of mine, mate of mine, love of mine, thank you for taking me as your wife, for keeping faith, for not giving up, for the immense joy of your body, and for the future happiness of our little family. Let's hit the scratcher. What say you, Mister Doyle?'

'Nice to be promoted at last from master to Mister Doyle. We'll most certainly hit the scratcher, Mrs Doyle, but not before I give you a bath in that enormous contraption, then I'll dry you and powder all those important little places. How about that then, sheila?'

'Well now, cobber, how's a girl to refuse such an offer on her honeymoon? We can play submarines. Any idea where we might find a periscope?'

With shrieks of laughter, they dashed inside, shedding clothes in a steady stream all the way to the bathroom.

Later, they lay entwined under the duvet of the 7-foot bed. As they drifted off to sleep, Julie spooned herself into Stephen's back. Stephen laughed aloud as he felt the kicks of his unborn child. Julie, already drifting off, turned over as Stephen snuggled behind her. He lay peacefully, listening to his new wife's deep, steady breathing.

They couldn't possibly hear the sound of the inflatable dingy bumping against the pillars in the water directly below or see the black-clad figure expertly taping packets of Semtex around the top of the pillars above the waterline or see him set the timers on the detonators or hear the whisper of the oars on the calm dark waters or see Joe Moran eventually pause and listen to the distant sound of laughter and music floating on the still night air, then check the second hand on his watch as it swept inexorably towards the hour.

Lightning Source UK Ltd.
Milton Keynes UK
UKOW04f2144151015

260627UK00002B/45/P

9 781514 461037